FitzDuncan's Gambit

JOHN J. SPEARMAN

ISBN: 979-8-9866058-4-5

DEDICATION

To the readers who enjoy my work and encourage me to write. To Alicia, my wife and my strength, who challenged me to pursue it further. To all those who offer me moral support—you know who you are and I cannot be more grateful. Finally, to you, the reader. You are the reason I do this.

ACKNOWLEDGMENTS

Dear Reader,
You are the purpose of this and all my books. Thank you for
reading. If you like what you have read, please leave a positive review
on Amazon.com or goodreads.com. If you did not like it, I'm sorry.

If you would like to stay abreast of my latest activity,
please visit my website: johnjspearmanauthor.com

1

At the beginning of the campaigning season, the horse nomads attacked at Oritur, in the center of the March's eastern border, and then Litchville, to the north. Between those two encounters, the nomads lost more than ninety men. We estimated that was roughly twenty percent of their force, perhaps more. While common sense would perhaps indicate to most leaders it would be wise to withdraw, I suspected the losses they suffered would only enrage them.

When I returned to our primary encampment at Bannock Hill after visiting our southern detachment—only a dozen men at that time—I pored over the maps. I quizzed my father and the three kersants at Bannock Hill— Bill Martin, Mike Dorne, and Gus Polever—regarding the size of the towns in the southern part of the March. My other inquiries centered on the behavior of the nomads. Were there patterns to their attacks, or did they choose targets randomly? Did they ever assault a town repeatedly, or did they always switch from one to another? Does the weather affect their choice?

My father and the kersants did not have many answers. My father, the earl of the March, was responsible for its defense—the eastern border of the kingdom of Aquileia—against the annual raids from nomadic horsemen who came from much further east, across a wide desert. None of us knew why they came, they just did and had been doing it since anyone could remember.

Our defense of the border towns had two prongs. The communities fronting the border area were all fortified by a deep ditch with a high wall and palisade inside. Foot soldiers, members of an annually drafted militia, defended the walls. My father led the armsmen—the cavalry—whose task it was to break up the nomads' attempts to scale the walls. The nomads always outnumbered our armsmen because the cost of keeping that many trained soldiers was prohibitive. Still, we could force them away from the walls and break up their attacks.

A kersant is what we call a sergeant in the Eastern March. Each kersant led a unit of twelve men, including himself. The previous two years, my father cut the number of armsmen due to financial difficulties. Three border towns were pillaged last summer—the worst it had ever been.

Where was I? you might be asking. I wasn't here. A year ago, I was living a carefree life in the capital, Aquileia. I had not seen my father to speak with in nearly two decades since I was sent away to school at the age of thirteen. Why? Well, I'm a bastard. Not that way—I strive to be a gentleman. I was the illegitimate product of my father's dalliance with one of the maids in the manor.

Not long after, my father married someone more fitting to his station, who turned out to be a shrew of the worst sort. When she delivered her firstborn, a son, I was sent away. The only time I was allowed to return was for my grandfather's funeral, and even then, I was kept at a distance. I was not allowed in the manor. Instead, I had to stay at an inn.

Skipping forward many years, this last year of my life was filled with one incredible adventure after another. I have documented most of them in previous writings. Some of those adventures brought me to the attention of the royal family—in a good way, mostly but not entirely. I met the love of my life, Lucille Austermain, daughter of the Duke of Gulick, and we recently married.

In addition to being the most beautiful woman I ever saw, Lucy has supernatural talents. If she lived in the country, the locals would have considered her a witch. In the city where we lived until recently, people like to pretend there are no such people. Now she is Lady Oritur (her new title). Through Lucy, I discovered my own connection to the supernatural, but I've already told those stories, so I'll skip them for now.

Immediately following my wedding, the king summoned me and decreed I was now officially adopted by my father and would be his heir. He then named me Lord Oritur, from a town in the march, which is how Lucy got her new moniker. The king then directed me to join the defense of the March. As I mentioned earlier, we enjoyed unexpected success this season.

Returning to my question regarding the behavior of the nomads. None of our men ever plotted a nomad offensive through a campaigning season—they waited for the nomads to mount an assault and then responded. All agreed that our efforts this season were more successful than any of them could remember from years past, despite our lack of men. However, the absence of information and being understrength made my task of trying to anticipate where the horsemen would strike next incredibly frustrating.

"Sir, from this point forward, if you are handling the logistical side of things, please keep a record of their attacks," I asked my father. "We should have a record of where and when they attack in order to determine if there is any pattern to it. We should know how they respond to defeat and how they follow up a victory. If weather affects their choice, we should also keep a record of that. It might turn out that there is no rhyme or reason to their choices, but, right now, we have no way of knowing that."

"Is this something you did in the Rangers?" my father asked.

"Yes. We had years' worth of logs on the behavior of the Rhetians," I explained. "I would not say they were a foolproof predictor of what they would do, but they did help us concentrate our resources in the most likely places. In addition, they helped us predict future activity levels. For instance, if we thwarted a Rhetian attack, but they could escape with limited casualties, they would usually try again in the same area soon after with greater numbers. On the other hand, if they attacked and failed, with large numbers killed, they would avoid that location for as long as several years. Indeed, suffering a grave setback would quiet the whole Western March for weeks and months. We have no information like this for the nomads. About all anyone can say is that they generally don't attack the same place twice in succession."

"That's true," he agreed.

"Smoke!" came a shout from the tower. "From Ostroot!"

The militia guarding the town of Ostroot had ignited a signal fire that could be seen from our watchtower. That was a sign they were under attack by the nomads. Ostroot was five leagues south of Bannock Hill. It would take us three hours to reach it without exhausting our mounts.

The kersants were calling for the men to saddle up. We had forty-one men, including me, who were fit for duty. My father was heading to his horse as well.

"You're coming?" I asked as I was jogging over to get my weapons and armor.

"You can't talk me out of it this time," he said with a smile. "Besides, I want to see you in action. I'm tired of hearing the men talk about it after the fact."

With my father, we would have forty-two. If Kersant Rissolo and the southern detachment rode north from Clearview, we would have over fifty men. That would still be only two-thirds of the men we would typically muster.

After strapping on my breastplate and donning my helmet, I grabbed two lances, my bow, and a quiver of arrows, then busied myself in saddling my horse, Andy. Everyone who could ride was mounted and forming up in their units within minutes. When everyone was ready, the kersants gave the order to move out.

"Are the men you brought from Easton ready?" I asked my father, edging myself next to him and his mount, Aster. I was referring to a group of armsmen he needed to dismiss a year ago due to the poor financial state of the March. With my resources, we could now afford to bring them back, but they just arrived a few days earlier.

"More than they were a couple of days ago," he replied. "Not as much as they should be."

"Tell me about the defenses in Ostroot," I asked.

"The town is similar in size to Oritur," he responded. "They have four towers and should have skorpios in all of them. The militia force is a hundred men. They will be able to hold them off until we arrive, though they will be plenty glad to see us by then."

Skorpios were roughly three times the size of the crossbows they resembled. They fired bolts as thick as broomsticks with iron tips. In the previous few days, I rode past Ostroot twice and knew there were no geographic features worth noting. There was a stream, but it had low, shallow banks that would not provide any cover. The ground was flat, and there were no trees. The flat ground was under cultivation, about half in oats and half in beans. In other words, the lay of the land was typical for the Eastern March.

Fortunately, Ostroot was protected by stout fortifications, as was every Aquileian settlement in the border area of the Eastern March. The outermost element of the defenses was the ditch—ten feet deep and about sixteen feet wide at the top. On the inside edge of the ditch, a wall is built up about ten feet tall above the original ground level. This meant the distance from the bottom of the ditch to the top of the wall was twenty feet—nearly straight up. Built into the top of the wall are palisades—pieces of tree trunk buried three or four feet deep, sticking up about four feet. The larger towns, like Ostroot, also usually had defense towers about thirty feet tall.

The nomads tried to breach these defenses in two ways. By far the most successful method was to throw bundles of sticks into the ditch to fill it so they could run across the top of the piles and then climb the wall. Their riders would provide covering fire with arrows to keep our militia crouched below the palisades.

The other way was to attack the main entrance to the town. Riders with grappling hooks would brave the hail of arrows and skorpio bolts to try to throw a grappling hook attached to a rope over the entrance gate. If successful, the rider would try to climb over the gate and open it. This rarely worked but the nomads continued to try this method. After a few unsuccessful climbing attempts, some nomads might try to retrieve the loose ends of the ropes attached to the hooks and use their horses to pull the gate open or down. It would generally take more than a half dozen embedded hooks to make this worth attempting. It was even less effective than a man trying to scale the gate.

My father speculated that attempting to climb over the gate was viewed by the nomads as an act of great courage. He reckoned that one who survived such an attempt was probably held in great honor among them. Father also wondered if it might be a method by which the attacker could erase some sort of stain in his background.

Though individually, their warriors were quite brave, as a group they tended to avoid close contact with our armsmen, even though they usually outnumbered us by a considerable amount. Our armsmen would arrive, and the nomads would scatter and then try to surround us in the open. We would not be foolish enough to follow them, staying in the shadow of the town walls and the covering fire of the militia with their bows and skorpios.

In their first two attacks this year, our armsmen caught the nomads bunched up, drew our lances and rode on them. The losses we inflicted were more than what the nomads might experience in a complete campaigning season.

Previously, they might lose five to ten men in each attack, either riding on the gate or attempting the walls.

In thinking about why the nomads allowed themselves to be caught packed together, the only answer I developed was overconfidence. As I mentioned, in the previous two years, my father reduced the number of armsmen because of financial problems. The nomads succeeded in sacking three towns the year before—the worst losses the March suffered in many decades. In the first two assaults this year, the nomads outnumbered us. They probably thought it inconceivable that our small force would risk charging them. I'll take credit for that. Allowing the enemy to control every engagement was against my experience and nature.

As we rode toward Ostroot, I doubted the nomads would allow themselves to group together so tightly. Of course, after their first attack, at Oritur, I believed they would have learned the lesson, but they made the same mistake at Litchville. I hoped they would be foolish enough to make the same error this time but did not think it likely.

We arrived at Ostroot just after midday. As expected, the nomads were gathered in two groups—one in front of the gate, another attacking a section of the wall on the fortification's opposite side. We rode on the group trying to climb the wall first.

Six dismounted men were trying to climb the wall. They were not having much success since the militia occasionally leaned over the palisades and fired arrows down on them. To stay away from the arrows, the dismounted nomads were hugging the surface of the wall. The still-mounted nomads were located just out of range of the skorpios in the towers at the corners of the fortifications. These nomads fired arrows at the militia, trying to protect their men clinging to the wall. When we rode up, the horsemen scattered before our arrival as I expected, leaving their men on the ground to their own fates.

The nomads abandoned by their comrades had no good choices. Without covering fire, the militia would unlimber sixteen-foot-long wall-spears and attack the men on foot. If the unhorsed nomads tried to run away, the militia would cut them down with arrows.

We continued on to the gate. As we approached, the nomads withdrew to the open fields. We reined in, stopping in front of the ditch at the town walls, facing the nomads. They stayed out of range of the skorpios. While we were glaring at them and they at us, Rissolo's unit rode up and joined us.

We stood there for hours. The nomads shouted at us—presumably insulting our courage for not coming to engage with them. But of course, the same could be said against them. I counted the nomads twice and asked my father and the kersants to count them. The number we came up with most often was three hundred and twenty-seven. We were only fifty-four—not nearly enough to consider pressing the issue.

Our stalemate lasted until nearly six o'clock that evening, as best I could figure from the angle of the sun. Then, on a bellowed call from one of the nomads, the insults ceased. They turned and rode away.

The gates of the town opened. A tall, thin man wearing a breastplate and helmet strode out and headed for my father. My father dismounted to greet him.

"Mayor Jenkins, I'd like you to meet my son, Casimir. Casimir, this is Mayor Jenkins," my father said.

Jenkins looked puzzled at my father's introduction. He obviously knew my father's sons by his wife—Edwin and Percival—but not me. My father noticed his bewilderment.

"Casimir is my first-born, mayor," he explained, sharing no further details.

The mayor still did not understand but was too polite to press the issue further. The conversation turned instead to the attack and the mayor's report of casualties (four lightly-wounded militia, the six nomads at the wall just after we arrived were killed). As for the armsmen, we would water our mounts and return to Bannock Hill or Clearview. It would be a late supper, but better that than risk travel as darkness fell.

When we went into the town, the mayor separated from my father and came to me. "First-born?" he asked.

"Yes, sir," I replied. "Before he married."

The light of recognition appeared in the mayor's eyes. "Oh," he said. "I guess that is why I never heard about you. Well, I'm pleased to meet you. Have you returned to the March for good?"

"I believe so, mayor," I responded. "Those are the king's orders."

"Huh," the mayor grunted, then he turned and walked away.

On the ride home, I rode with my father but slowed and allowed the rest of the men to pull away. My father matched my pace, figuring I wanted to talk. When the men were out of earshot, I began.

"Tomorrow, we should send Bill Sample and his men to Clearview," I said. "I'm sure it did not escape the notice of the nomads that only twelve men were with Kersant Rissolo. We'll need to look at the maps, but I suspect their next target will be as far south as Litchville was to the north."

"You think so?"

"From years ago, they know you cut back your numbers, then reduced them again last year," I explained. "And they've seen proof of that at Oritur and here today. They know you have a northern and southern detachment, and the numbers there are smaller. We covered for that at Litchville by guessing correctly, and we've now restored the missing unit there. We need to do the same again."

"What happens if you are wrong?"

"Trouble," I replied. "At least by replenishing the numbers in the detachments, we buy a little time. I hope it's enough. We'll still be terribly short of men at Bannock Hill for another week at least."

"How many do you think you'll get from the city?" my father asked. "Realistically."

"Ten," I answered glumly. "We could use thirty."

"We couldn't afford that many," my father stated.

I held my tongue. My father did not know how extremely successful I had been in my quirky "business." Before this, I helped people by retrieving lost or stolen items when the law was of no use. My fee was half the value of what I recovered.

Even with my lending the March ten thousand ducats, and after paying for Lucy's wedding present—a magnificent necklace, plus giving her eight thousand to spend on new furnishings for our house in the city, my assets totaled nearly one hundred and eighty thousand ducats, thanks to the generosity of the crown in the recent Spadewell matter. We could easily afford the extra men, and for years to come. So, I made up my mind.

"Yes, we can, father," I said calmly.

"No, we can't," he replied forcefully. "The March is bankrupt, thanks to that woman. Seven hells! The March owes you ten thousand ducats, and it will take careful management to ensure you are repaid over twenty years—with no interest."

"Sir, we can afford it. *I* can afford it," I clarified.

"I'm not going to allow you to impoverish yourself due to my mistakes," my father growled.

"Sir, I have been far more successful than you realize," I said quietly and calmly.

"Oh really?" he said sarcastically. "And how much money do you have in the bank right now—after that draft comes out?"

"I'll have somewhere around fourteen thousand ducats in the bank," I answered.

"That won't go very far," my father replied triumphantly.

"And just over one hundred and sixty thousand ducats invested in different ventures around the city," I continued.

I glanced at my father. His mouth was opening and closing like a fish out of water. I gave him a gentle smile.

2

"Did you ever venture out to investigate the nomad camps?" I asked my father later, after dinner.

"Not while they were present," he said. "Your grandfather took me to see them shortly after they returned home one year."

"What did you find?"

"He took me to the swath of cropped grassland next to the river that marked where they camped during their visit," he replied. "They started in the south. By the time they arrive every year, the grass is high and already mostly turned to hay. They need a great deal of fodder for their mounts and the food animals they bring. From the bones left behind, they drive cattle from their home. I don't know whether they bring them all at the beginning of the season or drive smaller herds every few weeks. As they exhaust the fodder in one area, they move north. For fuel, they send riders to the southern forest. We could see the path they've made over the years since the grass no longer grows there."

"From what remained, did their camps seem well organized?" I asked.

"Well enough. The latrines were well away from the river. They buried the bones from the animals they slaughtered," my father recounted. "They left behind three huge iron kettles. Dragging them from their home across the desert and all that way must have been quite challenging. My father and I rolled them into the river hoping that the spring flood would wash them away."

"Did it?"

"I believe so," he stated. "The following campaign season was notably mild. There were only a few dozen of them, and they were gone before the end of

Heyannir. The only other times I can remember numbers that small and their departure so quick were the four different years when we suffered droughts in the spring—the only time the eastern plains get water. The stunted grass was not enough fodder."

An idea was forming in the back of my mind. There was something in what my father shared with me that seemed to signal an opportunity. There might be some leverage we could use, but what form it would take remained hazy. I reminded myself to access my ability later, to see if Bellona could provide me with greater insight. But, for now, we needed to meet with the kersants and try to anticipate the next move the nomads would make.

They were standing around a table, looking at a map unfurled. When I arrived, the kersants made room for me. I studied the map and pointed to a town named Sudenvale. It looked to be six leagues south of where our detachment was based near Clearview.

"Tell me about Sudenvale," I requested.

"It's the southernmost village in the border area," Mike Dorne, one of the kersants, answered. "About the same size as Ostroot."

I turned to Bill Samples, another of the kersants. "Bill, take your unit to Clearview tomorrow. You'll spend the rest of the season there. Gus, you and Mike will bring your units to Ostroot with me. We will leave the wounded here to keep watch. I want someone in the tower from first light to nightfall. The men will light a signal fire if the nomads attack here or further north. We'll be out of position, but there's no help for it."

We adjourned. The kersants returned to their units and shared the plans for the next day with their men. I sat at the table and continued to stare at the map in the quickly fading light.

"You look troubled," my father said as he sat across from me.

"I am," I admitted.

"What's bothering you?"

"I don't have a strong feeling about this," I said.

"About?"

"Where they're going to appear," I stated. "In the first attack, I expected a feint, so when they hit Oritur, we were prepared—not too far out of position.

With Litchville, I was confident that was the target. Today, Ostroot seemed the logical place. I don't have the same feeling about Sudenvale."

"Then don't go," he said.

I looked up at him. "What?"

"Up to now, you've been very clever or damned lucky," he said. "It doesn't matter which. My advice, which my father gave to me, is don't outsmart yourself."

"Please explain," I requested.

"Sudenvale has perhaps the stoutest defenses of any border town," he explained. "That's because they are so close to the forest. It's one of the few towns in the March that is not entirely dependent on farming for income. They also have a reputation for making some of the finest furniture in Aquileia. Those talented woodcrafters also make skorpios. Sudenvale has eight in the same number of towers. There is no gap in the area the skorpios cover, as there was at Ostroot today. If there is any border town that could hold out waiting for the armsmen to arrive, it's Sudenvale."

"Do our 'friends' know this?" I asked, gesturing to the east where the nomads were camped.

"Yes. They make a token attack on Sudenvale every year, but I think it's more like a scouting mission," my father said. "They ride up with a couple of dozen, test the defenses, see that the town is as well-defended as ever, then leave."

"Why didn't you say something earlier?" I asked. "This is one of the problems with turning the entire defense over to me right away. I don't know these things. Majors and Minors, I don't even have a grasp on how ignorant I am—even our enemies know more about our defenses than I do. "

My father chuckled softly. "I did not speak up because you've been correct to this point," he replied. "Plus, I don't wish to disagree with you in front of the men. I wouldn't even have mentioned it now, except you admitted you're uncertain."

When I retired for the night, I pondered what my father shared with me regarding Sudenvale. I tried to consider things from the viewpoint of the nomad chiefs. They were aware we were short-handed. So far, I was clever enough (or lucky enough, as my father said) to move the limited number of men where they needed to be. They did not press their attack earlier in the day against Ostroot with their usual vigor. However, it did draw my attention south, which might have been their intention.

Suddenly, I understood. *They will feint again*, I thought, *like the sham attack on Norvost to pull us away from Oritur. This time they will try to lure me further away—to Sudenvale. I would wager they will hit Oritur again. They won't hold back the way they did today.*

I thought the thing through again, and when I finished, I was even more certain I knew what they were planning. In the morning, I would cancel the movements I ordered a couple of hours ago. I might also send a rider to Quinn's Ford to bring Doug Campbell and Paulie Florio and their units to Oritur. Sleep came quickly after that.

In the morning, I drew my father and the kersants together and explained why I had changed my mind. None of them objected. Mike Dorne, in fact, was nodding in agreement. It stirred me that they had given me their trust in such a short time. We sent a rider north to summon the two kersants. Tomorrow we would move to Oritur and sleep rough on the other side of the town from where the nomads would appear.

If what I envisioned came to pass, they would come around midday on the day after we arrived. They would stage their decoy attack against Sudenvale earlier in the morning, anticipating I would have moved my forces south. If I had shifted the armsmen to Ostroot, and we responded to the call from Sudenvale, we would be too far away to return to Oritur by the time we realized their ruse.

That afternoon, the two units from Quinn's Ford arrived, and we all set off for Oritur. Our numbers came to sixty-six who were able to ride. We left the wounded at Bannock Hill. We reached the town early enough to request dinner from the innkeeper. He grimaced when we told him how many we were, then nodded.

"Give me a couple of hours," he requested. "My kitchen is only so big. I'll need to feed you in three or four groups."

"Thank you," I answered gratefully. "I apologize for the lack of notice. And, if I may presume upon your good nature, breakfast in the morning would also be welcome."

"It won't be much," he said. "Bread and jam, most likely. I'll need to alert the baker."

The innkeeper did a credible job. He prepared a stew, or I should say, three stews, since he could only make enough at one time to feed a third of us. It took a bit longer than a couple of hours, but no one complained. Breakfast in the morning was, as he predicted, bread and jam. The bread was fresh, though, and there was plenty of it. Then, we waited.

The sun was near its zenith when a call was relayed to us from the tower on the other side of the town's fortifications. Riders were approaching. We had stowed all our gear earlier, so all that was remained for us was to mount and ride.

I shouted to the nearest tower, "Have them call out the distance."

The tower relayed the message to the other tower. The answer came back. "Half a league, now."

"Let us know when it is six furlongs and what their pace is," I hollered back.

"When they tell us the nomads are six furlongs away, Paulie, Doug, and Gus, take your units to the left. Mike, Bill, my father and I will go to the right. If we are lucky, we may catch them between us and be able to exercise our lances," I instructed. "After our first pass, wheel to the right, and we'll regroup."

When the tower yelled, "Eight furlongs! At a trot!" we took our groups to the corner of the fortifications. As we did, I searched within myself for the place where my power resides, a place that has no real physical location. When I found it, I pulled forth a small tendril of Bellona's energy. Bellona is the Minor Goddess of War and my dominant supernatural connection.

The tower shouted that the nomads reached six furlongs, still at a trot. We all set off at a gallop. We could see our enemies as we neared the front of the battlements.

They remained at a trot as they approached. We continued to close with them. I shouted the order for lances as I slid the one from under my right leg. The enemy's lead riders saw us, and their formation began to peel away to either side, picking up their pace. It appeared that we would catch only the last of them before they scattered far enough to make our lances ineffective.

I was the frontrunner on my side. Screaming my fool head off, I caught one of them with my lance in his ribs. The lance went so deep that his body pulled it with him when he fell. I circled to the right. My men followed me as I led them under the protection of the archers and skorpios on the walls. I reined Andy in at the front gate, both of us panting.

Surveying the scene, I counted nine men and six horses on the ground. One of the men on the ground picked himself up slowly and began to stagger toward us, an arrow in his chest. He was one of Mike Dorne's unit.

"On me, men," I shouted. "Bows!"

I squeezed Andy's flanks with my knees as I unslung my bow from over my shoulder. Andy heeded my instruction and began to run for our wobbling comrade. We were no more than halfway to him when the nomads brought him down with two arrows protruding from his upper back. He fell to his knees and then slowly toppled forward.

"Seven hells!" I cursed. "To the wall, men," I called.

As we headed to the right, the small group of nomads who killed our soldier loosed their bows at us. One hit me in the upper left arm. Another hit Andy on his left haunch. I muttered another curse, more concerned for Andy than myself. His usual smooth stride developed a noticeable hitch. We reached the safety of the covering fire from the town.

I dismounted immediately, taking care not to touch the arrow still lodged in Andy's side. Andy shifted uncomfortably as I clasped the reins tightly. My father rode up to see what was the matter.

"Hold him," I instructed, handing him the reins.

"Do we have any alcohol and salve?" I called out.

No one answered. I looked at my father. He had a puzzled expression.

"Pouring alcohol along the shaft of the arrow as I pull it out lessens the chance of infection," I explained. "There are salves that reduce the pain and swelling. Unfortunately, from your expression, we have neither."

He shook his head.

"When you return to Easton, buy some pure, clear alcohol—the kind no one would dare to drink," I instructed. "Also, find an herbalist and ask for a pain-killing salve. The ones based on cloves are the most expensive but worth it."

"Where did you learn this?" he asked.

"In the Rangers," I replied. "I can't believe every kersant doesn't carry a supply."

I went to Andy's head, spoke with him and stroked his neck, apologizing for the hurt I was about to cause. After signaling to my father to hold the reins tightly, I went to the arrow. It looked like it was three or four inches deep. After taking a deep breath, I grasped the shaft with my right hand and pulled it out in one continuous motion. Andy screamed and bucked, knocking me on my butt. I kept rolling in a reverse somersault, to get out of his way if he continued. He didn't. One was enough. Andy gave me a reproachful look. Falling and rolling on the ground made my own wound hurt worse as the arrow wobbled in my arm.

"What about you?" my father asked, nodding at the arrow still stuck in my arm.

"Mount first, then rider," I said. "Unless it's life-threatening, and this isn't. Care to do the honors?"

My father handed me Andy's reins and then sidled next to me. He bent down. He reached with his hand but did not touch the arrow.

"On three," he said. "Ready?"

I nodded.

"One, two—"

"Yeeeow!" I roared. "Seven hells!"

Clutching my upper arm, I turned to him. "What happened to three?" I demanded.

"You would have tightened your muscle on three," he said. "That causes more damage."

"Where did you learn this?" I asked, echoing his tone from a minute earlier.

"Your grandfather."

"Anyone have a bandage?" I called out.

This time the kersants responded. Paulie reached into the pack behind his saddle and handed me a roll of gauze. I tore off my shirt sleeve and used it to wipe the excess blood from my arm, then unrolled the gauze and wrapped the wound tightly.

Meanwhile, the nomads drew up just out of range. Today they did not linger to screech insults. They turned and departed.

The gates opened. We watered our mounts. After thanking the innkeeper and baker for feeding us, we left. Doug Campbell and Paulie Florio's units would head straight for Quinn's Ford. The rest of us were going to Bannock Hill. I rode double with my father, allowing Andy to return unburdened. When we drew closer, I sent Gus Polever ahead to alert the cooks to begin preparing dinner for us.

Two days later, in mid-afternoon, the lookout on the tower called, "Riders from the west!"

"How many?" I shouted up. I was expecting my father to return from town today but no one else.

"More'n ten, less'n fifty," came the response. "Too much dust."

That was welcome news. These would be the men, former Rangers, whom Carl Stensland recruited in the city of Aquileia at my request. I was expecting ten. Above that number would be a blessing. I wondered if my father accompanied them. He returned to Easton the day before. Part of me was tempted to climb the tower to see for myself, but my wounded left arm convinced me not to try. I would have to wait.

It took two more hours before they arrived. During that time, I was as anxious and excited as a boy at the winter solstice, waiting for Grandfather Frost to deliver presents in the middle of the night. I tried sitting but had too much energy to be still. Pacing back and forth made me feel like a caged animal, so I would try sitting again, with the same result.

Somehow, the time managed to pass until they rode into my sight. My father was at the head of the group, chatting easily with two or three others. I saw Hank, Robby, and Bert, who joined me for parts of some previous adventures. I recognized a handful of others—men I served with.

Some had helmets, others breastplates, and three wore both—all tarnished and spotted with rust. They must have visited the armory in the manor. Rangers did not wear armor, so none of them would have owned it before arriving. Those without breastplates appeared to be wearing the boiled leather jerkins with quilted linings that served as armor in the Rangers. In addition to my father, there were twenty-nine men.

"Thank all the heavenly beings!" I whispered.

I strode out to greet them. My first worry was remembering the names of the men who served in my unit. I took a deep breath and closed my eyes briefly.

Then, with my eyes shut, I searched my memory for the faces I knew. The names returned to me swiftly.

As the approached, I called out to the ones whose names I knew. With the reins of another horse tied to his saddle, my father reached me first. He swung down slightly ahead of the others. His face bore a grin the likes of which I never saw before.

"Casimir, I'd like you to meet Sarn't Rowan and Sarn't Langford. Sarn'ts, my son, Casimir," he said.

The two men with whom he was conversing dismounted and offered their hands to me. "Dick Rowan," said a lanky man with milk-white skin and carrot-orange hair. "Gary Langford," said the other, Rowan's opposite in build and coloring. Langford was short and stocky, with dark skin and close-cropped curly black hair.

"You are a most welcome sight, men," I said, clasping each of their hands in turn. "My father may have told you I was hoping to have ten men come. Only in my fondest wishes did I expect twenty-nine."

"Then perhaps I shouldn't tell you there are six more on the way," Rowan said, "two or three days behind us."

I laughed softly, shaking my head in amused bafflement. "Would you please introduce me to the men I don't know?" I asked.

They did. After introductions, we sent them to unsaddle their mounts and find a spot to sleep. There would not be enough room on the sleeping platforms, for which I apologized. Both Rowan and Langford looked at me with puzzled expressions.

"Sleeping platforms?" Langford exclaimed. "Well, la-di-da. None of us expected such luxury, milord. A piece of ground without rocks or roots is good enough. You should know that."

"I remember it well, Sarn't," I replied. "Or should I say, kersant? That's the title we use here."

"Your father told us."

"And if you call for me and use the term 'milord,' I'll turn my head, looking for my father. I was a captain in the Rangers. That's plenty of title for me."

Both men laughed.

"I need to ask since my curiosity is compelling me, how could it be that so many were willing to come?" I inquired. "Were none of you able to find steady work?"

"That was never a problem, Cap'n," Rowan replied. "Almost everyone had a job and a living. I can only speak for myself, but I figured out that the thing I was best at and enjoyed most, was being a Ranger. Sure, I'll miss sleeping in a cozy bed every night, but I know I'll be much happier otherwise. I was ready to listen when Carl spread the word about you needing men. I went to learn more. He said it was the same pay as the Rangers, plus quarters in Easton for my wife and little ones. That's the deal, right?"

"It is," I answered firmly.

"What about for them who ain't married?" Langford asked.

"They will be furnished with quarters as well," my father interjected. "We have a dozen rooms over the stable that are empty. They won't be on their own, like you, but we will feed them while they stay there."

"Like living at an inn, without paying," Rowan remarked.

"Well then, Cap'n," Langford said to me, "I think you just got yourself some new soldiers."

"Sarn'ts," my father said, "or kersants, please allow me to steal Casimir away for a few minutes. I have news for him, and then I will return."

3

A long with these fine men, your lady wife arrived. She requested your presence," my father said.

"Lucy is here?" I asked with excitement.

"Indeed, but she is not alone," he informed me. "The Deputy Master of the Royal Household is with her, as is a large hulking man named Theo."

"Theo? What in the seven hells is he doing here?" I inquired.

"He will be in charge of the manor, according to Lucy. He certainly was useful in running off the vermin Veronica hired," he said.

"What does she need me for?" I asked. My heart yearned to leave immediately to see her, but my sense of duty was interfering.

"I don't know that she *needs* you at all, boy," he smirked. "However, you were just married, and then your lives were uprooted with the move to Easton. I'm as certain as I can be that she would like to see you very much, though."

"But—"

"But, you're wounded. Even worse, so is your horse," my father interrupted. "You are of little use here until Andy is healthy enough to ride, and that will be ten days or more. I don't know that you'll be of much use to her either, but sleeping with her must be more enjoyable than a cot here in Bannock Hill."

"As you said, my horse is unrideable," I argued. "How will I travel to Easton?"

"On the nag I brought with me," he said, jerking his head at the horse that was earlier tied to his saddle.

"But—"

"But, nothing," he cut me off. "I've been doing this as long as you've been alive. The March will not fall in your absence. If you stay for ten days, the armor I ordered for the new men should be ready. You can bring it back with you. I'll ensure the new men learn what they need to know, and I'll send Bill Sample's unit to Clearview tomorrow."

Sense of duty satisfied, I grinned and trotted over to pick up my saddle. It took only a few minutes to get the old horse ready for my journey to Easton. I mounted and urged the horse to approach my father.

"Did you bring the alcohol and salve?" I asked.

"Yes. Lucy said that when she has the time, she will make something more effective than what the herbalist in Easton has to offer."

"You'll explain my leaving to the men—in a way that doesn't make me sound like a namby-pamby?"

"Your reputation will only be enhanced after the new men tell the others about your bride," my father said with a chuckle. "They met up on the road, and from the conversations I overheard after we left Easton, the men quite adore her."

"Of course they do. They're good men," I said with a grin, turning the horse and nudging her to move.

The poor horse was certainly in no hurry, even though I was. I thought I heard the bells from Easton ring five as I approached, but the breeze was from the west, and Easton was far enough south that I wasn't sure. Upon reaching the manor, I noticed a change immediately. The guard at the gate was standing and alert. His armor gleamed, and he carried a vicious-looking pike. He appeared to be older, but his helmet covered his hair and obscured his face just enough that I could not get a good read on how old he might be. Something about him seemed familiar, though. He stepped in front of the gate while holding his weapon at the ready across his chest.

"Hello, sir," he said crisply. "May I ask your business at the manor?"

"Lord Oritur," I responded, "to see Lady Oritur."

"Oh! I apologize, milord," he said. "I heard you might be arriving, but since I've never met you, I would not recognize you."

"Would you step a little closer, please?" I asked.

"Milord?"

"You say you've never met me," I said, "but I believe I've seen you before. If you come nearer and remove your helmet, I reckon I'll figure it out."

He moved his pike to his right side and took two steps forward. With his left hand, he removed his helmet, tucking it under his arm. He looked up at me. With the helmet off, I knew him immediately. From the front, his head was an almost perfect rectangle. He had been a kersant when I was a boy. To my eyes, he was old then. He must be over sixty by now, though he did not look it.

"I was right," I said. "Hello, Kersant Lewiston."

"Milord?" he replied, clearly puzzled. "I used to be a kersant, years ago. Now I'm a gate guard. How do you know me?"

"I would have been thirteen the last time you saw me," I said. "I did not have my growth yet, and my voice certainly had not changed."

He peered up at me. I decided to make it easier on him and dismounted. He stepped closer still and studied my face. The light of recognition came to his eyes.

"Pipsqueak?"

"That's one of the nicer names I remember you calling me, kersant," I said with a chuckle. "Let me try to remember—varmint, naughty puppy, snotty, devil, a plague of the seven hells, nuisance, scoundrel, wretch, hooligan, pest—"

"*You're* Lord Oritur?" he asked, his expression incredulous.

"Aye, kersant."

"Well, I'll be dipped!" he exclaimed. "How did that come to pass?"

"It's a long story, kersant, and I promise I'll share it with you, but now I am eager to see my wife. Before I go up, how did you end up here?" I asked.

"Lord Easton put the word out that he needed reliable guards and would pay a decent wage," he said. "I'm too old to go riding on the border, but my wife was tired of me sitting home. Me and a couple others heard that woman was gone, so…"

"I am glad to see you, kersant," I told him. "Quite a difference from the last time I arrived here."

"Aye, milord," he replied, pressing his knuckle to his forehead. "We have a proper lady in the manor now. There will be a lot of changes, and all for the better, I reckon."

He opened the gate, and I walked up to the manor. I was halfway there when the front door burst open. Lucy came out. I quickened my stride. We met at the bottom of the front steps. I switched the horse's reins to my wounded left hand and embraced her with my right. As I lifted her feet from the ground with my embrace, she began smothering me with kisses. I responded in kind as best as I was able.

"I've missed you, too," I said when she slowed down.

"That's part of it," she responded.

"Oh?" I stated, now figuring she saw my arrival in one of her glimpses of the future.

"Yes," she confirmed.

She clasped my hand and started tugging me to the house. I broke away to tie the horse to a post. She waited for me impatiently.

"There's an incredible amount to do," she said. "We've only been here since midday, and the place is a disaster. I'm sad to say we cannot stay here tonight. I have booked us a room at the inn."

"It's that bad?"

"Your father's wife mismanaged the manor horribly," Lucy said. "She kept cutting staff and their wages. The last few months, the two who were left were stealing everything they could carry away. Theo ran them off as soon as we arrived."

"I heard Theo was here. Please tell me he is not the cook," I added.

"Theo will not be cooking," she said, laughing as she pulled me further into the manor. "When we are established and know what we are doing, he will manage the household for me," Lucy explained. "Williston is teaching us."

"Who is Williston?"

"He is the deputy master of the royal household," Lucy said. "The queen sent him to help us get things under control and to instruct us since the manor is far larger than even our house in the city. My mother and aunt are also coming. They have direct experience in households of this size."

The first floor of the manor featured a central hall leading directly through the building, linking the front and rear entrances. The first room to the right, open to the hall, was the huge receiving room. Beyond it was the larger of two drawing rooms. Behind it was the staff dining room, which seated twelve. To the left of the main entrance was a small parlor. Through the parlor was a study.

Further down the hall past the parlor was the smaller drawing room. The dining room was next, featuring an enormous table. The kitchen was the last room on that side of the first floor, with the pantry next to it. Below the kitchen was a root cellar, and under the staff dining room was the armory.

Lucy took me to the smaller drawing room. A dark-skinned man with only a fringe of white hair around his bald head was seated at the desk writing. When he saw us, he stood up.

"Caz, I'd like you to meet Ellis Williston, deputy master of the royal household. Mr. Williston, my husband, Lord Oritur," she said.

Williston gave a slight bow. "Milord," he said.

"Mr. Williston, thank you for helping my wife gain control of this mess," I said.

"Aye," he grunted. "It surely is that."

"Do you think you can put things to rights?" I asked.

"Aye. We start in earnest tomorrow," he said. "I sent Lady Oritur's man Theo to town to buy cleaning supplies—brooms, mops, rags, buckets, soap, vinegar, and mineral spirits. When we booked our rooms at the inn, I asked the owner to spread the word that we are hoping to hire staff. We'll be offering the same wages as Manton and Gulick, and all found. Lady Oritur knew what the proper rate of pay is. I asked the innkeeper to tell folks who are interested to come to the manor first thing tomorrow."

"How many people are we hiring?" I asked.

"You have a master of the household in Theo. You need a groom, a cook, and at least three maids. Your father hired the gate guards. You will also need to hire some temporary labor if you want to be able to live here anytime soon. The stables aren't even fit for pigs right now. Neither is most of the manor," Williston said, shaking his head. "You also need a builder to come to look at the structures. There are roof leaks, broken windows, and the gods only know what else. It looks like no one spent even a wheathead on keeping the place from falling down."

"Not for about twenty years," I commented.

"It looks it," he agreed. "Oh! You also need to buy a terrier. You have rats. Maybe a cat, for the mice."

"We already have something for the mice," Lucy said.

"Tomorrow, if we have workers, we start on quarters for the maids, the cook, and the groom. The sooner we get those done, the quicker they move in," he said. "They can't stay here as it is now. After that, address your rooms and the public rooms. Then, the rest of the rooms above the stable. Plus, cleaning up once repairs are finished. You were right to send for me, milord. It would have been unfair to put this all on Lady Oritur, no matter how capable she is."

"Hearing the list you just rattled off, I'm grateful the queen was willing to give you leave to help us. What remains to be done today?" I asked.

"We've done as much here as we can for today," he said. "I suggest we return to the inn, have a nice meal and a good night's sleep, and prepare to tackle all this tomorrow. So you two go on ahead. I'll follow presently."

"I left Bella at the inn," Lucy said.

"This poor old horse can barely carry me, so riding double is out," I said. "I'll walk with you."

We said goodnight to Kersant Lewiston and continued down the street. Once out of earshot, I turned to Lucy.

"Were you able to get the house in the city organized?" I asked.

"Nearly," she replied. "I was still waiting on a couple of things to arrive. Greta is keeping an eye out for them. My mother sent a woman older than Betsy to stay in the house and keep it ready for us, whenever we return."

"That's good. Did I leave you enough money to furnish the house to your liking?" I asked.

"More than enough," Lucy answered. "I brought fifteen hundred ducats with me."

I smacked my forehead with my palm. "I forgot to have one of the banks obtain funds from my account in the city. Damme! I wanted to transfer ten thousand here for your use in putting the manor back in order. From what Mr. Williston said, you might need all of it."

"The biggest expense will be the builder," Lucy said. "And that can wait until the funds arrive. We will also need furniture. I think the people Theo ran off were too lazy to gather firewood and burned some tables, chairs, and dressers."

I groaned. "The bank should only take nine or ten days," I said. "Now, tell me how Theo came with you."

"I thought that would have been your first question," she teased. "Blame Freddy. He saw this as an opportunity to be rid of Theo. Father and Uncle David agreed, and, yes, they know how Theo feels toward you. They feel he is capable of running the household here, though. I must admit, I agree. He won't be the cook, so you shouldn't have to worry about him preparing his little surprises in your food. Theo was brilliant today in running off the two women who were living here in squalor. I think he will be an asset. Besides, he answers to me, not to you. That will make things easier. Plus, for at least the remainder of the year, he will be too busy to worry about you."

"If you say so," I grumbled.

"I do," she said. "Now it's your turn. Tell me what you have been doing. Your father said you have been busy but did not share many details."

For the remainder of our walk to the inn, I told her of the battles in which we engaged. Lucy was especially interested in how I managed to put our limited numbers in the correct place. I finished by mentioning that I was wounded and, more important, so was Andy. That was how I was allowed to come to see her.

"I noticed—your left arm?" she asked.

I nodded.

"I have something for that," she said. "I will also teach you some incantations that should allow you to make use of your affinity with Eir. That way, if you or Andy are wounded again, you can speed the healing."

"That would be wonderful," I said gratefully.

Lucy and I both were blessed with ties to some of our Minor Gods. We both have connections with Eir, the goddess of healing, and Njörun, the goddess of good fortune. Those are our lesser influences. However, our dominant links are different. Lucy's dominant is Freyja, the goddess of romance and sexual pleasure. Mine is Bellona, the war goddess. According to Lucy, the reason we are so compatible is the two connections we have in common. I knew nothing whatsoever about my latent affinity until I met Lucy. I still don't know much, though I traveled to the Temple of Bellona and learned more about my dominant and how to access and control that power. Those who have read my earlier tales have already heard about our religion, so I won't waste your time reviewing it again.

"Something else is troubling you," she commented.

"Many things are troubling me," I replied. "My father allowing the manor to fall into such decay, the reduced number of armsmen. If King Mark followed through on his plan to name Lord Weald as my father's successor, it would have been a disaster."

"No. There's something else," Lucy stated.

I thought for a few strides. "Everything we do is in reaction to the nomads. They dictate the action. They decide where and when to attack. I want to seize the initiative," I said.

"Then do it," she replied.

"We don't have enough men to attack them," I explained. "It would be at least three to one against us."

"Is that the only course of action available to you?" she asked.

My face fell. A few days before, I felt I was on the verge of a good idea, but it kept dancing away from me. I was going to access my link with Bellona to see if that would help me, but I forgot.

"Please remind me tomorrow to draw upon Bellona," I asked.

I explained how I had forgotten, then asked about her journey to Easton.

"It was pleasant. I rode Bella and Theo drove the wagon. We fell in with the men who went to Bannock Hill with your father today. They were a high-spirited bunch. They were happy to return to the kind of work they love."

"You brought a wagon?"

"How else was I to bring our clothing and other necessities?" she chided. "Not only did I need to pack my own things on short notice, I also had to gather yours!"

"I'm sorry, my love," I apologized quickly. "I wasn't thinking. A part of me hasn't yet grasped the idea that this is not a temporary assignment—it's my ... *our* life from now on. I'm glad you're thinking for both of us. Think of what a hash I would make of things if you weren't here. It's one reason why I asked you to hurry."

"One reason?"

"I'll show you another reason after dinner," I teased.

"If I have forgiven you by then," she taunted.

We arrived at the inn, the Rider's Rest. I took the old horse to the stable behind and turned her over to the groom. If it were Andy, I would have cared for him myself, but I did not know this horse, so I felt less guilty. Lucy waited for me patiently, and we entered the common room together.

Realizing I was the lord to Lucy being Lady Oritur, the innkeeper fell all over himself to greet us. I desperately needed a hot bath and was tempted to ask for one before dinner but I realized his people would be at their busiest right now. So instead, I asked for one after we ate.

"You're not so bad," Lucy commented. "A bit of sweat, leather, and horse, but not as gamy as I expected."

"I've been able to wash up in streams occasionally," I said, "but I feel filthy."

Lucy took me up to our room. It was in the corner of the building and quite large. With four windows wide open, it was airy and pleasant. Thinking of my bath later, I realized I brought no change of clothing with me from Bannock Hill. I mentioned it to Lucy.

"Well," she said with a naughty gleam in her eye, "you won't be needing clothes after your bath, but I can see how tomorrow morning might present a problem. The wagon is behind the manor. Now that there are adequate guards at the gate, we felt that was the safest place for it."

I left by myself. Rather than saddling the old horse for such a brief journey, I decided to walk. It would give me the chance to access my power and try to find out what idea was trying to get out of my head.

The streets were emptying as it was near dinner time. I searched within myself and tugged forth a tiny tendril of Bellona's essence. It was not even five paces before I knew exactly what to do. The answer was simple and straightforward—so much so that I wondered if it had ever been done before. Even better, I now had the men to implement this plan.

I tucked the tendril I grasped back into place. Even though I wanted to laugh out loud, there were still some people about, and I didn't want them to think me mad. Still, I almost felt like skipping back to the manor.

Kersant Lewiston was still at his post when I returned. After we exchanged greetings, I proceeded in, then stopped. I figured the kersant would know the answer to my question.

"Kersant, do you know where I could buy a terrier?" I asked.

He paused a moment. "For milady? Or a ratter?" he inquired.

"A ratter," I said. "The dog will probably live in the stable but have free run of the whole place. If Lucy wants a dog, we'll worry about that later."

"That woman of your father's," he spat. "What a plague she was upon this house! And her two weak-chinned, snotty whelps. Good riddance to all of 'em, I say. So, you have rats. In the stable, I'm guessing. In the manor, too?"

I nodded.

Lewiston shook his head sadly. "The old earl, if he knew…" he muttered, then regained his focus. "I know a fella," he said, addressing me. "He breeds and trains ratters. You'll be wanting a trained dog and not a pup. He generally has one or two he keeps out of every litter. I'll speak with him in the morning and have him come to see you."

"Thank you," I said.

4

I continued up to the manor and went around back. The wagon was packed with trunks stacked two high and tied down with rope. I recognized one of mine on the bottom layer. After untying the knots, I clambered up on top of the trunks, lifted the one above mine and placed it behind me. I jumped down and was able to slide mine out without making the rest topple.

The clothes inside were better suited for cooler temperatures, but I didn't want to linger. Dinner with my wife was waiting. I would return in the morning and find more suitable attire.

I hurried back to the inn with my clothes in a small bundle under my arm,. Lucy was waiting in the common room. I sped up to our room, dropped my clothes, and then returned to her. No sooner did I arrive when the innkeeper appeared and escorted us to the table.

"You don't need to remind me tomorrow about…" I said. "I did that on the way back to the manor. The idea I was unable to form came to me."

"Good. Care to share what it is?" Lucy asked.

"Not really," I said. "I need to discuss it with my father and some of the more experienced men first. It might be brilliant, but there could also be a hundred things wrong with it. So I'm trying to temper my excitement."

"Is there anything else I should remind you?" she asked, teasing.

"Yes. I *must* go to the bank," I replied. "Other than that, I'm all yours."

"Good. I have plenty to keep you busy," she said.

While we waited for our food, I mentioned that Kersant Lewiston might know of someone who bred terriers. I cautioned her that this dog would not be much of a pet and would probably live in the stable. Then, I asked her about the mice.

"Chauncey," she answered.

"Even inside the manor?"

"The rooms are large," she replied, "and the ceilings are high. As long as we keep the furniture well away from the walls at first, he can eliminate that problem quickly."

"We could always get a cat," I suggested.

"I don't like cats," she said. "They are too lazy and self-important."

"Huh," I grunted. "I thought you, being … you know…"

"A witch," she said with a smile. "You have never used that word, I've noticed. You can say it. Especially since no one can overhear us right now."

"I don't much like the word," I admitted. "You're so much more than that."

She blushed. "Thank you. Anyway, the whole thing about witches and cats is nonsense. From what I learned growing up, familiars—the animals that bond with people like us—are the ones who initiate the relationship. Chauncey found me. I did not find him. It was his decision to ally himself with me. Cats are among the least likely to do that. As I said, they are too self-important, self-absorbed, and less intelligent than people think."

After a moment's pause, I laid my most significant worry on the table. "Are you happy, my love?" I asked, clasping her hand. "I couldn't bear it if you weren't. If this way of life is not to your liking—"

"Don't be ridiculous, Caz," she scolded me. "Remember, I knew what awaited me when I agreed to marry you. I will admit that finding the manor in such a sad state was an unpleasant surprise but that will quickly pass and we will all feel a sense of accomplishment from putting it back to rights. This is the life I saw my mother lead, and she set a fine example. She does not spend her days in Gulick Manor. She spends them with the people of the duchy, helping wherever she can. I intend to do the same, and I have abilities my mother does not. I'm looking forward to getting to know the people of the March."

Not to sound soppy, but my heart swelled hearing her response. It filled me with gratitude that a woman so capable agreed to share her life with me. I sent silent thanks to Njörun for this great good fortune while I gently squeezed Lucy's hand.

After dinner, we repaired to our room and found a hot bath waiting. This was the first scrub I would be able to enjoy since leaving the capital. Lucy joined me in the tub as she wanted to wash after her journey. It was a tight fit, but I certainly didn't mind. Lucy admonished me when my hands began to wander, but it spurred us to complete our ablutions and commence other highly pleasurable activities.

Later, Lucy rummaged in her bag and retrieved a small jar. Dipping her fingers in it, she rubbed the salve on the wound in my left bicep. It hurt at first, but the pain was soon replaced by a warm, pleasant sensation. Before she started rubbing it in, she began to murmur something.

"Calling upon Eir?" I asked after she stopped.

She nodded. "Before you return to Bannock Hill, I'll teach it to you."

In the morning, I rose with the sun, dressing in the clothing I retrieved from the wagon. Lucy woke while I dressed. She stopped me before I put on my shirt and rubbed some more of the salve into my wound, again softly mumbling before she started. When I finished dressing, I left her and headed downstairs hoping to breakfast. Theo was there.

Theo was a hulk of a man. I'm not small, standing at six feet, two inches, but Theo had at least three inches on me. His shoulders were wider, and his chest was deeper. I pictured him confronting the slovenly woman and the insolent gate guard I encountered in the manor upon my arrival a few weeks earlier. I began to chuckle. Theo looked at me, expressionless.

"Thank you for clearing some of the vermin out of the manor," I said. "I was just imagining how it must have looked."

Theo's expression slowly changed. A ghastly smile grew on his face. Then, he began to laugh, a macabre sound I only heard once before—huh, huh, huh.

Lucy arrived, and the innkeeper immediately came to make a fuss over her. He led us into the dining room, where various breakfast offerings were already laid out. We filled our plates. Theo went to sit at a different table, but Lucy brought him to sit with us. Theo did not look happy to be sitting with me.

"Theo, are you mad because you couldn't prepare a special surprise for me in my breakfast?" I teased.

He looked—not quite at me, but just to the side of me—his face devoid of expression.

"Theo, I realize you probably still dislike me," I said. "I hope you still care for Lucy. Please understand that, in your new duties, Lucy is your employer, not me. You need to please her. If you still wish to disapprove of me, that's fine—as long as it does not interfere with whatever Lucy wishes for you to accomplish."

This time Theo turned his blank countenance directly to me and nodded slowly. I felt like breathing a sigh of relief but did not dare in front of Lucy. Theo frowned upon everyone except Lucy. He had stated before she was the only person he liked.

Mr. Williston joined us. After exchanging polite good mornings, I asked, "Mr. Williston, I need to open an account with a local bank, today if possible. Would you be able to make some inquiries this morning about which I should choose?"

"Yes. Our innkeeper is quite a chatty fellow and a bit of a gossip," Williston replied. "If he doesn't know the answer, he will be able to send me to someone who does."

After breakfast, Lucy and I walked hand in hand to the manor. Kersant Lewiston was not at the gate. However, another man of similar age was. Like Lewiston, his armor gleamed, and he wielded a pike. As we drew nearer, I thought I recognized him as well.

When we reached the gate, he bowed deeply, saying, "Lady Oritur." He opened the gate. When I tried to follow Lucy, he lowered his pike, barring my way.

"I'm under strict instructions not to allow hooligans past the gate," he said. "Kersant Lewiston warned me a certain miscreant would try to get past me, but I swore to do my duty."

"Are you still upset about the dancing lessons, Mr. Clausen," I asked. "That was my grandfather's doing. But, I will admit, they have been useful at times..."

Clausen lifted his pike out of the way, standing it up and tucking it in the crook of his elbow, then imitated my grandfather quite well, clapping in time and calling out, "One, two, three, four, and one, two, three, four."

Lucy looked on with amusement.

"I believe I told you my grandfather insisted I learn how to dance," I explained. "Mr. Clausen was one of the armsmen forced to be my partner. Paulie

Florio, one of the kersants I was riding with, was another. I'm pretty sure they found it every bit as embarrassing as I did."

"Yes, we did, milady," Clausen agreed. Then, changing the subject, he added, "I see you carry his blade."

"He left it to me when he died," I said. "It is the second-most valuable thing I possess."

"Aye? And what's the first?" he asked.

"The love of a woman who is far too good for the likes of me," I replied, nodding in Lucy's direction.

"Yes, I would agree that is more of a treasure," Clausen stated. "So, I get to call you milord now. My tongue will find it much easier to wrap around that word for you than for the other two. Good riddance to bad rubbish, I say."

"Well, they're gone now, and we have work to do," I said.

"Mr. Clausen," Lucy said, "there will be some people coming to inquire about positions here. So please send them up when they arrive."

"Aye, milady," he acknowledged.

About halfway to the manor from the gate, I told Lucy, "I'm going to change into more appropriate clothes and get started on the stables. Holler if you need me."

"Your other trunks are in front of the one where you found what you're wearing," she said. "Sorry. Since you'll need to move everything around, you might as well unload the wagon."

"Yes'm," I replied, knuckling my forelock.

"Stop it!" she protested, laughing.

I unloaded the wagon, trunk by trunk. Thankfully, it was still the cool of morning. I tried to arrange the chests, putting aside the three I recognized as mine. Some of Lucy's were quite heavy. I reckoned those contained some of her concoctions. The first I opened held clothes suitable for working in the summer heat. I stripped down right there and changed. Then I went to the stable.

I smelled it long before I reached it. The stench was so powerful that I needed to retreat. Entering through the kitchen, I found the odor there was also offensive but not as overpowering as the stable. I called out for Lucy as I progressed into the manor. When she answered, I determined where she was and went to her.

"Do you have any peppermint oil?" I asked.

"Yes. Why?"

"The reek in the stable is so bad," I said, "that I will need to cover my face with a handkerchief. Soaking it in peppermint oil will help mask the stink."

"I'm sure I do. Come with me, and I'll get it," she said.

Returning outside, she went to one of the heavy chests and opened it. Arranged neatly within were bottles and jars. She paused a moment, remembering, then dug inside. After moving some things aside, she pulled up a clear glass bottle.

"I can tell I'm going to need much more of this before we're through," she said.

"Lady Oritur!" came a call from the house.

Williston had opened a window and was leaning out.

"Yes?"

"Some people are here for interviews," he replied.

"On my way," she called back. "Go ahead and soak your handkerchief but leave the bottle here. We'll need it when we tackle the kitchen."

With the treated cloth in place, I returned to the stable. The smell of the peppermint oil did not eliminate the wretched stench. Still, it did make it possible to continue without gagging. Every stall appeared to be at least ankle-deep in manure. If there was straw laid down, I couldn't see it. There were odds and ends of tack, all needing repair or irretrievably ruined. I looked for a shovel and a barrow. Not finding either, I went outside and started to walk around the building until I found them. They were not near the building but had been left next to the remnants of the manure pile. I spotted them in the overgrown weeds.

Upon closer inspection, neither one would be of much use. Left out in the elements, the wood on both was beginning to rot. I heard the bells in town chime nine o'clock. The banks would be open, and I could see about buying a new barrow and shovel. Entering through the kitchen again instead of the more formal rear entrance, I followed the sound of voices until I came upon Lucy and Williston.

They were in the smaller drawing room that was almost presentable. The larger drawing room, the receiving room, the parlor, and the study were not fit for occupancy. There were five young women and one man standing in the hall outside. I nodded at them pleasantly and entered the room. Williston and Lucy were talking with a woman. Lucy looked up and saw me.

"Oh, good. You're here," she said. "The man outside is interested in speaking with you about becoming our groom. Would you please talk to him?"

I nodded and left the room. "Hello, Mr…?"

"Collinwood, sir, uh, milord," he stammered, "Tom Collinwood."

"Collinwood," I mused. "Collinwood… Any relation to the Collinwood who was the groom here twenty or so years ago?"

"My uncle," he replied.

"How is he?" I asked.

"He's well, milord. I'm sort of here for the both of us," Collinwood stated.

"The both of you?"

"Aye. My uncle and me."

"Where is your uncle?"

"He took on with Baron Winstonworth about twenty leagues west of here when he left Easton."

"Why did he leave?" I asked.

Collinwood looked uneasy. It was clear that he did not know whether he was allowed to say. I took pity on him.

"Was it because of Lady Easton?"

"Aye, milord," he said, obviously relieved that I brought it up. "He said she kept on 'forgetting' to pay him. When he went to remind her, she would screech at him. He told me he stood it as long as he could, but when she tried to cut his wages in half, he left. He's been with Baron Winstonworth since but has never been too happy there."

"And what about you?" I asked. "What experience do you have?"

"That's one of the reasons I'm here for the both of us, milord," Collinwood said, wringing his hands nervously. His words began to gush forth. "I don't know much about horses other than I love 'em. If you take me on, my uncle will come too, and he promised to teach me everything he knows. You wouldn't have to pay but one of us. The job is all found, right? That's good enough for me."

"That's correct—all found. Wages plus lodging and meals. Your uncle wants to leave Winstonworth?" I inquired.

"Yes, milord," Collinwood replied, still eager to talk. "Says Winstonworth is a prat and mistreats his animals. Beats 'em, he does. Uncle Ted says if things are back to the way they used to be, he'd be here in a minute."

"What are you doing for work now?" I asked.

"Fieldwork," he said. "It's alright, but I'd rather learn to be a groom, milord."

"When could you start?" I inquired.

"Me? I could start right away, milord," Collinwood answered quickly. "My uncle might need a few days."

"Here is what I propose, Tom. We'll pay you as a general laborer for now and your uncle as a groom. That's about twice your pay. When he decides you deserve it, you'll get paid the same as he does. It's actually a good thing your uncle can't come right away. The stable is disgusting, and it would break his heart to see it. Our first job, you and me, is to clean it up. How does that sound?"

Collinwood's eyes and his mouth opened wide. "Cor, milord! That's better than I hoped!"

"You won't be able to live here until we get things cleaned up," I cautioned. "Where are you living now?"

"With my folks," he said. "That won't be a problem, milord."

"And you need to inform your employer that you're leaving."

"That's no trouble neither. It's the slow time, and he ain't had work for me for a few weeks."

"Nevertheless, you owe him advance warning," I said. "You'll need to do that today."

"Aye, milord."

"Good. Let me tell Lady Oritur and Mr. Williston about you, then you can come into town with me."

I stuck my head through the door of the drawing room where Lucy and Mr. Williston were. After telling them that Tom Collinwood was now a member of the staff, I informed them we were heading to town. I was going to the bank while Tom would be searching for a barrow and two shovels.

Mr. Williston excused himself to the young woman with whom he was speaking and came to me. "The sense I got from our innkeeper is that Farmers and Mercantile is the largest bank here, but they are strictly local. Bannister

Brothers would be a better choice if you have interests elsewhere in the kingdom."

In a previous adventure, Bannister Brothers provided tremendous assistance. That was enough to convince me to establish my account with them. I gathered Tom, who was chatting up one of the women waiting to see Lucy and Mr. Williston, and we headed to town.

5

s we walked into Easton, I instructed Tom to find a sturdy barrow and two shovels suitable for scooping manure. When he saw them for sale, he was to meet me at Bannister Brothers. Once I was inside the bank offices, a young man quickly rose to greet me and ask if he could help. He invited me into an office.

"Your name, sir?" he asked.

"Casimir FitzDuncan," I replied, "though I was just granted the title of Lord Oritur."

"Oh," he said. "You're the one. I'm sorry, milord. I'm afraid I cannot help you. Mr. Bannister will insist on working with you himself. Would you please wait a moment while I ensure he is free?"

Many times in the past, the class structure in Aquileia annoyed and frustrated me. But, since being named Lord Oritur, the few times I mentioned my title, the reactions mostly amused me. I was still the same bastard I'd been since birth, but—Majors and Minors!—the difference in how I was treated!

The young man scurried in two minutes later. "If you'll come with me, milord," he said.

I followed him to a significantly larger and more grandly appointed office. A well-dressed, distinguished-looking gentleman greeted me with a slight bow of his head. His appearance was similar enough to the man I met in Newcastle that I could see they were family.

"Please come in, milord," he said expansively. "May I offer you some refreshment?"

Deciding to play with him a little, I asked, "Would you by any chance have some qava?"

I managed to keep from laughing out loud when the man's face fell. "I'm sorry, milord. No. I can offer some tea?" he asked hopefully.

"No, thank you," I responded in a disappointed tone.

Mr. Bannister looked crestfallen. Here I was, perhaps the largest potential customer in Easton, and he was already falling short of my desires. I was willing to wager that the next time I visited this office, they would have qava available.

"How may I be of service today, milord?" he asked.

I explained about needing to transfer money from my bank in the city of Aquileia to his. He knew my bank and assured me there would be no difficulty. I gave him my account numbers and asked for him to obtain ten thousand ducats as soon as possible. He excused himself and stepped to the door.

"Roger!" he hollered. "Bring the account ledger!"

This was a part of Aquileian culture that always amused me. Most people believed that the nobility and the upper class were genteel and refined. They thought their social betters would surely summon servants in a polite and refined manner. As a result, thinking they were acting properly, members of the aspiring middle class bought little silver bells that they would ring to call their staff. The reality was that the upper classes had no need for delicate tinkling silver bells. Instead, they yelled for their servants like a dockside innkeeper would bellow at the serving wenches.

Roger came huffing and puffing a minute later, bearing a huge leather-bound ledger. He set it on the corner of Bannister's desk. Bannister then waved him out.

Sitting down, Bannister slid the ledger to the center of his desk, then used the ribbon to open it to the current page. He took a quill and dipped it into his inkwell. First, he copied the account number onto a small piece of paper on his desk. Then he wrote my name in the ledger next to that number.

"Is there anyone else you would allow to access this account?" he inquired.

"Yes, Lady Oritur," I replied. "She will have more need of these funds in the near future than I."

Bannister wrote that in the book. He rotated it on his desk and held the quill out to me. "Please sign," he asked, pointing to where he needed my signature.

"Lady Oritur will need to come to sign the ledger as well," he instructed. "I will draft the letter immediately and get it in the express post before midday. Today is Onsday. I should have confirmation from the city a week from today, if not the day before."

"That's faster than I expected," I commented. "I would not think it so easy to transfer that amount of gold as quickly as that."

Bannister looked at me with a smile. "Oh, Lord Oritur," he said, "no gold will move back and forth. That would be cumbersome and risky. So instead, they will mark their records that ten thousand ducats of the gold in their vaults is actually owned now by Bannister Brothers. Similarly, we have gold in our vaults that is the property of other institutions. If the numbers ever reach a point where there is a serious imbalance, I suppose they or we might demand the physical transfer of gold. As it is, there is enough commerce and interplay between us that the amounts we hold for one another are roughly equal."

"So if I wanted to rob a bank, all I would need to do is fiddle with the account ledger?" I asked.

"The only problem with that," he replied smiling, "is that I would have no memory of the transaction. All sizeable transfers and disbursements go through me. This piece of paper has your account number. We can always look it up in the ledger if you lose it or forget it."

We finished our business, and Bannister himself escorted me out the door. Tom Collinwood was waiting for me. After Bannister and I shook hands, I let Tom lead me away. He'd found a hard goods merchant who sold barrows and shovels.

We went to the store. I ended up buying two barrows, four shovels, and four pitchforks. While there, I asked the merchant who the manure dealer in Easton was. He gave me the name. I would need to schedule him to come collect in a few days once we cleaned out the stable. Straw would be another thing I would need to order. The merchant suggested coming to the city market on Njordday.

"Straw, hay, feed—you'll find sources for all of it," he said.

Tom and I returned to the manor, each pushing a barrow. When we neared the stable, I asked him if he had a handkerchief or sweat rag. When he produced the dirty piece of cloth from his pocket, I poured peppermint oil on it and refreshed mine as well.

"Tie it over your nose and mouth, or you won't be able to stand it," I said. "Our first order of business is to clear out the manure."

Tom nodded. I threw the main stable doors open, and we entered. Even with the peppermint oil, I knew we would not be able to stay inside long. Following me, we pushed our barrows to the left end of the stable. It did not take long for us to fill our barrows. Before we even filled the barrows, we encountered rats. We pushed the filled barrows out and around back to where the manure pile was. After dumping them, we retreated. I took the rag from my face and gulped deep lungfuls of air. Tom did the same.

After a minute, I began to chuckle. "Do you think that someday, you'll tell your grandchildren, 'I used to shovel shit with Lord Oritur,' Tom?"

"Aye, milord," he said with a grin. "Maybe I tell them, 'Lord Oritur weren't so bad, kiddies. He put his breeches on one leg at a time and weren't afraid to wade ankle-deep in manure, just like a regular fella.' What do you think, milord?"

"I like it, Tom," I said. "Oh well, back to it."

We kept working. I was not able to keep pace with Tom. My wound began to ache. As the sun climbed higher, it grew hot. Neither of us dared to strip off our shirts due to the flies. We kept going until I heard a clanging noise from the back of the manor. I signaled to Tom, and we broke off and went outside. Lucy saw us and stopped banging an iron triangle.

"Mr. Williston went to get lunch," she called. "He should return any minute. You both need to wash before you eat."

Lucy handed me a cake of soap. Tom and I took turns on the pump. We even dunked our heads under the water. Nevertheless, Lucy refused to sit anywhere near us. With her were Theo and four of the women from the morning.

One was older, a round-faced plump woman with a winning smile. Lucy introduced her as Laurie, and she was to be our cook. The other three were younger and cute in a fresh-faced way. They were Rose, Hazel, and Gladys. None of them seemed particularly interested in me. Tom, however, was the target of shy glances and giggles from all of them.

Mr. Williston arrived while Tom and I were finishing washing. He brought food from the inn. Tom and I ate quickly and returned to our unpleasant task. From overhearing conversation, the job of cleaning the kitchen was nearly as unpleasant as the stable. Before I returned to work, Lucy treated my arm again.

At five o'clock, Lucy banged on the triangle again, telling us the workday was over. She asked the new members of our staff to return no later than eight in the morning. I grabbed some more clothes from one of my trunks, then Theo, Mr. Williston, Lucy, and I returned to the inn. Thanks to Lucy, a bath was already waiting for us in our room.

"I'm going first," she said, "since you are far filthier."

The next day we started right away. Just after nine o'clock, Tom and I were interrupted by the arrival of a man driving a small pony cart. The cart was full of cages.

"John Joiner," he said, extending his hand. "Jed Lewiston tells me you have a rat problem."

"Casimir FitzDuncan," I replied, taking his hand after I wiped mine on my breeches. "We do. I'm not ready for you to help me here in the stable. You've caught a whiff, and I wouldn't subject a dog to that stench. They can use you in the manor, though."

"You understand that I may need to pull up floorboards and open up some walls to get at 'em?" he asked.

I nodded. "Let me help," I suggested. "While my wife will probably not be too fussed, some of the staff might."

"All we'll need you to do is keep 'em from scurrying away and occasionally brain one," Joiner said. "Dogs'll do the rest."

"I'll warn them we're coming," I said.

There was a growing pile of refuse outside the rear entrance. I walked past it and over to the kitchen door. No one was there, but from looking at how improved it was, they were clearly ready to move to another room.

"Lucy!" I called.

She came gliding in. The grace of her movement always struck me. Her hair was pulled back, but some tendrils escaped and clung to her cheeks, which were flushed from exertion. To me, she looked magnificent.

"Yes, Caz?"

"The ratter is here," I announced. "We're not ready for him in the stable, so he will start in here. I wanted to warn you in case some of the staff are squeamish. He might need to open the floor and walls too."

"Thank you," she said. "I figured he would. His dogs will find plenty in the pantry and root cellar. We were clearing out the pantry but needed to stop. I'm surprised you didn't hear the girls screaming."

Suddenly, I heard the scrabbling of paws on the kitchen floor. I turned and went to watch. By the time I cleared the door to the kitchen, I could already see two dead rats. All six dogs were in the pantry.

"I'm hoping there was nothing in there you wanted to keep," Joiner said as the dogs were digging through the sacks and tins in search of their prey.

A rat escaped the dogs and tried to make a break for it, but Joiner bashed it with a stick at the threshold. One of the dogs came and shook it vigorously. When it determined the rat was dead, the dog return to the hunt in the pantry.

Another rat was flushed out. One of Joiner's dogs was on it in a flash. The dog's jaws snapped on the rat's back. The dog gave it a furious shake, then tossed the dead rat aside. One of the dogs had jumped up to the third shelf and was nosing along the wall, toppling sacks, tins, and jars out of his way and onto the floor. A rat jumped to escape but was caught in midair by another dog. Joiner picked up a dog and put it on the highest shelf. He then took another for the second-highest. They began prodding and poking their way along the shelves, unconcerned with the things they were knocking to the floor.

"Sorry about the mess," Joiner apologized.

"Better a mess than rats," I replied. "We can clean up the mess. Getting rid of rats is something only they can do."

It did not take long before the dogs had killed or chased away all the rats in the pantry. Joiner found the door to the root cellar. He whistled, and the dogs came bounding over. I could sense their excitement and happiness. For them, this was fun. The dogs jumped down into the cellar, not bothering with the steep steps. Looking down, I observed the same controlled frenzy I witnessed in the pantry. Since I was serving no useful purpose, I asked Mr. Joiner to find me when he finished.

It was nearly midday when he left the manor with all six dogs on his heels. He opened the cages on the back of his pony cart, and the dogs jumped in. Joiner came to me with a smile on his face.

"We only needed to get into the floor twice and the walls once," he said. "We'll return in a few days when you have the stable cleared out. We'll go through the manor again, too. Jed said you're looking to buy a dog, too."

"I am. There's no sense going through this over and over again," I said.

"True enough," Joiner replied. "Now, if I sell you one of my dogs, you have to understand it's not a pet."

"I do," I assured him. "He'll probably live here in the stable. We'll fix a cozy corner, but this will be his home—not the manor. When the time comes, I'll want you to teach our man Theo, and Tom here, how to work with him. We'll want him to come through the manor every so often to ensure the rats don't come back."

"That sounds good to me," Joiner agreed.

"What do I owe you for today?" I asked.

"Nothing. We'll settle up when I come back," Joiner said.

Shortly after Mr. Joiner left, Jon Sinchak, the third gate guard, summoned me. There were six men on horses at the gate. Looking up at them, I recognized two from the Rangers.

"Mr. Sinchak, please let these men through," I said.

I greeted Al and Ike, whom I remembered. The other four introduced themselves to me. I welcomed all of them and gave them the directions to Bannock Hill. They should arrive by nightfall. Though all wore blades, none had armor beyond the boiled leather jerkin the Rangers wore. I took them to the armory below the manor. There was not much remaining, but they did find six serviceable bows and quivers. I sent them off and told them I would see them again soon.

That evening, Marta and Susannah were waiting for us at the inn. Marta is Lucy's mother, and Susannah is her aunt. Dinner that night was lively, as both women were peppering Lucy and Mr. Williston with questions. That evening,

Lucy taught me the incantation or charm she muttered when rubbing the salve into my wound. I'd repeat it, but you wouldn't understand.

The next afternoon, my father appeared. He looked morose. I took a break from shoveling manure to see what was wrong.

"They came to Norvost yesterday," he said. "We lost three men and their mounts."

"Who?"

"Part of the group with Gus Polever," he said. "It's my fault. I didn't recognize what the enemy was planning, and the three of them got caught in range when the nomads wheeled on us. Then I come back here to see you shoveling shit. You shouldn't have to do that—also my fault. I've—"

"Father," I interrupted, "what's done is done. If you want to sit there and moan about it, go ahead. I prefer to move on and spend my energy putting things back to rights."

The reason he came back was to check with the smith who was making the armor and to add six more breast plates and helmets. He also needed to make arrangements with his bank to collect the men's pay at the end of the month. Finally, he wanted to check on our progress.

I showed him what we accomplished so far. Seeing it darkened his mood further. He left to make his calls. I went to Marta and Susannah and asked them to sit with him at dinner that evening, telling them what sort of temperament he was in.

When I said goodbye to him in the morning, he seemed to be in a better frame of mind but not by much. Since today was the first day of Heyannir, some of the armsmen would arrive by midday to escort him back to camp. They would drive a wagon with the pay chest to Bannock Hill. The armsmen on duty when I arrived would also be receiving the back pay my father had withheld earlier due to lack of funds. Everyone else would receive a full month's pay, even the men from the capital who had just arrived. That was my decision. The detachments from Quinn's Ford and Clearview would ride in, collect their money and return to their encampments.

The next day was also Njordday—market day throughout the kingdom of Aquileia. I took a break from moving manure and went to the market with Lucy. I was searching for someone who would deliver straw and someone with hay.

When I found each one, I arranged for delivery in two weeks. Then I went to look for Lucy. As on earlier occasions elsewhere, I had no difficulty spotting her in a crowd. It was as though the Gods shone a special light on my wife.

As we returned to the manor, she remarked, "This is a surprisingly rich market."

"In what ways?"

"Variety of wares, quality, and abundance of the produce," she said.

For the balance of our walk, I explained to her what I knew of the richness and fertility of the soil here in the March.

It was Onsday again before the stable was cleared enough that the stench began to subside. The manure dealer had come earlier and taken away the huge pile we created behind the stable. He complained that it was unusable. Since I agreed, we agreed on a charge of ten florins for him to dispose of it.

Though the manure was cleared out of the stable, there were small heaps of straw and hay that had long since gone bad and feed sacks with holes, most more than half empty. Mr. Joiner came back with the dogs, and they had an absolute lark. The rats were hiding in the hay and straw. Tom Collinwood and I were forking it into our barrows while the dogs were clawing their way deeper into the piles.

When we eliminated the last of the straw and hay, the dogs gathered at a spot on the back wall. Mr. Joiner used a prybar to pull away the rotted board, and the dogs charged in. Ten more rats were dead in seconds, joining the dozens the dogs dispatched earlier. With that done, the animals sniffed around some more but then returned to Mr. Joiner.

We went upstairs to the quarters above the stable. There were a dozen rooms of decent size. Each had a bed, a dresser with a wash basin atop, and a small table with a chair. The dogs went room by room. In one, they tore open the mattress, only to find the remains of an old nest. The dogs found more prey in the linen closet where sheets, blankets, and towels were stored,. Two of the dogs burrowed into the closet, and rats came bolting out. The other dogs snapped them up. The two who went into the pile of bedclothes each came out with one in his mouth. Mr. Joiner lifted the pile of sheets with his stick, and there were two other dead rats there.

On our way out, Tom and I opened the window in each room and left the doors open. If there was any sort of a breeze, it would help clear the odor. The mattresses would all need to be replaced. The linens would need to be sorted to see what was still usable, and the ones that were salvageable would need to be boiled clean.

When I returned down the stairs, Joiner had crossed over to his cart and opened five of the cages. When he whistled, the dogs began to leap to their spots. One was left, looking curiously at Mr. Joiner. His cage was shut.

"Tom," Mr. Joiner said, "meet Toby."

"I'll get Theo," I said and trotted to the manor.

I opened the back door and hollered for Theo. He appeared quickly from around the corner. I explained he was needed to learn how to work with the dog. When we returned to Tom and Mr. Joiner, Tom was on his knees, and Toby was sniffing him up and down.

Toby was all black, with a close coat that seemed wavy. When Theo approached, Mr. Joiner asked him to let the dog smell him, too. Theo sank to his knees. Toby took two sniffs of Theo, then jumped up at Theo's chest. Theo reacted, catching Toby in his arms. The dog began licking Theo's chin.

"Majors and Minors!" Joiner exclaimed. "Would you look at that? I have never seen that before."

Toby continued to lick Theo's face. Theo wore an expression I'd never seen him display before. For the first time since I met him, Theo looked happy.

"How much do I owe you, Mr. Joiner?" I asked.

"Twenty florins for Toby and twelve for the ratting," he said. "So, one ducat, eight florins."

"A bargain at twice the price, Mr. Joiner," I said as I retrieved the money from my pouch.

6

With the stable now empty, I wanted to rinse it out. I looked all over but did not find a hose. That required a trip to the merchant from whom we bought the barrows. I returned an hour later and attached it. Tom, Theo, and I took turns on the pump. One of us held the nozzle of the hose, and the third swept the filthy water out. We were just finishing when a man with skin as black as night strode up, carrying papers in his hand.

"I'm looking for Lord Oritur," he said.

I laughed. My current state, sweat-stained, half-wet from the hose, and marked with streaks of grime, certainly did not present a lordly appearance. The man could hardly know which of the three of us was the noble.

I wiped my hand on my breeches and offered it to him. "Casimir FitzDuncan, recently named Lord Oritur. You can see I don't stand on ceremony much."

His laugh was deep and rolling. Even if I were grumpy, I think that sound would make me smile. He shook my hand.

"Greg Pruitt," he said. "Mr. Williston has engaged my services to do some repair work. I've been through the manor and made notes."

"The stable and the rooms above it probably need attention as well," I said. "Would you like me to accompany you or leave you be?"

"If it's all the same with you, milord, I'll come to see you in the manor when I finish," he replied.

"Good enough," I said.

After unfastening the hose from the pump, Theo, Tom, and I took turns washing up. When I finished, I went looking for Lucy. As I approached the rear entrance, I noticed the first pile of rubbish had already been collected, and a second had grown to take its place.

In just a week, Lucy and her group made significant progress. The kitchen was clean enough to use, as was the pantry. In the process of cleaning, we discovered several pots and pans were missing. The china and glassware were mostly intact, but all the silverware was gone, as you might expect. All the serving utensils, trays, and bowls, which I remembered being silver, had also disappeared. Marta told us not to worry. She inherited her family's silver, and it was sitting in storage. She sent a message home asking for it to be shipped and said it would please her if we put it to use.

The public rooms on the ground floor were clean, but some of the few pieces of furniture that remained were marked for replacement. There were odd stains, and even stranger smells on the upholstery. The bedrooms on the second floor were clean. The women were currently working on the third floor, where the staff would live. Once they were clean, Theo would remove all the mattresses. Mr. Williston had been taking measurements and would be ordering new mattresses as soon as he measured the beds above the stable.

When I found the women on the third floor, they were all hot, sweaty, and dust-covered. Just as Mr. Pruitt had difficulty picking Lord Oritur from the three of us outside, he would have been equally hard-pressed to identify which of these seven were Lady Manton, Lady Gulick, and Lady Oritur. I told Lucy that Pruitt was inspecting the stable and would return to review his findings soon. That seemed to be a good enough reason for the women to break off from what they were doing.

When I reached the ground floor, I heard Lewiston bellow for me. There was no one at the gate, so I was puzzled. He waved some paper at me.

"Post, milord," he shouted.

I trotted to the gate and took two envelopes from him. One was from Bannister Brothers. The other was from Pierre Luin, the financier in the capital who managed my investments for me.

The note from Bannister was short. It informed me that my bank in the city acknowledged transferring the ten thousand ducats to Bannister. That meant Lucy could begin drawing money from our Bannister account.

The letter from Pierre was more complicated but also bore glad tidings. First, my investments' quarterly share of income came to just under eleven thousand ducats. The other item was to inform me that one of the buildings of which I was part owner recently sold. My share of the sale was over fifty percent more than I paid. Pierre wanted to know what I wanted to do with the money.

I had forgotten about the quarterly disbursements. With the prospect of expensive repairs and the necessity of replacing ruined or missing household equipment, I was worried that the ten thousand ducats I transferred to Bannister might not be enough. With nearly eleven thousand ducats more coming, there should be plenty. Regarding the proceeds from the building sale, I would write Pierre and ask him to invest all of it in something. The quarterly income he should send in a draft to my account with Bannister Brothers here in Easton.

Lucy saw the letter in my hand and my pleased expression. "Good news, my love?"

"Timely good news," I replied and explained what both letters said before handing them to her.

While she was reading them, I heard a "hallo?" from the kitchen. Figuring it was Mr. Pruitt, I went to collect him. I brought him to the smaller drawing room where my father had moved his desk. He, Lucy, and I sat down, and he went over his notes. It was not as bad as I feared, but neither was it as good as I hoped. When he finished, I asked him how much he thought the total would be.

"Well, milord," he said, "I'm hesitant to give you a number for fear that when we get deeper into the job, we find damage we weren't expecting."

"Mr. Pruitt, Mr. Williston selected you from all the available builders in Easton. You may not know this, but Mr. Williston is the deputy master of the royal household."

Pruitt's eyes widened. He did not know that.

"Mr. Williston did not choose you based on cost. He made his decision based on your reputation. I trust his judgment completely. We recently renovated a house in the city of Aquileia that was in the same state of neglect as this but without the filth. If you are like Mr. Cullion, who did that work for us, you expect to find certain things. I'm well aware that there might be damage no one could foresee behind the plaster, above the ceiling, or below the floor. If that is the case, your original estimate no longer applies. I'm just trying to get an idea of where you think things will fall, based on what we know at this moment, so I have enough money transferred to Bannister Brothers."

"As long as you understand…" he replied.

"I do, Mr. Pruitt," I assured him.

"If you'll give me a minute," he requested.

I stood and offered him the use of the desk. He took his papers and sat. Then, with a stick of graphite, he began to write figures down. He wrote a number on the lower corner of each piece of paper. On the last piece, he totaled the numbers from each page. After he checked his figures, he looked up.

"Near as I can figure, based on what I saw today and what I expect to find that's hidden, repairs to the manor and the stable will come to around ten thousand ducats," he said.

"When can you start, how long will it take, and will you give me a contract?" I asked.

"I can have my people begin erecting the scaffolding that we need to repair the roof tomorrow, but actual repairs won't begin until Maniday. If all goes well, we should finish before the snow flies," he said. "And I have a standard contract that I can provide you."

"Please get me the contract but do not delay in beginning the work," I requested. "My solicitor is in Aquileia, and I do not yet have one in Easton, so it will take some time to get the contract returned to you. If there is any problem with the contract that would cause us to stop work, you have my word that you will be paid in full for anything you do up to that point."

"Milord," he said with a smile, "it's a fairly standard contract. I doubt your solicitor will object to much of it if he objects at all."

"I didn't think so," I replied, returning his smile. "You'll find I'm not one to look over your shoulder. Neither is Lady Oritur."

"We know the work gets done more efficiently if we stay out of your way," Lucy added. "Just tell me when you need a certain room cleared so you can work in it, and I will see to it that it is done."

"One last question, Mr. Pruitt," I said. "We can go to the bank right now and withdraw funds to help you get started. Then, when you deplete them, come to me or Lady Oritur for more. How much would you like to begin?"

Pruitt looked pleasantly surprised by this. "Um, normally milord, no one gives me money in advance."

"I'm aware, Mr. Pruitt. Yet I also know that providing you with funding in advance eliminates your need to borrow from your bank and the charges associated with that. You would, of course, pass that charge along to me. I would rather spend that money on the finest quality workmanship available in Easton," I said.

"Then four thousand will see us well begun," Pruitt said.

I told Lucy I was going to the bank and would not return. While there, I wanted to write letters to Pierre Luin and my solicitor, Graham Throckmorton. Pruitt waited patiently while a clerk wrote out a draft for four thousand ducats. When Pruitt left, I asked the clerk for the courtesy of a desk, a quill, and some paper.

When I finished, I went to the inn. Lucy arrived not long after. Again, they prepared a bath for us. This time, Lucy was willing to share the tub with me. Knowing I was departing to return to the border the next day might have played a part.

When we dried off and dressed, I gave her the letter for Throckmorton. After Pruitt delivered the contract, she would add it to the letter and send it off. I also reminded her to go to Bannister Brothers and sign the ledger.

I was not looking forward to the next day. The bodies of the three men who were killed returned to Easton that day. The following day would be their joint funeral. I would attend it before returning to Bannock Hill.

In the dining room later, I noted Theo bearing a strange expression. Lucy saw where I was looking. She smiled and leaned forward.

"Did you see Theo with the dog?" she whispered.

"I did."

"He looks so sad now," she commented.

"Even though Mr. Joiner said the dog was not a pet, I don't think he told the dog or Theo that. I planned on having the dog live in the stable but I'm willing to bet that after we can move into the manor, that dog will be sleeping with Theo," I said quietly.

"It won't take that long," Lucy said. "Theo will sneak the dog in here. Did you see how happy Theo was and how that dog just worshipped him?"

"We'll need to make sure Theo lets Toby do his job," I said.

"Toby is the dog's name?" she asked.

"It is. Just make sure Theo walks Toby through the stable every day. I reckon he will cover the house by himself."

The next day, I bundled some clothes and retrieved the old horse from the inn. I dressed somberly and went to the first funeral. My father was there, having arrived from Bannock Hill moments before. He brought my horse, Andy, with him. That put a smile on my face even in such gloomy circumstances.

My father said a few words on behalf of each man. It was clear to everyone how moved he was. When the service concluded, he wrapped me in a hug. It was only later that I realized I had no memory of him ever hugging me before.

After paying our respects to the families, I pulled my father aside and told him about my idea. I wanted to know if we had ever tried anything like it before. He looked at me with a stupefied expression, then shook his head.

"We've never done anything like that before," he said, "and now that you mention it, I'm amazed we didn't try it long ago. I can't think of a single reason why you shouldn't make the attempt."

7

Andy seemed fully healed. I think he was as happy to see me as I was to see him. We headed to Bannock Hill.

When I arrived, I gathered the kersants. There had been no attack today, so there would almost certainly be one tomorrow. The previous attempt was at Norvost. I admitted to them I had no idea where the next would be.

"It doesn't matter, though," I said.

They looked at me with puzzled expressions.

"Tomorrow, when the nomads return to their camp, I'm going to take the former Rangers with me. As we follow the nomads, we'll stay just out of sight and begin fanning out to the north. We'll try to keep an even distance between us, so those heading north must ride much harder to get into position. I'll be closest to their camp," I instructed.

"What are you going to do?" Kersant Rowan asked.

"We're going to light the damned fields on fire," I said. "They depend on that pasturage to feed their mounts and the cattle they eat. We're going to destroy it. We will cross the river to the eastern shore and begin lighting grass fires. Each of us will continue moving north until we reach where our neighbor began. Once you make it to that point, cross west, travel about two leagues, and begin again, only heading south. We should finish by daybreak, then return to Bannock Hill."

"Why are you taking only the new fellas?" Gus Polever asked.

"One thing we did quite a bit of in the Rangers was moving at night and preparing ambushes," I said. "I certainly do not wish to offend anyone and absolutely want to avoid creating a rift between the two groups, but this is something the armsmen are not accustomed to. In the future, we will train, so everyone feels comfortable traveling quietly at night. For this raid, I will take the men with experience. To make it fair, the group I take to scout the east bank of the river the next morning after our return will be only armsmen. My trust in all our men is equal. Will that be acceptable?"

Gus grunted his acceptance. The others nodded agreeably. I looked to Kersants Rowan and Langford. They were both grinning.

"Make sure all of your men have a flint and take extra water," I cautioned. "Does anyone have any concerns?"

"Do you really think this'll work, Cap'n?" Mike Dorne asked.

"If they can't feed their cattle and their mounts, they have only two choices," I said. "They can come west to find fodder, which brings them close enough to us that we can keep scouts on them and bring all our men to battle—including Quinn's Ford and Clearview. Or they go home. This has been a bad campaign for them so far. We've cost them between a fifth and a fourth of their men. If I were in command, I'd head home."

"Has anyone ever tried this before?" Rowan asked.

"My father didn't think so when I asked him after the funerals today," I said. "He was surprised we hadn't tried it. I'll tell you what—if this works, we'll be doing it again, maybe even before they show up after the summer solstice. It all depends on how quickly the grass dries out."

"If we succeed in keeping them away," Gus asked, "what happens to us?"

"I don't see any reason to disband the armsmen or ever cut their numbers again. The only reason my father did that was due to circumstances that will never be repeated. The nomads have proven to be persistent as the seven hells over the decades, maybe even centuries. They'll keep trying," I said. "I just want them to react to us instead of us always letting them make the first move."

The following morning, I made sure I was carrying a flint and filled two extra waterskins. I called the former Rangers together and explained what I wanted to do, showing them the map of the region.

"I reckon they have moved camp to somewhere near here," I said, pointing to a spot opposite Clearview. "After they break off their attack today, I'm going to follow their trail. It won't be hard—a couple of hundred horses will leave clear evidence in the grass. I'm going to stay out of sight until well after dark. Then, I'm going to light the hay on their side of the river on fire. I'll work my way north about a league, where the next man should begin setting the grass ablaze as soon as darkness falls. Each man should work north for a league, then cross the river. Come west about two leagues and start lighting the grass, this time working south until you reach where the next man started. If this works, they won't have fodder."

The men had questions, which I answered to the best of my ability. One pointed out that torches would be very helpful in getting the fires started. I resolved to ask whichever town we defended that day to provide us with them.

Around ten o'clock, judging from the sun, the lookouts reported a signal fire coming from Arpsfield. This town was between Bannock Hill and Clearview. We saddled up quickly and rode toward the signal. I was excited for two reasons.

The first was that we would have just shy of a hundred armsmen riding against the enemy. If I managed them well, we would inflict casualties. That is if the enemy engaged. They might just be out for show. The other reason was my plan to burn the fields. It should work. There was a good breeze from the west, as there was nearly every day. Once we started the hay burning, there would be nothing to stop it.

Gus Polever sidled next to me as we rode. He spoke softly to avoid being overheard. "I didn't want to bring it up in front of the others, Cap'n, but I'm happy you're back. Your father made a few bad decisions back-to-back at Norvost, costing us three men. What's worse is, he knows he messed up. The men all saw it, even the new fellas. It hurts my soul to speak against your dad— he brought me on in the first place—but we'd all be a lot happier if you was to lead us from now on."

I didn't want to say anything, but I had my own sense of things.

Gus continued quietly. "A coupla years ago, your pa would greet every signal fire with a grin and a 'let's go get 'em' but the last two years, he just seemed tired. Plus, he had to cut our numbers, and I know it like to killed him to do it. You got the right attitude, Cap'n. Made me real happy to hear you say it's time for them to worry about what we're doing instead of it always being the other way. I don't even care if your plan works, you understand?"

"Gus, I appreciate what you are saying," I replied, keeping my voice down. "You have to remember—I went for a long time without seeing him—since the old earl's funeral. When I saw him for the first time about a year ago, he didn't look like I remembered. He looked beaten down. Now, he's told me some of it, and some of it my wife and I have figured out, but that woman he married…"

I paused and sadly shook my head. "He spent as much time away from her as he could, trying to hide from the problem. About two years ago, he couldn't hide anymore, and things only got worse. The king was about to take the March away from him."

"Was he really?" Gus asked in disbelief.

I nodded. "Even worse, up until the king chose me, he was planning on sending someone here who would really cock things up. The king was going to do it to discredit the man's whole family. Fortunately, that family did a good enough job of disgracing themselves that the king didn't need to. He's had his eye on me for a while. Just before I returned, he ordered my father to adopt me and made me Lord Oritur. A couple of months ago, I was still a bastard."

"Pardon my saying, Cap'n, but you had to be doing something right," Gus said, "especially to marry so well. The new fellas was traveling here with your wife, and to hear them tell it, she's like to one of the Goddesses."

"I think so, too," I said with a chuckle. "Anyway, from the time I left the Rangers, I needed to make my own way. I was lucky to have a good friend show up at the right time, and it started me off on a path that's been more successful than I dreamed—especially in the last two years. He also introduced me to Lucy, my wife. When my father finally came to see me, I was doing well for myself, and he was feeling beaten. It must have driven home all the mistakes he made."

Polever was silent in thought. "Aye," he said. "The son he had to send away makin' something of himself, and the two he was stuck with being turds. That's a sure recipe for heartache."

Gus pulled away and rejoined his unit. While I was glad to learn the men already held confidence in me, it saddened me to learn how they viewed my father. When I returned to the March, I hoped it would rekindle his spirit. Instead, it seemed to be reminding him of the mistakes he made and couldn't undo. I thought about asking Lucy to speak with him. She might find a way to free him from the malaise that was afflicting him.

When we arrived at Arpsfield, it looked like the militia were hard-pressed. The nomads were split into two groups, one on either side of the fortifications. It looked as though there was fighting at the palisades on the top of the wall, and the mounted nomads were pressing closer to provide covering fire for their men who scaled the wall.

Fortunately, I could see the detachment from Clearview approaching from the south. I ordered Gus Polever to take his units and the former Rangers to the north side. That left me two units, and we would join with the two units under Colin Rissolo and Bill Martin and hit the south side.

Perhaps the nomads were emboldened by their success in the last encounter when they managed to kill three of our men and so were attacking with more than their usual vigor. Whatever the reason, our enemies had not been this close to scaling our fortifications all season long. I lost sight of Polever and his group as we neared the corner of the walls. The Clearview men were coming on the gallop. I ordered mine to match their pace and shouted for lances. As I slid the one from under my right leg, I could see Rissolo and Martin give the same command.

I searched within myself for the link to Bellona and pulled forth a wisp of her power. As soon as I did, time seemed to slow. I could see how things were about to unfold, and I grinned.

With what looked like more than a dozen of their men atop the wall, the nomads were slow to abandon their position. They finally started to move, but it would be too late for them to completely escape. My group rode up on the rear of their formation while the Clearview detachment slammed into them from the side.

Lunging forward in my saddle with my lance outstretched, I pierced one of the nomads between his shoulder blades. He toppled slowly from his mount. My next target was too far away for me to reach his body, so I jabbed my weapon in his horse's rump. The animal immediately faltered. As Andy and I overtook him, I quickly buried my lance in the man's ribs as he fell. The rest of the mounted nomads were pulling out of reach.

"On me, men," I shouted. "Double back. Bows!"

We returned to where the dismounted nomads were fighting with the militia. Riding to the edge of the ditch, we were so close our arrows could not miss. In less than a minute, the threat was ended. A weary member of the militia gave us a wave.

I ordered the men to reverse direction again and head to the front gate. As I rode, I tried to count. Between the men on top of the fortifications and those fallen outside, there were more than thirty we slew. If Polever's unit and the Rangers had as much success, we just hurt the nomads badly.

Our enemies were well out of range when we reached the front gate. They were riding away in retreat. I pushed the tendril of my power back into its source. As the main gate to town began to open, I dismounted. A barrel-chested black man who looked eerily similar to Mr. Pruitt the builder was striding toward me. He was wearing a breastplate but carried his helmet under his arm.

"That's a timely arrival, sir, I must say," he called.

"I'm glad we made it," I replied. "How did they get on the wall?"

"My fault," he said. "I noticed yesterday that the ropes in the skorpios were frayed and needed to be replaced. Unfortunately, we didn't have them today and the bastards were able to crowd close like that. I'm Vic Pruitt, the mayor."

"Casimir FitzDuncan," I said, shaking his hand. "Do you have a brother who is a builder?"

"Oh! You're that Lord Oritur fella. Heard about you," he said. "Greg is my cousin. Have you met him?"

"He's going to be doing some work on the manor in Easton," I said. "How are your people?"

"We have two dead, another three wounded bad enough that I'm worried about 'em, plus some others I haven't counted up yet," he answered. "You?"

"I haven't checked with the unit that went to the north side, but I think we came through pretty clean," I said.

"How many of theirs?" he inquired.

"Just over thirty, I think, on the south side. The north is probably about the same," I responded, then changed the subject. "Mayor, would you have three dozen torches in Arpsfield that we could have?"

"Probably not three dozen, but we could make some real quick," he stated. "Why?"

"I have a little mischief planned for our friends," I said, jabbing my thumb over my shoulder in the direction of the retreating nomads. "And I need three dozen torches to do it. Would you please see to it while I talk to my men?"

Mayor Pruitt turned and began shouting for torches. I walked to where Gus Polever and the former Rangers were waiting. All of them were smiling.

"We got thirty or so of 'em," I said. "How did you guys do?"

Gus looked over at Kersant Langford. "Thirty-eight," Langford stated.

I totted up the figures in my head. Earlier, we killed roughly ninety. With more than sixty today, that came to at least a third of the force they brought. It might be an even more significant percentage if they arrived with fewer. At most, I reckoned they had three hundred remaining.

I turned and faced the east. Setting the fields on fire was a good idea, but I had an annoying thought we would not need to do it right now. Reaching back within myself, I summoned some of Bellona's influence. I reconsidered my plan and thought about the casualties we inflicted upon our enemy. Suddenly, I knew we should hold off on setting the grass ablaze. That would be something to do before the nomads arrived. We could try it next summer.

The idea of a nighttime action stuck with me, and a gambit perfect for the situation was clear to me. Though the armsmen were not accustomed to operating at night, I had thirty-five men out of one hundred and sixteen who *were* experienced. They could help direct the others. The thought of riding on the nomad camp in the darkness and surprising them seemed more attractive by the second. Even if the nomads kept pickets on watch, we would be in the middle of their camp before anyone could respond to the alarm. Since I had never heard of the armsmen riding on the enemy encampment before, the nomads might not even set out a watch.

I returned the tendril of my link with Bellona to its place. Then, turning to the men, I announced, "Change of plans."

I trotted into the town to find Mayor Pruitt. When I did, I thanked him and informed him we would not need the torches after all. He looked disappointed for a moment but then said, "We already started making 'em, but don't worry. They'll come in handy sooner or later."

I found Kersants Rissolo and Martin and instructed them to return to Clearview to gather what they would need for two or three days, then come to

Bannock Hill the next morning. Finding Andy, I swung back into the saddle. I told the kersants we were returning and not implementing the plan I discussed. When they gave me puzzled looks, I promised to explain at Bannock Hill.

While we were returning, I asked Gus to send a man to Quinn's Ford and tell the whole detachment to come to Bannock Hill in the morning. When we arrived back at camp, I gathered the kersants and sat with them away from the men. They looked at me expectantly, puzzled that I had changed the plan.

"Men," I said quietly, "the idea of burning the fields and destroying their fodder is still a good one, but it's an arrow I think I want to keep in our quiver for now. We enjoyed another success today, and that changed my thinking. So far this season, we've killed over a hundred and fifty of them. At most, they have three hundred men left—perhaps less. With all our forces, we number a hundred and sixteen."

"That's still nearly three to one against, Cap'n," Rowan stated.

"It sure is," I agreed but did not allow my grin to falter. "We have never attempted a gambit like this. No one can remember a time when the men of the March rode on the nomads. As a result, I doubt they even set pickets. Not that we're any better, we don't do it either."

"They never attack at night," Gus said.

"And neither have we, until now," I said. "Tomorrow night, we'll follow the trampled grass from Arpsfield back to their encampment. We're going to kill as many men, horses, and cattle as we encounter. By the time they understand what is happening, we'll already be heading home."

"It sounds dangerous," Langford remarked.

"It *is* dangerous," I agreed. "Every single time we ride out to meet them is a risk. But hitting their camp at night is less risky, even though we will be outnumbered. We will catch them by surprise and bash them so hard that their only rational choice will be to go home early. I know the armsmen aren't used to traveling or attacking at night. Kersant Rowan and Kersant Langford's men are. They can guide the others."

"You make it sound so easy, Cap'n," Gus Polever said, "but it ain't."

"I know that Gus, but tell me, which did your men like more? Today, where we rode on them? Or a couple of weeks ago when we sat outside the town and traded insults?"

"Seven hells, Cap'n! That's not fair," he complained. "Everyone knows the answer."

"Gus, you've been riding for the March for over twenty years," I said. "Haven't you ever wanted to ride across the river and jam your boot up their backsides?"

"Well, sure. Lotsa times."

"Then let's do it. Let's grab the reins for once."

That night, I checked the heavens. It was a quarter-moon, waning. *Perfect,* I thought. *Just enough light to follow their trail, not enough to give us away at a distance.*

8

When the detachments from Clearview and Quinn's Ford arrived the next day, I called all the men together. I climbed on top of a table and called for their attention.

"We're leaving right after dinner, men," I instructed. "Before we go, everyone who knows how to use them should have two lances. We'll head to Arpsfield. There, we'll pick up the trail to where the nomads are camped. Night will fall while we are on the way. Here is the best advice I can give you about traveling in the dark—trust your mount. Your horse can see in the dark far better than you can. Let them worry about their footing—they'll do a much better job. Keep chatter to a minimum after night falls. When we reach the river, spread out and hold. We'll cross all at once when you hear me enter the river—the camp should be just on the other side. Draw a lance and wait until you see the kersants light their torches. That will be the signal. If you're clumsy with a lance, use your sword. When you see the signal, hit the camp at full speed. Feel free to make as much noise as you want. Hollering, yelling, screaming, whooping—they're all good. After you make it through, wheel around, come back through the camp, and across the river. When we get a league distant from the river, Kersant Polever will light another torch. Head to it."

I paused and took a deep breath. "Anyone or anything on the ground is your target. The kersants will have torches, and they'll toss them into whatever they encounter that will burn and provide some light. You have all noticed by now we have some new fellas," I said. "I'm a new fella too. All us new guys have one thing in common—we served on the other border in the Rangers. I'm not saying, and I better not hear anyone say, the Rangers are better than our armsmen because that is *not* true. The Rangers are just used to a different style of fighting, that's all. One of the things they're good at is moving and fighting at night. That's something no one has ever asked the armsmen to do. So, starting tonight, and in the future, we're going to move at night when it suits our purpose. Since it's new to so many of you, it's a good thing we have three dozen of us who are used to it. One of the things the new fellas aren't so good at is lance work. All the armsmen excel at it. So, the one bunch will help us get there, and the other will demonstrate how deadly a lance in the hands of an armsman can be. I expect both groups to pay attention and start learning the things you don't know so well."

Some of the men looked troubled. Others, including all the former Rangers, were smiling. I didn't want any of them to be scared.

"Why *are* we doin' this, Cap'n?" came a voice.

"Aren't you tired of fighting when and where *they* say?" I asked. "Haven't you ever wished we could force them to do what *we* want?"

Murmurs of assent rose from the group.

"We're going to cross the river and hit them like a thunderstorm of death. We're going to kill as many of their men and animals as we can on one pass through and back. Don't waste time trying to chase someone or something down. If we do it right, we'll be across the river and heading home by the time they realize what just happened. We're not going to stand toe-to-toe with 'em and slug it out. Seven hells that would be stupid. They outnumber us. Just one pass through and one pass back and leave. That's all I need. If that doesn't convince them to go home, maybe we'll just have to do it again some other time. And don't worry, we'll be back tomorrow in time for breakfast."

The men laughed at that. I stepped down from the table I was standing on. I gestured to Rowan and Langford. They approached me.

"I meant what I said. If your men aren't comfortable with lances yet, have them use swords. Of course, it limits their reach, but that's better than getting tangled up and falling on their asses," I said. "Understood?"

Both men nodded and went to make sure the former Rangers understood. If this attack worked as I hoped, we would definitely need to train the armsmen to be more comfortable moving at night. The former Rangers would need to learn how to use lances.

My excitement level was high. I found it hard to be still. The hours seemed to drag. I took my two lances and stood in line at the grindstone, waiting to sharpen their bladed tips. The other men waiting seemed anxious.

"Men," I said, gaining their attention, "I would never ask you to do the impossible. The reason I want to do this is because we should not have any difficulty accomplishing it. When we're successful, I expect the nomads to head for home—more than four months early. But you know what the best part is?"

Several of them shook their heads, not wanting to speak up.

"The best part is," I teased, "that you still get paid those four months, even though the nomads will have left. It's more work for me, though. I'll need to come up with worthwhile things for you to do to keep you out of trouble."

That generated some chuckles.

"What sort of 'worthwhile things,' Cap'n?" asked one.

"Training, mostly, I guess," I replied, shrugging my shoulders. "I'll worry about that tomorrow if that's alright with you?"

After my turn at the wheel, I took my lances back to the sleeping platform where my cot was. I sat on the edge of the decking and considered what was coming. My connection with Bellona indicated this was the right thing to do under these circumstances.

Still, men would die tonight. We might lose as many as ten, though I hoped it would be fewer. Many more of the enemy would die if things went as planned.

I am not bloodthirsty. Slaughtering my enemies was not my goal. I had no special relish for it. My aim was to convince them to leave as soon as possible. The only method of persuasion I knew would be effective right now was reducing their numbers. I prayed to the Three Major Gods for success tonight, for the safety of my men, and for the souls of the nomads we would send to the afterlife. When I finished that, I prayed to Bellona, thanking her for blessing me. I prayed to Njörun, asking for her good fortune in this endeavor, and I thanked Eir for allowing me and my horse Andy to heal so quickly.

After a hearty meal from our complaining cooks, who whined about having extra mouths to feed, we set off for Arpsfield. There was noticeable energy in the men. Some of it was excitement, some was nerves, but I hoped the length of our ride would have a calming effect. I noticed none of the former Rangers brought lances. We would remedy that when we returned.

Each of the kersants had a torch and a flask of flammable spirits. Gus Polever had two. When we crossed the river, each one would drench the head of his torch. A single spark would then light it. I instructed them earlier to throw their torches into something that would catch fire quickly—probably whatever portable shelters the nomads used—and to spread them out to provide better visibility through the whole encampment. When those shelters burned, they would provide more illumination for our raid.

An hour past Arpsfield, and twilight was upon us. The route the nomads took to their camp was like a broad highway of trampled grass. It was easy to follow. Another hour passed, and we had only the light of the quarter-moon and stars.

"Remember, let your mount pick his or her own path," I called out quietly. "They can see in the dark. You can't."

"Got that right, Cap'n!" came a jibe from one of the men. Quiet chuckles lifted in response.

Sometime after the third hour of our passing Arpsfield, we reached the shallow bank of the river. At this time of year, the river was only two feet deep. We could see the glowing coals remaining from the campfires. I heard one of their horses nickering not too far away. When I judged everyone was gathered, I nudged Andy forward into the water. While we crossed, I withdrew a plume of my power and pulled the lance from under my right leg.

Hearing Andy's hooves entering the river, the rest of the men followed. To me, the noise seemed deafening. But, in reality, it was not loud at all. When we reached the far bank, I stopped. I heard the rasp of seven flints on steel, not all at once. Seven torches bloomed into flame. That was the signal.

Squeezing Andy with both knees, he sprang forward. I heard myself screaming at the top of my lungs as we sped toward triangular shapes of what I guessed was light-colored canvass in the dim light from the torches. One of the torches flew end over end into one of these canvass shelters. It immediately burst into flame and brightened the area around it.

Andy and I passed the first two of these, but at the third, a man was trying to scramble out from under the canvas on his hands and knees. I quickly switched the lance to my left hand and skewered him before he could stand. Then, out of the corner of my eye, I saw another torch fly, engulfing another shelter in flame. I thought this was good—the kersants were trying to broaden the illuminated area by spacing out the fires they started.

At the next canvass shelter, there were two men. One was standing, and the other was rising from his knees. One of my armsmen spurred just ahead of me and took the one who stood. I contented myself with the other.

By now, our enemies were on their feet and running, trying to escape. Andy and I rode some down. There were four armsmen near me, and we seemed to be having a contest to see which of us could send more of our foes headlong to bleed out their last into the dust. I dispatched four more of our enemies.

Andy and I reached the end of the encampment. I could see men running into the darkness, but my own orders were not to pursue. Instead, reining Andy in and turning him, I shouted, "Double back when you reach the end! Double back!"

Once Andy turned, it did not take long for him to reach full speed again. On our way back through, there were fewer of our enemies, but there were still some. Everywhere I looked, I saw fallen nomads, and that was just in the row of the canvass shelters we were riding along. Andy and I rode down two more victims as the light from the burning canvass began to fade away.

We reached the river and crossed, along with many of our men. I pulled Andy to a stop and turned to see what I could in the fast-dying light. As their commander, I would wait until all my men were back on this bank.

"Continue on the canter, men," I called out. "Continue on the canter for a league, then rein in."

When Kersant Polever judged he was at least a league past the river, he would stop and light his second torch. That would be our rallying point. By now, there was no more light to see anything in the camp. There were groans and cries of wounded men. I heard no more hooves enter the river, so I turned Andy, and we set off. While I stowed my lance under my leg, I accessed my connection with Bellona. I was not seeking more energy—I wanted more knowledge. My most pressing concerns were how many of our enemies remained, and how they would react to our attack.

As Andy loped along, I tried to … Oh, Seven Hells! I can't rightly find the words for what I was trying to do. The closest I can come is that I was trying to *feel* whether the nomads were pursuing us or too shocked to move. After trying to stretch my senses out, I had a hunch that they were not riding after us, but it was only a hunch.

Far ahead, I saw a torch flare into light. As I drew closer, the kersants began calling out the names of their men. I heard some of the responses. Andy and I slowed as we reached the group and shouldered our way to the light that Gus was holding. As I neared him, the kersants were finishing their roll. When I reached the light, I called the kersants by name.

"Rissolo!"

"All here, Cap'n."

"Martin!"

"All present."

"Campbell!"

"One missing."

"Who?"

"McSweeney, Cap'n."

"I'm here," came a whining voice.

"Then why didn't you answer, muttonhead?"

"Sorry, kersant," he called as the laughter of the men rose.

By the time we finished, two others were reported missing. When their names were called again, both piped up. The last was the funniest.

"Why didn't you answer, numbskull?" Gus Polever inquired.

"I thought it were McSweeney's job," came the voice.

That crack caused the men to roar. Meanwhile, I immediately thanked all the Majors and Minors for seeing my men safely through the evening. When I returned to Easton, I must visit the Temple and make suitable offerings.

We were on the path we followed from Arpsfield. It was a simple thing to retrace our journey. By the time we reached the town, the gray light of false dawn allowed us to see the riders closest to us. We continued on, reaching Bannock Hill in time for breakfast, as I promised. I asked the kersants to sit with me.

I made sure all the men were fed before I collected my food. The kersants were mostly finished eating, talking excitedly among themselves. They quieted when I arrived.

When I sat, I asked, "Any idea how we did last night?"

Langford looked at the others, then answered, "More'n two hundred, Cap'n."

With my mouth occupied with a piece of bacon, I mumbled, "How do you figure?"

"A dozen shelters from the river to the edge of their camp," he said. "Twenty files of 'em from north to south. We had four or five men riding in between each file. I reckon we got at least one man from each shelter—sometimes both of 'em when there were two. So, more'n two hundred. From what I could see of 'em running away, less than a hundred left."

"Does that seem right to you?" I asked, looking at the other kersants.

They nodded.

"That's what we were yakking about when you came, Cap'n," Paulie Florio said. "I mean, no offense, but you gotta be touched by the Goddess of good fortune or something, Cap'n. I thought it would be a good night if we lost only five or six men. Not a single one even took a wound! And I rode past at least a dozen bodies on my way back to the river. Jack's got it right—more'n two hundred."

"Well, I think we're going to ride out and see tomorrow morning," I said. "We're going to take a wagon and stop at Oritur and Arpsfield on the way and get as many shovels as we can."

"Shovels?" Campbell asked.

"If we were as successful as we think we were," Rissolo said, "I'm betting the survivors left for home in one hell of a hurry this morning. They wouldn't stick around to bury the dead."

"So, we gotta?" Campbell complained.

"I don't know what gods they follow," Gus Polever said, "and I don't rightly care. Our Gods, though, just gave us the kind of victory they make songs about, and I reckon they wouldn't be too happy if we left that many bodies unburied. So, yeah, we gotta."

"Didn't think of it that way," Campbell admitted.

"If they're gone, what are we going to do?" Bill Martin asked.

"Train, for now," I answered. "There is still a lot of the campaigning season left. It's possible they come back."

"Think they will, Cap'n?" Rowan asked.

I laughed. "I don't have the faintest idea," I admitted. "It's possible."

"I don't think they will," Polever said. "But the cap'n is right. We need to be ready if they do."

Most men tried to find a spot out of the sun to sleep. We had been awake all night, and now that the excitement was over, fatigue took command. Before I found my own piece of shade, I made sure all the horses were in order. I was pleased to see all the men took care of their mounts before succumbing to their own needs.

I found the cook and pulled him aside. "Pete, tomorrow morning after we leave, I want you to go to Easton and buy as much beef and ale as you think it will take to satisfy everyone—including yourself. Last night was a great success, and we should celebrate it."

I handed him ten ducats. "That should be enough to make sure you can afford the very best. If I hear anyone complain about the quality of food or drink tomorrow night, it will be on your head," I warned.

I found a patch of grass where the shadow of the watchtower blocked the sun. Stretching out, with my hands behind my head, my mind reviewed the whirlwind my life had been since Lucy and I married less than two months before. I couldn't even remember what I expected life to be like once we were wed. Things changed so dramatically, so quickly, that it almost seemed as though it happened to someone else. Before I could begin to unravel that thought, the comforting fingers of sleep pulled me into their embrace.

The next morning found everyone in a lively mood, considering the chore that lay before us. I reminded the kersants to make sure everyone had his armor and a bow with a full quiver. Though we expected the nomads were already heading for home, they might still be in camp. However, we would outnumber them, so I was not especially concerned.

I drove a wagon with Andy tied behind. With the Quinn's Ford detachment, we went to Oritur to ask for shovels. Gus Polever would take all the rest of the men, stop in Arpsfield and ask for shovels too.

When we reached Oritur, the mayor, Otis Scarledge, was already waiting, having seen us coming. He met me at the gate. When I asked for shovels, he wanted to know why, of course. So I explained to him what we did.

"Do you think they'll come back?" he asked.

"There is a lot of the usual campaigning season left," I said. "So, it's possible. I don't know how big their tribe or nation is across the desert. Their losses might matter as little to them as a gnat bite."

Mayor Scarledge managed to find us thirty-two shovels. We loaded them in the wagon and headed across the plain to where the nomad encampment was. There was still a trail from the last time they came to Oritur, so we followed it back.

9

When we reached the encampment, the rest of the men were already there. I drove the wagon across the river and found Gus Polever. He was supervising as men were using their horses to drag the dead bodies to the side of the camp furthest from the river. There were still several dozen of the shelters standing. Looking to the north, I saw some cattle and horses grazing.

"Two hundred and eleven, Cap'n," he said. "That's the count of the dead. There was wounded, too, but they aren't here. Can't imagine them making it far, though."

"We aren't going to waste time searching for them," I said. "What else?"

"Looks like nearly a hundred head of cattle wandering close by. Some horses, too."

"Detail some men to gather everything from the camp worth taking," I ordered. "There should be some large kettles we want to take and some cooking spits. Look for sheaves of arrows as well. Put the kettles on the wagon first. Then we can fill them with the other things. I don't want to leave anything behind that would be useful to them when they return next. The rest of the men will dig, taking turns. Once we make a big enough hole, send some men to round up those cattle and the horses and start to drive them back to Bannock Hill."

"How many shovels?" he asked, peering into the wagon.

"Thirty-two."

"Arpsfield could only spare nine. If you drive to the far side of the camp, we'll hand 'em out and get the grave started," Polever said.

When I reached that end of the encampment, I saw nine men already digging. They were cutting hunks of sod first and stacking them behind the trench they had begun. That would have been my suggestion as well. The sod was thick. The roots of the grass extended six inches into the soil.

Gus Polever whistled and handed out shovels to the men. He spoke with the other kersants and relayed my instructions. Soon, there were groups of men starting to comb through what the nomads left behind. Gary Langford asked me to move the wagon to the center of the camp.

I did, then set the brake and climbed down. Already a group of men was hoisting a huge iron kettle into the wagon. I could see another group dragging a second toward us.

The kersants had everything under control, so I allowed myself to wander, looking at what was left behind, trying to learn more about what kind of people these nomads were. There was no gold or silver that I could see. Instead, I found clothing and bedding, bows and arrows, waterskins and some tack that was being repaired. There were some knives with decorative carvings in the handles. It certainly did not appear that they brought much in the way of material possessions.

I returned to the wagon. The three kettles filled most of it, arranged in a triangle to make them fit. There were a bunch of iron rods. Langford explained these were cooking spits. The kettles were completely filled with sheaves of arrows. The arrows we could not fit were being burned. We heard Gus whistle again and returned to him.

He called for a new group to take the shovels. There was now a trench about a hundred feet long and just over six feet wide. The sod that was stacked behind had been pulled away from the edge. With the sod cut, the digging proceeded more quickly, especially with forty-one men on the shovels. They were tossing dirt out in front of the piles of sod. Other men began dragging the bodies to the other side of the trench.

The bodies smelled. Flies were swarming already. Most of the dead loosed their bowels when they expired. That stench, combined with the coppery smell of blood and incipient rot, produced an unforgettable odor.

Polever called Bill Martin over and discussed something. I wasn't close enough to overhear. Martin left and gathered the men of his unit, then they departed. I saw them mounted a minute later, heading to where the nomads' cattle and horses were grazing. They rode away from the river, leaving the animals undisturbed for now, circling around them. I understood they would try to find any animals that scattered and herd them toward the others and eventually to the river.

Gus whistled again, and new men took over digging. The trench was about four feet deep. The depth, combined with the height of the dirt tossed out, made for slower progress as the diggers needed to throw each shovelful higher. I returned to the wagon where Gary Langford was waiting.

"There really isn't much worth taking, Cap'n," he said. "We got all the iron. The canvass isn't worth much. We might as well burn it as carry it, along with the sticks they use to prop it up."

"As long as we take or destroy anything that would be useful to them," I said. "Go ahead and burn that stuff."

Gus whistled again a short time later. By now, the trench was so deep that the men digging needed to be pulled out by their comrades. Gus waved me over.

"Deep enough?" he asked.

I took a look, then nodded. Gus started shouting orders to drag the bodies and put them in. The men responded. Two would take each body by the hands and pull it to the edge. Then they would yank the corpse forward and launch it so it would lie flat at the bottom of the trench. Once the bodies were deposited, they began to shovel the dirt on top. Again, with so many wielding shovels, it did not take long. The last step was to put the hunks of sod on top of the mound. I didn't know if the sod would grow again but I wanted to give it a chance.

With this done, the men washed themselves in the river, clothes and all. They were whooping and splashing each other like the boys they once were. Minutes earlier, they were burying the corpses of their slain enemies.

Bill Martin rode down the bank to where I was watching the men. "We're about to drive the animals across, so you might want to tell the men."

"How many?" I asked.

"Fifty-four horses, a hundred and five cattle," he replied, "Where are we taking 'em?"

"Bannock Hill," I said, "eventually. Concerning the horses, if any man thinks one of those will be a better mount than he has currently, let him swap.

He'll need to train the new horse, though. After that, we'll take the horses to Easton and sell them. Every man will get a share of the proceeds."

That brought a smile to Martin's face.

"I have something different in mind for the cattle. I'll tell the men to stop playing. Go ahead and take the animals across," I said.

As he rode away, I walked to the edge of the river.

"I hate to ruin your fun, gentlemen," I called out, "but Kersant Martin is about to muddy your water. He's got over a hundred and fifty animals about to cross upstream."

The men scrambled out. Most wore sheepish grins, knowing that I saw them acting like children. It didn't bother me at all. On the contrary, I thought what they did was probably a good way to cleanse both body and soul from the intimacy with death we just experienced.

I took the wagon with the kettles and thirty-two shovels back to Oritur. Again, Mayor Scarledge was waiting for me. He opened the gate, and I drove the wagon in.

"I brought the shovels back," I said, "and I thank you for lending them to us. I know you would never ask for any compensation, but I thought you might be able to use the iron in these kettles and other hardware. The kettles are full of arrows as well."

"Milord, that's generous of you," he said. "I take it the nomads are gone?"

"They are," I confirmed. "We buried two hundred and eleven just now."

Scarledge looked at his feet for a moment. When he returned his gaze to me, he said, "Milord, my expectations two months ago were bleak. I thought this would be the roughest and most dangerous campaigning season of my life so far. In fact, I thought we would lose the town. What has happened instead is so completely opposite that I can scarcely comprehend it. Thank you, Lord Oritur. I'm proud that you go by our name."

When I returned to camp, I saw the men had made temporary enclosures for the animals we brought back, using poles and ropes. It wouldn't stop them if they were determined to leave, but if they were content, as they seemed to be, it would keep them together. A couple of the men were in one paddock, looking at the horses. I parked the wagon, unhitched the horse, unsaddled Andy, and took both animals back to the corral. When I finished with the horses, I checked with the cook to ensure he obtained what I asked. I could smell the beef roasting but could not see the kegs. He nodded with a broad grin before I could even open my mouth, jerking his head behind to indicate where things were.

I went to a table near the center and climbed on top. I asked Gus Polever to whistle. He was one of those people who could stick two fingers in the corners of his mouth and generate a scorching shriek of sound. His blast captured everyone's attention.

"Men, as Kersant Polever said, 'the Gods just gave us the kind of victory they make songs about.' I would encourage all of you to give thanks in your own way—especially McSweeney."

That drew a laugh.

"I want to show my appreciation to you in *my* own way," I continued. "Before we left, I asked Pete to buy as much beef and ale as he thought we needed to satisfy everyone here. I can smell the beef. Pete? Where's the ale?"

With a bit of a flourish, Pete's two assistants came pulling a cart. On the back were four kegs of ale. The two at the end were on their sides and already tapped. There were two more behind them.

With a roar, the men jumped to their feet and went searching for their cups. When they grabbed them, they ran to the kegs. There was a bit of jostling, but all in good humor. Meanwhile, Pete and his men began carving the huge chunks of beef they roasted all day and putting them on plates. There were vegetables and roast potatoes as well. I climbed down from the table and watched.

As men passed me, I heard, "Thankee, Cap'n,'" or "Blessings, Cap'n." A few called me "milord," and others began using it. I stood, taking in the sight. Never in my wildest imaginings did I ever see something like this in my future. I remembered the summers when I was left behind at school—the only student without a home. I recalled the years of reluctant handshakes I received or the outright shunning I suffered from my schoolmates because of my illegitimate birth.

Thinking of those dark days and how different my life was now could have made me gloomy. It didn't. Instead, I marveled to myself how everything in life seems to happen for a reason. I'm no great philosopher, but I understood that my life to this point shaped me and led me to who and where I am now. And that, to me, seemed pretty damned fine.

I ceased my ruminating and trotted off to find my cup. I joined the line at the kegs when I had it in hand. Men offered to step aside for me, but I refused.

"Milord, we're all on our second or third," one man protested.

"I'm in no hurry," I replied. "Someone has to keep a level head—at least, level enough that I can extract the full amount of enjoyment from tonight."

No one ended up getting *too* drunk that night. Most of the men seemed to be pleasantly sozzled. Then, after dark, the singing started. I was content to sit in the shadows and listen. Some of the men had beautiful voices. Others couldn't carry a tune even if you put it in a rucksack for them, but that didn't stop them. Blending them together in an atmosphere of such good spirits made it sound like a choir—albeit one that sang a lewd and humorous repertoire.

No one woke with the sun the following day. I made it to my cot the night before without difficulty, but many didn't. Though I could tell I'd been drinking the night before, I felt reasonably well. That was not the case with more than a few. Indeed, there were bodies scattered all over Bannock Hill when I rose. I found Dick Rowan and Gary Langford among the few awake and moving,

"I'm going to Easton to share the good news," I said. "I should return before lunch tomorrow. Set up the quintains and rings for lance training. We'll start that when I return. Get the other kersants to help, since you won't know how to do it. I'd ask them, but they're still sleeping it off. Other than that, let everyone have an easy day of it today."

They grunted their acknowledgment. I went and saddled Andy. Together we set off on the three-hour journey to Easton.

Along the way, I considered how I wanted to present the news to my father. He spent decades defending the border against these nomads. In my one month here, I accomplished something he never did. I forced them to leave. While pondering, I reflected on how my time with the Rangers influenced my approach. My father had known only the March and managed the defense the way my grandfather taught him—the way things had always been done.

We started the campaigning season shorthanded. Despite that handicap, we inflicted casualties upon our enemy. My aggressive approach was one reason for our success. My link to the Goddess Bellona aided me in identifying opportunities on the field of battle and exploiting them. In the end, though, my unwillingness to allow the nomads to always dictate the course of action led us to that final assault.

I hoped my father would revel in our success. My fear was that my success would push my father deeper into the malaise he seemed mired in. Andy and I trotted through the gates of Easton just after I heard the bells in the town center ring eleven. We worked our way through the streets, ascending the gradual rise that culminated in the manor. When we reached the gate of the manor, Clausen was on guard. While he opened the gate, I asked if my father was there.

"He is, milord," he replied.

"Good. I have some news to share," I said.

"Pleasant news?" he asked.

"The best," I said. "We rode on the nomads the night before last. They were all asleep. We killed a few, and the rest decided to go home the next morning."

Clausen looked at me with his mouth hanging open. "They left? It's still Heyannir," he said. "How many is 'a few,' if you don't mind my asking?"

"Two hundred and eleven," I said.

"Majors and Minors, milord!" he gasped. "That's like half their number!"

"We were having a successful campaigning season before that," I added. "We figured we already dispatched around a hundred and fifty—not all at once, mind you."

"Cor, milord!" he said. "Your old man is gonna be so proud of you he'll bust. I want to hear more about it, but you're probably aching to tell your pa."

He nodded, and Andy and I rode through. Scaffolding surrounded the manor up to the roof. I saw men clambering about up there, replacing sections of tiles—hot work in the late mid-summer. Andy and I rode around the manor toward the stable. What a difference from the sight (and smell!) that greeted me when I arrived a few weeks earlier.

I could see fresh straw in every stall. When we drew closer, the only thing we smelled was the straw. The stench from before was gone. There was a bit of tack hung neatly from hooks on the wall. The trough was full of clean water. I dismounted happily and tied Andy so he could drink. For the time being, I left him saddled, not knowing whether I would need to ride soon.

Entering through the kitchen door, my nose was greeted by wonderful odors. I thought I smelled some sort of berry pie and roasting fowl. Laurie, the cook, was facing away from me. She appeared to be mixing something in a bowl, humming to herself.

"Hello, Laurie," I said. My entrance startled her, and she jumped an inch off the floor and whirled around.

"Oh, milord!" she yelped, with the bowl tucked under one arm and patting her chest with the other. "You gave me a fright just now."

"I'm sorry. I didn't mean to. Whatever you have in the oven smells divine. May I see?" I asked as I was reaching for the oven door.

She slapped my hand away. "No, you may not," she replied indignantly. "Too many cooks spoil the broth, milord. This is *my* kitchen, and you are not to poke around in it."

"Yes, ma'am," I said meekly. "Will you at least tell me what you are making?"

"Raspberry pie and roast chicken," she said. "The chicken is for lunch, the pie for dinner. Will you be here for both?"

"I certainly hope so," I replied eagerly. "Raspberry pie is one of my favorites, and it's been years since I had any."

"Then you best not give the cook such a fright," she admonished cheekily, shaking her wooden mixing spoon at me.

"It will never happen again," I said. "In the future, I will make as much noise as possible before entering your domains. Can you tell me where my father and wife are?"

"The last I knew, they were in the small drawing room with Mr. Williston and the ladies," she said.

"Thank you, Laurie. I'm sorry for startling you," I said.

"I know you didn't mean to," she replied, "and since you seem properly regretful, I'll let you have a raspberry."

She nodded at a bowl on the counter to the left. It was full to the top with plump, red raspberries. I plucked a handful up with my fingers and put one into my mouth. It was tart, sweet and delicious. When I said it was years since I had raspberries, I wasn't fibbing.

One-by-one, I popped the others I took into my mouth on the way to the small drawing room. I heard their voices as I approached. When I reached the threshold, I swallowed the last of my raspberries.

"Hello, everyone," I said. "I apologize for interrupting, but I have some news. Would you like to hear it?"

Everyone expressed eagerness.

"We won a huge victory," I announced.

"You didn't burn the fields," my father pointed out. "We would have known if you did."

"No. Three days ago, they attacked Arpsfield," I recounted. "By the time we arrived, they had men on the top of the wall on opposite sides."

"Seven hells! How did that happen?" my father demanded.

"The mayor told me they were in the process of repairing their skorpios when the nomads attacked. Without the skorpios, the nomads were able to pull in close. Their archery forced the militia to keep their heads down, and their men were able to climb and reach the palisades," I explained. "When we arrived, the nomads were close enough to success that the horsemen were slow to abandon their men atop the wall. We drew lances and rode down more than sixty of them. When I realized that, I changed the plan."

"So, you decided not to torch the fields. What did you do instead?" he asked.

"I sent riders to Quinn's Ford and Clearview, bringing both detachments to Bannock Hill. The next night, we departed after dinner and followed the trail back to the nomad encampment. We caught them sleeping," I said. "It was a slaughter."

"And you say they left? How do you know?" my father asked.

"We returned to their encampment yesterday morning to see," I explained, "and to bury the dead if we needed to. We needed to."

"Majors and Minors!" my father breathed. "How many?"

"Two hundred and eleven, sir. We borrowed shovels from Oritur and Arpsfield and buried the corpses. Then we collected anything worth taking—three large kettles and some iron rods they used for spits, plus sheaves of arrows—and returned to Bannock Hill. They also left behind fifty-four horses and a hundred and five cattle. We'll drive them into Easton soon and sell the horses. I plan on sharing the proceeds with the men. For the cattle, I have something else in mind. Also, while we were taking care of the bodies, I sent Pete out to buy as much ale and beef as it would take to satisfy everyone, and we celebrated last night."

"I wish I'd been there," my father said.

Already I could see the excitement over news of the victory was fading and a gloomy malaise returning to him. It's unusual to think of a son needing to give his father a stern talking to, but I intended to do just that. I was tired of feeling pity for my father.

"It's what to do next that puzzles me, sir," I said. "If it's not a bother, may I steal you away for a few minutes?"

Seeing my father slipping into despondency, the others not only granted their permission but also seemed to urge me to take him. He rose uncertainly. I gestured him out of the room.

I led him around the corner to the stairs. "Sit!" I commanded.

He sat.

"Look at me!" I demanded. "Not at the floor!"

"Since you returned to my life, you have acted as though a black cloud was hanging over your head," I growled through gritted teeth. "Any happiness you experience disappears within a second. You have been wallowing in self-pity over what you did and didn't do years ago. Well, you can't change any of it! For better or worse, all the things that happened have led us to this place and made us who we are. And I am pretty damned happy about who and where I am. I've been blessed beyond my wildest imaginings. Instead of dwelling on your past mistakes, can't you join Lucy and me in preparing a wonderful future? Together, we have the chance to make the March stronger than ever before. Lucy and I could use your help, but if you're more interested in punishing yourself over the past, we'll move forward without you."

My father looked as though I slapped him hard. In a way, I suppose I did. I think my experience of being sent away to school, never to return, helped shape my outlook. I learned that dwelling on my circumstances, which I could not change, was unproductive and made me feel worse. Focusing on what I *could* do generated results, and I was able to take some satisfaction from what I accomplished.

"Now, if you're finished moping about the past, I could use your advice," I said.

My father shook himself like a dog coming in from the rain. "What?"

"It's still Heyannir," I said. "They could still return. I don't dare allow the armsmen to split up or dismiss the militias. How do I keep everyone happy and productive? Can we scout the route the nomads follow? Is it worth posting a watch? That's just a start. I don't know the answers. You might not either, but I figure if both of us are trying to figure it out, we will be better off."

"If you really think so—"

"I do," I snapped. "And for now, I'm kicking you out of the manor. You're to stay in Bannock Hill until we finish the repairs. Seeing all the work we need to do is probably making you even more gloomy. You can return to the manor when everything is back in order, and we can all pretend it has always been that way. Understood?"

"But—"

"But you ordered armor for those who had none, didn't you?" I asked. "Is it ready yet? If it is, let's take it to Bannock Hill. I would appreciate it if you would go check on it right now, then return for lunch. I need to speak with my wife. Then, after we eat lunch, I need to stop by the Temple. The Gods granted us this victory, and I will ask the priests to make a sacrifice in thanks. Once I finish that, we can ride together to Bannock Hill and hash out how we will keep the men busy and out of trouble."

My father looked as though I slapped him again. He said nothing but rose and headed toward the stable. I watched him go, letting out a deep breath after he disappeared.

10

I returned to the others and asked where the maids, Theo, and Tom Collinwood were. Lucy told me they were finishing the cleaning of the second floor. I asked for a progress report, and Mr. Williston took the lead.

"When they finish the second floor, every room will have been cleaned and aired out," he said. "The mattresses have been removed from every bed. We have ordered new ones. There were not enough available locally, so the rest are coming from Newcastle and Aquileia. Mr. Pruitt's men are working on the roof, the attic, and the third floor. The roof repairs should take another nine or ten days. In the attic, there is evidence of water damage and rot in some of the roof beams and trusses. A crane is due to arrive tomorrow to lift the replacements up while the roof is still open. Pruitt says a handful of the load-bearing beams on the third floor show rot. He will need to open the walls and ceilings to replace them—the beams will be lifted up to the attic by the crane and then lowered into place."

Williston paused as he lost his place on the list Pruitt had provided.

"Ahem," he said, resuming. "The chimneys have all been swept and inspected. They are all in need of repair. The masons will be here tomorrow to begin work from the ground floor up. They will need to go through the walls to make their repairs in two places, but the main part of the work is in the attic, where roof leaks followed by freezing weather loosened the mortar. Theo and the maids cleaned the bottoms of the hoist shafts—full of garbage. Pruitt inspected and repaired the tackle for the hoists, installing new rope. Both are operational now. Pruitt has also opened inspection holes in the plaster on the second and first floors but saw no signs of rot. That damage is limited to the attic and third floor. There is water damage on the floors of all the lavatories, and we needed to replace three of the tubs. Lady Oritur instead ordered tubs of a new design for all the lavatories, including the two in the stable. She also ordered new furniture to replace the pieces missing throughout the manor. The tubs and furniture will be arriving over the next few weeks."

"What about the stable?" I asked.

"When the roof of the manor is complete, they will shift the scaffolding to the stable," Williston said. "Mr. Pruitt will need to replace roof beams and trusses, and some of the load-bearing beams on the second floor. The two lavatories have water damage on the floors, and they are getting new tubs, as I said. The chimneys have both been swept and inspected, and they need some repair. The masons will begin when they finish here. The lower boards on the sides and back of the stalls need to be replaced. All the load-bearing beams have rot from the bottom, and Pruitt will change those out as well. The hay, straw, and feed storage area is surprisingly undamaged."

"Mr. Williston, when will the third floor be ready for Theo and the maids to move in?" I inquired.

"Less than three weeks, milord," he responded. "There's also the question of the ballroom."

I had forgotten about the ballroom on the third floor. Maybe my mind didn't want to remember because of the dancing lessons my grandfather insisted upon. However, I certainly did not remember it being used for a party while I lived in the manor.

"What needs to be done in the ballroom?" I asked.

"There is water damage to the floor, milord," Williston said. "Mr. Pruitt suggests that replacing the flooring would be cheaper than repairing it. The same for the lavatories."

"We will do what he suggests, but the ballroom is the lowest priority," I said. "The kitchen was the first on the list, but from what I saw, it is restored."

"The last of the pots, pans, and utensils we ordered should be here soon," Marta said.

"We restocked the pantry and root cellar as much as we could," Lucy added. "Some things are missing because they are out of season now."

"Since the kitchen seems to be finished, the next priorities should be the servants' quarters and the lavatories," I said. "After that, the stable and the rooms above. Then the first floor. Our quarters, on the second floor, come after those. The ballroom is last, I think."

Mr. Williston was making notes. When he finished and looked up, I asked, "Sir, if you would please excuse me, I would like to speak with the ladies."

I nodded.

"I'll check on their progress upstairs," he said, rising from his chair and departing.

I shut the door behind him. The women looked at me curiously. They were wondering why I wished to speak with them privately.

"From what I saw, would I be correct in assuming my father has been as morose as ever?" I asked.

Susannah and Marta looked at one another before answering. Some hidden signal must have passed between them. Marta was the first to speak.

"Yes," she confirmed. "Susannah and I have been trying to tell him the same things we just overheard you say, though not as harshly."

I was embarrassed. I did not think I raised my voice that much. Marta saw my expression and waved it off.

"You're correct to pull him away from here. He's been fretting about everything."

Susannah and Lucy nodded in agreement.

"Lucy, do you have any insights?" I asked, hoping her more developed magical abilities would have given her some idea of how to get my father back on his feet.

She shook her head, her lips pursed together. From her expression, I sensed she knew more than she felt she could tell me. Lucy possessed a limited form of clairvoyance, but her grandmother had told her that sharing her knowledge of what she foresaw would jeopardize it. Though Lucy had long since realized her grandmother was a bit more than slightly mad, the warnings and limitations she placed on Lucy remained.

Sensing we needed privacy, Lucy's mother Marta took Susannah by the hand and said, "We'll go check on lunch."

When they left, I took Lucy's hand. "I apologize for dumping all of this on you, love," I said.

She smiled. "But it's not all on me," she protested. "Mr. Williston has been amazing. My mother and Aunt Susannah have been an enormous help. Theo has shown a completely different side—one I never would have guessed. He is demonstrating he will run the manor well. Of course, it helps that Mr. Williston is here to guide him. Theo is also in love."

"One of the girls?" I asked anxiously.

"No, Lucy replied dismissively, as though I were a dunce. "Toby—the dog."

"Ohh."

"Toby can't stand for Theo to leave, and Theo hates being separated just as much, so Theo sneaks him into the inn, as I predicted," Lucy explained. "He sleeps on Theo's chest. Toby follows Theo around and can't tolerate being on the wrong side of a closed door from him. Because of this, it means Theo needs to go through every room, so Toby can do his job. It is part of Theo's job anyway, so it just helps remind him."

"Has Toby found any more rats?" I asked, concerned.

"No. Only mice that Chauncey didn't eat already," Lucy said.

"Chauncey is here?"

"Of course," she said nonchalantly. "I leave a window or two open every night in the manor and the stable for him."

"Where is he staying?"

Lucy shrugged.

"I was hoping to stay the night," I said, "especially when I learned Laurie is baking a raspberry pie. But, instead, I need to return to Bannock Hill with my father."

"I miss you too," she said, leaning forward and kissing me softly. "You'll be back soon enough."

"It might be weeks," I complained.

"Only three," she said, then clapped her hand over her mouth and blushed.

That was her way of sharing a minimal amount of information regarding something she foresaw. She probably thought it over carefully before deciding to let it "slip" out. I didn't know whether to be happy it was only three weeks or be frustrated that it was three weeks and not less. The best option was to be happy.

"Would you consider visiting?" I asked.

She laughed. "Where would I sleep?" she inquired.

"Well, that *would* be a problem," I admitted. "Perhaps you could just come for lunch and bring me a piece of raspberry pie?"

"That would hardly be fair to your men," she teased. "I would need to bring enough for all of them. That reminds me. I unpacked your qava things. Do you want to take them with you?"

"*Yes!*" I replied. "That will be something fun to introduce to the men."

"Simple minds are so easily entertained," she muttered as though talking to herself.

We were interrupted by the return of Marta and Susannah, announcing that lunch was nearly ready. Then we heard footsteps coming down the stairs from the upper floors. It sounded like a group.

"I don't know how you have been dining, but I would like everyone to eat together today," I said.

"That is what we have been doing while the manor is being repaired, Lucy explained. She called upstairs, "Theo, lunch is ready. After you all wash up, please have Rose, Hazel and Gladys set the dining room table and help Laurie plate the food. Then, we will all eat together."

Lucy took me to the dining room. It was dominated by the enormous table I remembered from boyhood. I was never allowed to eat there. The table was big enough to seat thirty-six people. Unfortunately, only thirteen chairs remained. The sight struck my funny bone, and I chuckled.

Lucy maneuvered me to stand at the head of the table before she sat down. I thought to question her, but she whispered, "The way your father has been acting, he needs to earn his place back. You should tell him that."

Rose and Gladys began bustling in and out, setting places for everyone. Instead of silverware, there was a hodgepodge of various spoons, knives, and forks. At least the water goblets were all the same.

Marta and Susannah joined us, seating themselves, then Mr. Williston came in. My father then entered. Susannah stopped him immediately.

"Wash up, Duncan," she ordered.

"I will," he said. He handed me a letter. "This is for you."

He turned on his heel. I looked at the letter. Flipping it over, I saw the royal seal. I set it on the table. Lucy raised an eyebrow, questioning why I did not open it immediately.

"I am about to have lunch with my family," I said. "It can wait."

Marta smiled, pleased with my response. Theo entered, with Toby trotting at his heels. When Theo stood at his place, Toby sat attentively five or six feet directly behind him. Hazel, Rose, and Gladys began delivering plates to all of us. My father and Tom Collinwood came in.

My father definitely noticed I was standing at his place at the table. I ignored him. The three maids brought in their own food last and sat down.

"Laurie," I called out, "will you be joining us?"

She bustled to the door. "Oh, no, milord," she responded. "I've already eaten, and my pies are about done. I need to pull them out any minute."

"Perhaps next time," I suggested.

Then I turned back to the table. "Thanks to all heavenly beings for the table set before us. As we enjoy this meal, let us not forget the needs of others."

When I finished, I nodded to the men, indicating they should sit. I waited until they did, then sat myself. As soon as my butt hit the chair, Lucy picked up her fork, the signal that everyone was allowed to begin eating.

This room was producing the oddest feelings in me. The grand table, the missing chairs, the mishmash of utensils, and now, even though I never ate in this room, remembering how my grandfather insisted that I learn proper dining etiquette.

The meal itself was simple—roast chicken with an herb crust, green beans, and a roll. Despite its simplicity, it was prepared near-perfectly. The chicken was moist, not dry. The green beans were thoroughly cooked but still crisp. The rolls were steaming, fresh from the oven. With butter, they tasted marvelous.

There was no conversation while everyone began eating. After a few minutes, though, I sensed everyone was waiting for someone to say something. I realized that sitting at the head of the table made that my responsibility.

"Father, was the armor ready?" I asked.

"It was," he replied. "They finished the last pieces yesterday. I hired a wagon from the livery and asked them to drive it to the smith so they could load it. We can leave after we finish."

"That will be fine," I said, "though it means we miss out on the raspberry pies that Laurie is baking. I haven't had raspberry pie in years and years."

"I'm partial to strawberry pie, myself," Mr. Williston offered.

"Blueberry for me," Marta added.

"Any kind of fruit pie is my favorite," Tom Collinwood blurted. He suddenly turned red, thinking he shouldn't have said anything.

Lucy jumped in to reassure him he was not overstepping. "I agree with Tom," she said. "I've never encountered a fruit pie I didn't love. And the best thing is fruit pie for breakfast."

"Tabby always did spoil you rotten," Marta commented. "Tabby was our cook when Lucy was a girl."

"Tabby made good pies," Theo remarked.

You could have knocked me over with a feather. I had never heard Theo put together a sentence of four words unless it was in grudging response to a direct question. To hear him volunteer an opinion was astounding. I tried to mask my amazement since I did not wish to embarrass him, but Lucy and Marta both noted my astonishment.

"Did you have a favorite, Theo?" Marta asked.

Theo nodded. "Mhm. Cranberry-apple."

"Oh!" Lucy sighed. "I remember! All Tabby's pies were good, but that might have been the best. We must make sure Laurie knows how to make one this autumn."

"I always thought her pumpkin pie was her best," Marta remarked.

"I haven't had pumpkin pie in years," my father said wistfully. "My father used to insist on having pumpkin pie on the first day of Gorman."

That kindled a happy memory. My grandfather did indeed love pumpkin pie. He often used me as an excuse to wheedle a couple of slices from the cook. We would eat them sitting on the back steps to the kitchen door.

"I'm most fond of mince pie," Mr. Williston stated.

Susannah and the three maids had not yet said anything, so I attempted to draw it out of them. The three maids mostly blushed and giggled, never stating a preference. Susannah admitted she preferred sour and tart tastes to sweet, with a preference for gooseberry.

The remainder of lunch passed quickly in a lively conversation. Theo did not say anything further, but I was still astounded by his comment. I did learn that Tom Collinwood's uncle would be arriving in a few days. At that point, Lucy would move Bella from the inn to our stable and Susannah and Marta would also move their horses if they were still here. They felt things were well in hand and would be returning home soon.

I made a point of thanking Laurie for lunch. Lucy retrieved my qava pot, grinder and beans, and I fastened them to Andy's saddle. It was then I remembered the letter. I'd left it on the table, so went to fetch it. It was indeed from the king. I broke the seal with my finger and opened it.

Lord Oritur,

Gulick and Manton both informed us that you are aware that they correspond with us regularly. We would like you to do the same. Your father provided regular reports in the past but none for three years now. We would value your assessment of the state of the March and any information you have from elsewhere. In particular, we are concerned with the current defense of the March. Please provide us with your evaluation as soon as is convenient.

-M

I took the letter with me, stuffing it inside my shirt. Lucy was saying farewell to my father near the stable. I allowed her to finish, then said my own goodbye. Not many words were involved, but we did use lips and tongues. I swung into the saddle and set off with my father.

He went to the smithy. I detoured on the way and visited the Temple of the Three Major Gods. After dismounting and tying Andy to a post, I went inside looking for a priest. When I found one, I asked if I might see the head priest, as I had some important matters to discuss.

The priest scurried off. He returned shortly with a younger man, about my age. That surprised me slightly. Usually, head priests were older. He glided over to me.

"How may I help you?"

"Hroth," I said, using his formal title, "my name is Casimir FitzDuncan. King Mark recently named me Lord Oritur—"

"Ah. Yes. I am aware of you. Your lovely wife has made quite an impression already in Easton," he said.

"I apologize for not introducing myself or Lady Oritur before now. The defense of the March commanded my immediate attention, and repairs to the manor have consumed her time," I explained.

The head priest smiled. "Again, I'm aware. People talk, and like them, I am delighted to see matters changing for the better. How may I help you?"

"Hroth, you may soon hear that we won an amazing victory," I said. "We routed the nomads, and the remainder of them have fled for wherever it is they come from. Of course, such a thing can only happen if the Gods will it. I owe them a worthy sacrifice. When is the next major feast day?"

"In three weeks," he replied. Lucy's "slip" now made sense. "It is the feast of Andvar."

Andvar was not one of the Three Major Gods. Instead, he was a Minor God, responsible for smithing and crafting. Still, any God's feast day was a worthy occasion.

"Would you usually sacrifice cattle?" I asked.

"Yes."

"Would it be more pleasing to the Gods if these cattle were taken from an enemy?"

"Most pleasing," the priest answered, beginning to smile.

"How many would you require to satisfy not just Andvar but also the other Minor Gods and the Three Majors?" I inquired.

"Are you meaning to make this a festival for more than just Easton?" the priest asked.

"Our victory benefits the border area the most, but also the entire March," I explained. "I would like the word to be spread to invite anyone who wishes to come."

"That will certainly be welcomed by everyone," he said. "We have not had a celebration like that since I have been here. I will check the records to be sure, but it might require as many as a hundred cattle."

"I will have a hundred and five delivered to you in a few days. Where would you like them?"

"Oh, my!" he said. "I suppose to Williamson. He operates the biggest stock business in Easton. I will need to warn him they are coming."

"I imagine you would have other expenses to make this happen," I said. "Would a thousand ducats as a donation help?"

"That should be much more than enough," he replied. "This will certainly be a wonderful way to introduce Lady Oritur and yourself to the March."

"My intent is to honor the Gods first, for the victory they granted us," I said. "If doing so carries with it other benefits, I shall welcome them, but that is not by design."

"I understand, milord," he said. "Would you like me to spread word of this?"

"Please."

"Would you like to participate in the ceremony?" he asked.

"In what way?"

"When I have been present at other events like this, the sponsor usually wields the hammer for the first sacrifice," the priest explained. "This is done on the altar in front of the participants."

"I would like to be present when the animal is blessed and sanctified at the altar, but my strong preference would be for any slaughter and the butchering to take place out of public view," I said. "I have no desire to wield the hammer."

"That is easily arranged," he said.

11

The wagon was loaded and waiting. My father was already seated with reins in hand, and I dismounted and tied Andy to the back, next to Aster, my father's mount. My father seemed slightly surprised I would sit with him on the wagon. The unsprung wagon would be much harder on our bottoms than riding. I want to talk with him, though, and that would be accomplished more easily sitting next to him.

When we passed through the city gates, I turned to him. "I apologize for speaking so harshly before," I said, "but I do not apologize for what I said since it is all true. We cannot change the past. But we *can* shape the future. Plus, I want the father I missed—the one whose company and approval I longed for—not a broken man, old before his time."

"I'm sorry—"

"Don't be sorry!" I said with force. "Turn the page on the past. Relish today. Events have led us to this point where we are reunited. You are finally rid of Veronica. We have more than restored the number of armsmen under the banner. Seven hells, we just chased the nomads home, and it's still Heyannir!"

"*You* did that," he replied. "*You* restored the armsmen, not me."

"Sir, the Gods work their wonders in mysterious ways," I said. "The path my life took generated the monetary wherewithal for me to be able to restore the armsmen. The greatest part of my assets came to me in the last year, as did meeting Lucy. I know which one of those is a greater sign of good fortune, and it isn't my finances."

"You *are* exceedingly lucky to have Lucy as your companion in life," he commented.

"And I try to remember to thank the Gods regularly for it," I replied. "As far as my financial affairs, the Gods saw fit to put me in the way of that money. As events have unfolded, it seems to me their intent is far better served by employing my windfall in service to the March."

"Hmm," was his response.

"As far as what I have accomplished on the border," I said, "I attribute much of my success to my experience in the Rangers. In dealing with the Rhetians, our worst losses came when we allowed them to seize the initiative. However, when *we* dictated the course of events, we prevailed. In that way, my different experience was a benefit here."

I attributed most of my success to my aggressive approach. The abilities Bellona blessed me with, in terms of seeing opportunities in the middle of battle, helped me make the most of every opportunity. This was not the time to share that information with my father. I hope to be able to do that someday, but not today.

"But I have failed—"

"You have stumbled, father," I countered. "Perhaps more than once. But the race is not yet over. Last fall I went to the Queen's Cup with Lucy. The evening before, Lucy's cousin Freddy, Lord Rawlinsford, gave us a detailed explanation of odds and betting. Lucy teased him, saying that he always threw that careful analysis to the winds whenever he saw an attractive gray horse—he always bets on the gray. At the race, Lucy and I decided to bet on the attractive gray, even though the odds were one hundred fifty to one. Freddy bet on the favorite because Lucy had twitted him the night before. As the horses came to the starting line, I began to think I had wasted my money. The gray could hardly have looked less interested. Even worse, he started poorly. He nearly threw his rider on the first high fence. He jumped short on the water obstacle following. He was five lengths behind the nearest horse and at least a dozen from the leaders. Then, all of a sudden, the gray, whose name was Trooper, woke up and realized he was in a race. I won't bore you with further details, but Trooper won, nosing out the favorite at the wire. No one really cares how Trooper began the race.

Everyone remembers how he finished. Be Trooper, father. Be the man whose approval I wanted. Be the man who used to greet every signal fire with a grin."

"I did, you know," he said quietly after a few minutes passed.

I looked at him.

"I used to see every signal fire as an opportunity," he clarified. "But then—"

"But then I showed up, and the two of us, and Lucy, put things back the way they should be," I said. "That's the way that story should read. So, we'll glue those other pages together."

A couple of miles passed in silence. When I looked over, I could see the faint trace of a smile. He noticed.

"Perhaps the story isn't over yet," he said.

"I also apologize for my delay in arriving at the smith's," I said. "I was arranging something at the Temple."

"What?"

"A victory like this does not come without the will of the Gods. So I met with the head priest to find out when the next feast day was," I explained. "The Feast of Andvar is in three weeks. We will thank all the Gods and invite anyone who wishes to come."

"Majors and Minors!" my father breathed. "The last time that was done was before you were born. It was expensive. I remember my father complaining."

"The nomads are donating the cattle for the sacrifice," I said. "I am donating a thousand ducats, so not so awful."

"I didn't realize you were so religious," my father commented.

"I have a healthy respect for the Gods," I explained, "but my attendance at Temple is not frequent."

"Will you allow the armsmen to attend?"

"Of course! I would hope they would all want to be there and receive the praise they are due. Now, how are we going to keep them out of mischief in the meantime with no nomads to scrap with? I have lance training scheduled for tomorrow. The former Rangers have no idea how to use a lance."

The two of us spent the rest of the journey to Bannock Hill devising a regimen for the men. We would teach the Rangers how to wield lances. The armsmen would learn more about night maneuvers. We would visit every town on the border and work with the militia. By the time we could see the camp at Bannock Hill, we had most of the next six weeks mapped out. It was only then that my father remembered the letter.

"What did the king say?"

I handed it to him and let him read it.

"I hope you have paper and a quill hidden away somewhere," I said when he handed it back.

"I do. You should attend to the king's request immediately," my father said. "I will conduct the training tomorrow. After all, I have much more experience than you do."

When we pulled into camp, the armsmen began swarming around the wagon. They weren't coming for the armor since it was under a tarp and not yet visible. The men were eager and excited to share the news of our victory with my father. I slid from the bench of the wagon. My father was trapped by the press of men, all trying to speak at once. Their enthusiasm and high spirits were beginning to infect him.

Eventually, the crowd of men backed away enough for him to climb down. They followed him to a table where he sat to listen to them tell their stories. The announcement that dinner was served did not disperse the throng immediately. A gaggle of the older men who served with my father the longest stayed with him, even in the mess line.

My father and I both tried to be the last in line. He tried to wave me ahead. I returned his gesture.

"Age before beauty," I insisted.

He took the place in front of me, muttering, "Pearls before swine."

I laughed. He meant for me to hear his quip. I took it as a good sign.

When he collected his food, the kersants of the armsmen waved him to their table. I searched for Rowan and Langford and went to sit with them. There was still a division between the armsmen and the former Rangers. With the training my father and I planned, we would begin to eliminate that difference. In addition, we would be shifting men from unit to unit. While we would lose the familiarity and cohesion each unit developed over the years, new bonds would form. With at least a month before the nomads might return, this was the time to shuffle the deck, so to speak.

My father was not finished eating when he noticed the men beginning to rise. He clambered onto the top of the table. Gus Polever whistled and stopped everyone in midstep.

"Men," my father called out, "there are breastplates and helmets in the wagon. Those of you who lack one or both, please try some on until you find one that fits. I am worried in particular about the helmets. From what I have seen this evening, some of your heads seem to have swelled recently."

The men laughed at this.

"In the morning, we will take count of who is still lacking which piece and whether we need to have the smith make larger or smaller items," he continued. "We also have lance training tomorrow. I noticed the quintains and rings have been set up—good. Lest any of you believe we are persecuting you for a particular weakness, we will also begin training on night actions quite soon. Finally, we will be changing unit assignments. We will post the new units next week. Any questions?"

"Why, milord?" came an anonymous voice.

"Because I said so, you impudent pup!" my father retorted with false indignation, which he dispelled by laughing after he uttered it. "Why to which part?"

"Why to shaking up the units, milord?" came the voice.

"Because I have noticed some division in our ranks," my father replied. "There is no room for that. We all ride under the same banner. The only 'us' and 'them' is the 'us' who attack nomads and the 'them' who ran away home. Besides, a change is as good as a rest."

"If the riders went home, milord, won't that give us some rest?" called another.

My father adopted an incredulous expression. "Rest? *Rest*? I'm afraid you're mistaken, young man. Their absence gives us a long overdue opportunity to engage in intense training. The best part is that we won't be interrupted for at least a few weeks, so we'll be able to get serious about it. By the time those bastards return, they'll be facing the finest soldiers who *ever* rode for the March."

The following day, my father took charge of training. Though lance training was aimed at the former Rangers, some armsmen also needed a brush-up. I made a few passes just to demonstrate I knew what I was doing, then retired and went to write King Mark.

My letter began with the news of our putting the nomads to flight. Then, I summarized the earlier battles briefly and informed him of the addition of the former Rangers to our ranks. That section of the letter ended with an accounting of our current strength.

I opened the second part of the letter by thanking him and Queen Liliana for lending Mr. Williston to us and informing him that Marta and Susannah had come to help. The task of establishing a household was made an even greater challenge due to the state of disrepair we encountered. However, the experience of the two women and Mr. Williston had been invaluable. I listed all the repairs that needed to be made to the manor and their progress as of my visit the day before.

Finally, I thanked him for the opportunity and the trust he placed in me. When I finished, I read it over, checking for any errors I might have made. Finding none, I folded it. Then, using a candle I found with the paper and quill, I sealed it. I did not own a signet ring, so I did not have a crest to impress in the hot wax. Of course, I could write to the College of Heraldry and ask them to design something suitable for "Lord Oritur" but balked at the idea. In time, when my father died or decided to step back from his duties, I would become Lord Easton. I was perfectly content to wait.

After finishing that letter, I quickly wrote a note informing Lucy of the arrangements I had made with the head priest. I asked her to find something suitably "lordly" for me to wear and to provide a thousand ducats to the head priest. In closing, I noted the date of the Feast of Andvar, reminding her she had told me I would be returning at that same time. It occurred to me that the Feast of Andvar took place on the same day as the Queen's Cup steeplechase, though perhaps it would be better said in the opposite order—that the race was held on Andvar's feast day.

After addressing both letters, I gave them to Gus Polever. My father had assigned him to return two breastplates and four helmets that fit no one, with instructions to replace them with pieces that were larger. I gave Gus a ducat to pay the Royal Post for the letter to King Mark, needing to send the letter the quickest way possible. The other he would deliver to the manor himself.

That evening, my father excused ten men from tomorrow's training. They were thrilled to hear this and began celebrating and teasing their fellows. Then he informed them they were to drive the captured cattle to Easton and deliver them to Williamson's stockyard, and their celebrating ceased. The horses we took would remain at Bannock Hill until we made arrangements to sell them.

The next three weeks flew by. Heyannir gave way to Twiman. My father retrieved the pay chests full of ducats and brought them to Bannock Hill for the pay muster. By now, the former Rangers were as proficient with the lance as the best of the armsmen. As promised, my father and I reassigned men within the units so that all were a mix of armsmen and former Rangers. By this point, calling them former Rangers no longer felt appropriate. Shuffling the men between units helped erase that distinction quickly, as did their swift mastery of the lance.

I introduced qava to anyone interested or brave enough to try it. Thirty-four of us now enjoyed it and I taught Pete how to make it. He found equipment like mine on one of his trips to Easton and now served it every morning.

With the new units, we left Bannock Hill and began traveling around the border area. We took this opportunity to tell the mayors that the militia should be allowed to attend the Feast of Andvar. Every other night, I picked units belonging to two kersants, and we departed camp after dinner on horseback. We would try to return to camp in the middle of the night to "attack" it. This required teaching the men new duties. The armsmen never stood watch before, though the former Rangers had.

The first few attempts were comical for the blunders made on both sides. Guards fell asleep. The "attacking" party would make so much noise that the men in camp would be able to intercept them along their way. Eventually, I felt the men mastered the basics.

I was about to teach them some new tactics when the day neared for us to return to Easton for the Feast of Andvar. Before we broke camp, my father and I insisted on inspecting everyone's armor and appearance. At the ceremony opening the proceedings, I wanted the armsmen to be arrayed in front of the altar. It would not be acceptable for anyone to wear tarnished or rust-spotted armor or to present an unkempt appearance.

On the morning of the feast, I departed at sunrise. My father would lead the rest of the men shortly afterward. I was pleased with how my father was responding to my challenge. He seemed to be his old self, which Gus Polever confirmed. He had a nice manner with the men, and his sense of humor appeared to have returned. Watching him, I noticed how similar my leadership style was to his.

Riding through Easton, I noticed a profusion of flowers everywhere, with orange as the predominant color. I wondered if that was due to the festival. When I arrived at the manor, I saw further evidence of progress. The scaffolding no longer surrounded it. When I went around back, there was no scaffolding at the stable either. I would need to ask if this meant roof repairs were finished.

Arriving at the stable, another pleasant development greeted me. Tom Collinwood came trotting out and took Andy gently by the head. Behind him, I saw his uncle. I dismounted and thanked Tom.

"Milord," he said, "it would be my pleasure to groom your horse and make him ready for the public."

"And will you be doing this yourself?" I asked.

"Well," he admitted, "I'm still learning, so my uncle will be watching what I do."

"That will be just fine, Tom," I said.

I started to approach his uncle. The older Collinwood met me halfway. He wore a broad smile.

"Well, young varmint," he said, "it's nice to see you made something of yourself after all."

"It's nice to see you as well, Mr. Collinwood. Welcome back."

"Glad to be here," he said, "especially with your lady wife in charge. Now you go see her and get ready for the festival. Don't worry about your horse. We will have him ready."

At the door to the kitchen, I called out, remembering my promise to Laurie not to surprise her. She laughed and bade me come in. As I crossed through, I smelled what I hoped was raspberry pie. I was reaching for the oven door when she rapped the back of my hand with a wooden spoon.

"That just won't do, milord," she said. "Them's the last raspberries of the season, and I'm baking 'em in a pie just for you. Now scoot. Get out of my kitchen before I call Lady Lucy!"

I scampered out of range of her weapon and toward the door. On the way, I spotted a bowl with only a few raspberries left. I quickly plucked them out and scurried out the door laughing before she could scold me.

When I reached the main hall, I hollered for Lucy.

"Up here," she responded.

I climbed the stairs. "Up here, where?" I asked.

"In here."

Her voice came from what I remembered as my grandfather's room. Upon entering, I saw the sizeable four-post bed of Lucy's I remembered from her rooms in the city, which had been the site of some exceedingly happy times. But, even better, I saw Lucy in the bed, with the sheet pulled up to her chin.

"Shut the door and bolt it, my husband," she said quietly, reaching for me. "We don't have much time, and I've missed you awfully."

After that exceptionally welcome interlude, we bathed together in the lavatory. It contained a porcelain tub with a drain that took the used water through a pipe and out of the house. The tub was new, and I did not remember any sort of a drain from before and asked her about it.

"Mr. Pruitt and I made some improvements," is all she would say about the decision, though she did explain the process. "The water is heated in the kitchen. Then the buckets are placed on the hoist platform and lifted up to the hall. That is much easier than carrying them up the stairs, especially for the girls. When you're finished with the bath, you pull the plug, and the water drains out through a pipe that empties outside. You can also pour the water basin out through that when you finish with it. Simple."

We returned to the bedroom, and Lucy laid out clothing for me. They were my wedding clothes—buff breeches and a sky-blue coat, a paisley waistcoat in the same buff and blue colors and a cravat to match. Lucy had also found my suede boots that perfectly suited the breeches. She retrieved her own clothing from one of the armoires. She also would be in her wedding dress, buff and blue to match, though the order of the colors, top to bottom, was reversed compared to my outfit. We dressed quickly.

Looking around the room, I saw it was not finished. There was a jagged gap in the plaster along one wall, from the floor to the ceiling. The floor needed to be sanded and polished. I made a mental note to get a report on Mr. Pruitt's progress later. Also, the windows were different from the rest of the manor. Instead of opening by sliding the frame up, these in our bedroom now opened out. Then I remembered Lucy's rooms in the city had similar windows to allow Chauncey to come in and go out more easily.

As soon as Lucy noticed I was dressed, she shooed me out and called for Rose. As I descended the stairs, I heard the clock in town chime ten. The ceremony was to begin at eleven.

Reaching the bottom of the steps, I heard voices from the study. Marta, Susannah, and Mr. Williston were there. When I was last here, we did not use the study because all the furniture was missing except for the desk, which my father moved to the small drawing room. It was now completely and comfortably furnished into a cozy room with a sofa and chairs, and the desk was in its rightful spot. Both ladies and Mr. Williston were dressed nicely. I said my hellos.

"We were originally planning on leaving a few days ago," Marta said, "but when we learned of the festival you are putting on, we decided to stay to see it."

"Are you leaving as well, Mr. Williston?"

"Aye, everything seems well in hand," he said. Then, after a moment, he added, "That Theo is a puzzle. He says next to nothing, but he understands everything. I never needed to tell him something twice. He'll do a fine job here. And that dog…" he laughed, shaking his head. "That dog… Anyway, along with the ladies, I wanted to see this festival."

"I have no idea how it will turn out," I admitted. "I left things in the hands of the head priest."

"Well, he has been running back and forth between here and the Temple since you left," Susannah stated, "coordinating things with Lucy and Mr. Williston."

"I did notice flowers all over as I rode up," I said.

"Aye," Mr. Williston confirmed. "That's a part of it."

"Is there anything else I should know?" I asked.

"No," he replied. "Most of what the head priest needed was in the nature of organization. He's never done anything on this scale, and no one in Easton has either. Fortunately, I have, so I was able to help them arrange things properly. Other than the flowers, this won't be fancy, but people will be well fed and should go away happy."

"Mr. Williston, can you give me a report on Mr. Pruitt's progress?" I requested.

"Aye. The stable is nearly finished. Pruitt has painters working on the walls and ceilings of the upstairs quarters there. All the lavatories are complete with the enhancements Lady Oritur wanted to add. The staff quarters on the third floor of the manor are finished. The ballroom has been painted, but the floor still needs to be replaced. The chimneys have all been repaired. The first floor is finished, including the painting. The second floor needs plastering in spots, the floors sanded and finished, and then the walls and ceiling painted. Most of the furniture has been delivered, including all the mattresses. Lady Gulick's silverware arrived two days ago."

"That is encouraging news, Mr. Williston. How much longer do you think Pruitt will need, and do I need to withdraw funds for him?" I asked.

"Lady Oritur has withdrawn money as needed," Williston said, "about eight thousand so far. That includes Pruitt, the furniture, and the Temple donation. She also signed the contract with Mr. Pruitt in your absence. Your solicitor, Throckmorton, had no difficulties with it. He also recommended a local attorney if you need one. Pruitt reckons ten days will see him finished, with everything but the ballroom floor completed in a week."

12

Lucy appeared in the doorway then. The sight of her took my breath away. I don't know how it was possible, but I thought she looked even more lovely than at our wedding.

Her golden hair was arranged in braids that encircled her head like a crown. Woven into the braid were tiny yellow and blue flowers to match the colors of her dress. Around her neck was a garland of the orange flowers I had been seeing. Underneath, she wore the necklace I gave her as a wedding present.

"Close your mouth, Caz, or flies will come in," Susannah teased.

"You look beautiful, Lucy," I sighed. "How did you get your hair…?"

"Rose," Lucy responded. "Isn't she a marvel? Now, you and I must leave since we will be right there at the altar. The rest of you can dally for a little while but don't wait too long, or you might get crowded out."

Lucy waited for me and took my arm. We walked through the house and out the rear entrance. Tom Collinwood stood there with Bella's reins in one hand, and Andy's in the other.

What he accomplished in the short time since I arrived was astounding. Andy's coat gleamed. His mane was braided with blue and buff ribbons matching the colors of my clothing. His tail was wrapped with a weave of the same ribbons. In addition, he had a garland of orange flowers on his neck. Bella was similarly adorned.

"Wow!" I exclaimed. I couldn't help myself. "Did you do this? By yourself?" I asked.

"Uh, not by myself," Tom answered bashfully, kicking the ground slightly with his foot. "Uncle Ted showed us what to do, and Hazel and Gladys helped a lot with the braids and the tails. I mostly just kept Andy and Bella calm while they did it."

"Tom, don't demean yourself," Lucy scolded him gently. "You groomed both of them and keeping Bella and Andy calm while two strangers fuss with their hair is no easy task. It shows that both animals trust you, and that is a gift."

"That's what my uncle says—"

"Then you should listen to him," I added. "Where are Gladys and Hazel?"

"They went to get cleaned up, and then we are all heading down together," Tom said.

"Excellent. Please pass along my thanks until I can do so personally. And thank you, Tom. Andy has never looked better. His coat is more glossy than I have ever seen."

"Bella, as well. Thank you, Tom," Lucy confirmed.

Tom, blushing, offered Lucy a hand up. She did not need it, swinging herself into the saddle with the same gracefulness she displayed in all things. I climbed into my saddle and leaned down to give Andy a pat. The strangest feeling came over me. I don't know how I knew this, but I sensed Andy was tremendously pleased, as though he enjoyed being fussed over and knew he looked good. When I had the chance later, I would need to ask Lucy about it.

We left the manor. Jed Lewiston was the guard that morning. He overreacted to our appearance, staggering backward as though overwhelmed. "You look mighty fine for a pipsqueak, milord," he teased.

"I was just going to say that after everyone left, you should lock the gate and come enjoy yourself," I retorted. "Now, I'm wondering if that was a bad idea."

"Pay no attention to him, Jed," Lucy said, leaning in front of me. "Lock the gates and come have fun."

"Thankee kindly, milady," he said, knuckling his forelock. Then, for me, he lowered his hand, touched his thumb to his nose and wiggled his fingers. Lucy and I both rode away laughing.

When we reached the square at the center of Easton, thousands of people were already present. I could already smell cooked beef. In order to prepare for a crowd of this size, the priests could not wait until the "official" sacrifice to begin roasting the meat. The armsmen were already there and formed a corridor to keep a path open for us. As we passed, they reassembled in formation in front of the altar of the Temple's impressive steps. Lucy and I dismounted, tied our horses to a post, and then climbed the steps to where the head priest was waiting. He looked relieved to see us. We exchanged greetings, and I asked him what our role was in the ceremony. He looked to Lucy.

"Our role is mostly decorative, Caz," she explained. "He will ask 'who presents these animals as sacrifice,' and you respond."

"Is there a standard response?" I inquired.

"Um, no, not really," the head priest replied. "You can say whatever you wish."

"Well, it's Andvar's feast day, so I should mention him," I mused. "The whole purpose of today is to offer thanks for our recent victory to all the Gods, Major and Minor, so I will say that. Will that be acceptable?"

"Yes."

We could see the entire square from our vantage point atop the steps. When we arrived, I would guess it was half full. As the time neared eleven, the crowd kept growing. The armsmen were arrayed in ranks and files in front of the steps, and I must admit they looked damned impressive. Their helmets and breastplates flashed in the sunlight. I searched and found my father. He was in breastplate and helmet like the others, so it took me a minute. I beckoned him to join us on the steps. He refused initially, but I gave him a stern look. Kersant Polever also said something in his ear, so my father left the group and headed for us. I clasped his hand and pulled him to where Lucy was.

"I figured out how we will respond when the head priest asks 'who presents these animals as sacrifice,' and I need you both," I said. "In response to his question, we all will say, 'we do.' Then Lucy will say, 'In honor of Andvar, whose feast day this is.' Then I will say, 'To thank the Three Major Gods and all the Minor Gods for their assistance in our recent victory.' Finally, father, you will say, 'And to ask for their continued blessings for the people of the March.' That way, we all have an important role, and we cover the things that most need saying."

The head priest then asked us to move to the right side of the steps, to the audience's left. A group of priests wearing wreaths of orange lilies came from the Temple. Lucy told me orange lilies were associated with Andvar. I'd seen a spectacle like this once in Aquileia for a different Minor God, and I was tickled to be a part of this one. My father looked slightly anxious. Lucy seemed serene.

As the clock on the tower on the opposite side of the square began to chime eleven, two priests wearing orange wreaths appeared from behind the other side of the Temple from where we stood. They were leading a bull with more orange garlands hung on his horns and around his neck. As they neared us, I saw the bull's tail wrapped with buff and blue ribbon to match our clothing and our horses. I nodded my approval to Lucy. She winked back at me.

The priests led the animal to the top of the steps. While they did this, the crowd fell silent. The bull was given rice cakes earlier, treated with a potion to keep him docile. When the bull was standing behind him, the head priest began the invocation for the feast day of Andvar. He asked his question, and we responded in our various parts. The crowd responded with a murmur of approval. That made me feel pleased with myself, I must say.

The head priest then announced the acceptance of the sacrifice on behalf of Andvar and of the Three Major Gods and remaining Minor Gods. He repeated the three different purposes we proclaimed. He was concluding the ritual when there was a ruckus behind us.

I turned to see a man, sword in hand, charging up the steps toward me. My first thought was Lucy, and I swept her out of danger with my right arm. The man aimed his sword at my heart, screaming, "Die!" All I could do was parry his blade with my left arm, deflecting it downward and to my left.

I felt the burn as the blade sliced through my sleeve and along my forearm. Then the impact of the tip punched into my left thigh, followed immediately by an excruciating tingle and then a bloom of intense heat. His sword was buried in my thigh, and my own blade was still in the scabbard. Rather than reach for it, I punched the man in the jaw with my right hand as hard as possible.

He crumpled, losing his grip on his sword, and tumbled down the steps. The armsmen surrounded him immediately. They would have killed him, except my father yelled for them to stop and seize him instead. I could not reach the grip of the sword to withdraw it. Instead, someone grasped it and pulled it out smoothly. I looked to see whose hand it was. Aloysius Fenwick stood there smiling.

"Sorry, Your Lordliness," he said cheekily, "I recognized him too late, or I would have prevented it."

Fenwick turned to look at my attacker, being held by two armsmen. I followed his gaze with my own. My father stomped down the steps, stopping in front of the man. Then my father delivered a vicious backhand slap to the man's face, first with his right hand, then with his left. Then my father spat in his face.

"Is that...?" I started to ask.

"Edwin," Fenwick confirmed.

The crowd was uneasy and on the verge of panic. The head priest was frozen in place. Lucy was beginning to rip the hem of her dress to make a bandage. I leaned on Fenwick and turned to address the crowd.

"People of the March!" I called out. The crowd turned to look at me. "People of the March! I will be fine," I shouted. "It will take more than this to prevent me from giving deserved thanks to the Gods. So, enjoy the Feast of Andvar, as I intend to do."

"The only person here for whom the omens are bad," added the priest, "is the degenerate knave down there. Be assured the king's magistrate will deal with him harshly, but he will also face the judgment of the Gods for attempting to defile this sacred feast day. His intent was to ruin this day of celebration. Do not make his wish come true. Stay. Honor Andvar. Give thanks to the Gods for the recent victory and seek their blessings for a prosperous future."

Fenwick stepped forward when the priest finished. I wondered what he was doing. No one in Easton knew him.

"Three cheers for Andvar!" he shouted, "and three more for Lord Oritur! Andvar and Oritur! Hip Hip—"

"Hurrah!" came a somewhat mild response, though the armsmen bellowed.

Fenwick did it twice more. The second response was louder. The third sounded *almost* enthusiastic. He winked at me as he turned to face us. The noise of the crowd began to rise. It sounded gossipy but no longer fearful.

Meanwhile, Lucy had ripped my sleeve up to my shoulder. She wrapped the cut on my forearm with fabric torn from her dress, binding it tightly. She then ripped the leg of my breeches to inspect the wound in my thigh. Marta and

Susannah arrived, accompanied by Mr. Williston. At the same time, my father came from the other side.

I scanned the crowd. No one was leaving, which I took as a positive. A group of armsmen was taking Edwin to the Easton Gaol. You could hear his progress as people were hissing at him. Some darted up to spit in his face as my father did.

Lucy beckoned to the head priest. When he crossed to her, she said, "We need to get some stitches in his arm—the sooner, the better. Both of us need to change clothes. Neither of us can leave right now without spooking the crowd. We will return quickly. What can we do to divert their attention right now?"

"Start feeding everyone and bring out the ale and cider," my father interjected. "Food and drink will distract them. Do it now!"

The head priest nodded nervously and hurried away to set things in motion. My father returned to the armsmen, most of whom were still immediately in front of the steps. He told them something which I did not hear. However, their response, a raucous cheer, was clearly audible. They began marching in formation to the right of the Temple and started singing "The Farmer's Larder" at the top of their lungs (there was, of course, a much more naughty version of the song by the name of "The Farmer's Daughter").

People nearby started to ask what they were doing. The armsmen on the edges of the formation replied they were going to eat, drink and be merry, as the Gods intended. They stated that meat was being served, ale and cider were now available, and they planned to fill themselves with both until they burst. Watching the crowd, you could see the spread of the information like a wave approaching the shore. As soon as people heard, they began moving in the same direction as the armsmen.

Lucy saw the movement of the crowd and pulled my arm. I hobbled after her. Though she judged the wound in my thigh less severe, it sure didn't feel that way. I would not have been able to mount to Andy's saddle, except Fenwick gave me a boost, putting his hands under my butt and lifting.

"Come with us," I ordered Fenwick. "The gate might be locked, and I figure you will be able to open it."

His horse must not have been far away since he caught up with us before we reached the manor. He dismounted at the gate and soon had it swinging open. "Don't try to dismount until I can catch you," he said, "unless you want to fall on your tookus."

Recognizing the truth of his statement, I waited for him. Indeed, I would have fallen. Instead, he caught me and steadied me on my feet.

"Caz, strip!" Lucy commanded. "Fenwick, the pump. Help him wash the blood off and then keep the arm under the cold water. It will slow the bleeding, and the cold will make it hurt less. I'll be right back."

She dashed into the manor. I began taking off my clothes. Fenwick helped with my boots. The suede was now blood-splattered. I cursed softly.

"What was that for?" he asked.

"I could say it was due to seeing you, which would ordinarily be enough reason," I said. "In this case, it's because this handsome set of clothes was what I wore for our wedding. They're ruined. The boots are ruined as well. The king bought them for me, remember? Lucy also ruined her wedding dress to bandage my arm. Damn Edwin to the seven hells!"

"He'll wish for that before this is over," Fenwick said. "He assaulted a member of the nobility and drew blood. That means he must be tried in the capital, not by a local magistrate. I would not be surprised if the king tries his case personally."

Fenwick worked the pump, and I sluiced away the blood as best I could with one hand. Lucy was correct that the cold water helped lessen the pain in my arm. Once most of the blood was gone, Fenwick told me to hold the wound closed with my fingers.

Lucy came flying out. She beckoned us to the back steps. When we arrived, she handed Fenwick a towel.

"I'm going to pour some alcohol on it to reduce the chances of infection, then I will sew the edges of the cut together," she said. "I need you to keep dabbing the blood away so I can see."

While telling him this, she was threading a large needle with thick black thread. When she accomplished this, she tied a knot in the long end and put the needle between her lips. Then, she took my hand and put it between her knees, clamping it there.

"You know this will hurt?" she asked, mumbling through her sealed lips.

I nodded.

"A lot?"

I nodded.

"Very well."

She unstoppered a glass bottle filled with clear liquid—alcohol, I gathered from what she said. She poured it over the gash in my forearm. Seven hells, it stung! Then, she began stitching the wound together. Fenwick dabbed where and when she demanded. I gritted my teeth and muttered a wide and colorful variety of curses as tears flowed from my eyes in a stream.

After twenty stitches, she told Fenwick to start pumping again. She took me there and rinsed the wound again. She grabbed the towel from Fenwick and used both hands to press it to the wound and took me back to the steps. As soon as she released the towel, she started to wind gauze cloth snugly around my forearm. Blood seeped through the first couple of layers, but eventually, the wrap stayed white—at least for now. When she tied off the gauze, she picked up the glass bottle again.

"You know how this will sting," she said. "After doing this, I will pack the wound with this brown paste." She gestured at a jar next to her. "The alcohol is bad enough, but this will hurt worse at first, like the worst hornet in creation," she warned. "After a minute or two, though, it will take all the pain away for a time."

She was right about the sting. It brought my tears pouring out again. She stuffed the goo into the hole in my thigh. Not content with only reaching the surface, she used her thumbs to force it in as deeply as possible.

When she finished torturing me, she quickly wrapped gauze around my thigh and tied it off. She washed the blood from her hands, then darted back inside. Thankfully, she was correct about the brown stuff taking all the pain away.

Fenwick looked at me with his hands on his hips. "How did you get so lucky? Not only is she one of the prettiest women I've ever seen up close, she is just as pretty on the inside, which is even more rare. On top of that, she is talented. She dressed your wounds as quickly and competently as any physician I ever saw."

"I'm not lucky. I'm blessed by all the Gods," I replied sanctimoniously. "It's because I lead a pious life and think only clean thoughts, Fenwick."

He laughed so hard he needed to sit down and was still chuckling when Lucy returned. She was wearing a different dress and carrying a bundle of my clothes. With both of them helping, I dressed quickly.

"Let's get back before we are missed too much," she ordered as she crossed to Bella and swung into the saddle.

Crossing to Andy, I was able to walk almost normally. Whatever she packed into my thigh was effective. Fenwick stood at the ready if I needed his help, but I was able to get into the saddle, though not gracefully. About halfway up, the muscle in my left leg decided to relax suddenly, leaving me in the awkward position of having my right knee on the saddle and no way to push myself upright. I wriggled on the rest of the way.

After pausing while Fenwick locked the gate, we trotted back to the Temple. The square was still full of people, but they were thronging on the other side where the food was. We dismounted and tied our horses, then strolled to join the crowd.

People noticed Lucy and I had changed clothes but seemed happy to see us. Mumbled "milords" and "miladys" followed us. I still was not used to having a title. In this instance, it made me uncomfortable. When the armsmen began using it, I was not bothered because I saw it as a sign of respect that I earned. With the rest of the March, I did not think I had earned it yet.

As we neared the corner of the Temple closest to where the priests were serving portions of the cattle we captured, I saw Marta, Susannah, Mr. Williston, and my father on the topmost steps. They saw us and waved to get our attention. Through gestures, they indicated we should get some meat and something to drink, then join them.

Lucy leaned close and whispered, "Not yet. We need to mingle with the people and let them see us. This is an incredibly significant opportunity. We cannot waste it. Try to hide how much your wounds may hurt."

The more we wandered through the people, the friendlier they became. It is said that familiarity breeds contempt. In our case, familiarity generated goodwill. A few asked about my wounds. I would smile and admit that they hurt, but not enough for me to miss this festival and spend time with the people of the March. Lucy approved of my answer if the gentle squeeze of her hand on the inside of my right elbow was any indication. We encountered some people Lucy had met since arriving. They greeted her using the term "Lady Lucy." That made me smile.

It was interesting when I was able to hear some of the comments people made after we passed by. A few were about me, but most were about Lucy, commenting that she was as beautiful as people said or, even better, that she was as nice as they heard. I sent a silent prayer to the Gods, thanking them for putting her in my life and asked for their blessings upon my friend, her cousin Freddy, who introduced us.

There was still a line of people waiting to be served, but it was quite short. Then, Fenwick appeared, seemingly out of thin air. During the brief time we waited in line, I asked Fenwick, "To what do I owe the honor of your presence?"

"Good question, that," he commented. "This is neither the time nor the place to divulge that knowledge. However, I noticed you did not ask, 'To whom?' Is that because you are clever and already know?"

"Of course, I know, muttonhead," I replied. "You only take orders from one person. And while I am quite aware I possess a scintillating personality, the likes of which you have never before experienced, and we did work well together on our recent southern adventure, I have not forgotten that you tried to kill me twice and nearly succeeded the first time."

"Oh, Your Lordliness," he responded. "Can't we let bygones be bygones? Why, you and I are almost chums now. Besides, I couldn't bear to hurt your wife in any way. Not only would it break my cold, dark heart, but she would turn me into a newt."

"Have you been speaking with Ollie?" I asked.

"Ollie?"

"Sir Oliver West, Principal of the City Watch."

"No. We try to avoid one another," Fenwick stated. "Why?"

"Ollie has mentioned to me more than once his fear that Lucy might turn him into a newt," I explained.

"Ah," Fenwick remarked, "that explains it."

"Explains what?"

"Where another friend of ours came up with the phrase," Fenwick replied. "It's not fair, you know."

"What's not fair?"

"You consider Albert your friend, but not me," Fenwick whined in an exaggerated way. "He also tried to kill you, but you've forgiven *him*."

"Albert?" I queried. "Did he tell you this?"

"He did but shared no details."

"Albert was not a serious threat to kill me."

Fenwick wagged his finger at me. "His intent was certainly serious, perhaps even more than mine."

Lucy was listening to our entire exchange. She clasped Fenwick by the elbow and pulled him close, giving him a kiss on the cheek. Fenwick's face turned scarlet.

"I'll be your friend, Fenwick, even if Caz won't," she said. "But if you do him harm…"

Fenwick nodded. "Newt. I understand."

"Or worse," Lucy said gaily.

"He's already planning on doing me harm," I complained. "Without a doubt, he is bringing a 'request' from the king that will send me away again. Why is it that we cannot enjoy married togetherness and must instead endure forced separations, one after another?"

"If you weren't so capable," Lucy answered, "no one would request your involvement. Be flattered."

"I would be, but I miss you too much."

"I would miss her too," Fenwick quipped. "My enjoyment would be greatly increased if I could take her on these assignments instead of you."

13

Wₑ took our food and wooden cups of cider up to where the others were sitting. Along the way, Fenwick disappeared again. Before I could sit, my father rose and crossed to me. He enfolded me in an embrace. I could not return it as I had my hands full.

"What's done is done and can't be undone," he whispered, "no matter how much we might wish it. I would like to build a brilliant future with you and your wife if the offer is still open."

"Of course," I said quietly in reply.

As he backed away, I saw the glistening of tears in his eyes. "Marta, Susannah, Mr. Williston," he said, his voice surprisingly strong and steady, "I must go check on our armsmen and make sure their virtue is still intact."

They laughed at his crack.

"Thank you all for your help in restoring the manor," he said. "And Marta and Susannah, my thanks to you for helping to restore this stubborn old man. Hard to say which project was more difficult. I'll see you back at Bannock Hill, son."

He departed, walking down the steps, and fading into the crowd. Marta asked about my arm and leg, and I assured her I would mend. Susannah then spoke.

"So that was Edwin?"

"I suppose," I replied. "I haven't seen him since my grandfather's funeral, but, from my father's reaction, I would say yes."

"He has a weak chin," Mr. Williston proclaimed, "and he could peer through a keyhole with both eyes open. Both are physical manifestations of weak character and poor moral fiber."

I caught myself before laughing out loud when I realized he was serious. For someone's moral and ethical disposition to shape one's physical appearance was ludicrous to me. In my opinion, Edwin was simply his mother's son, and her influence over him was undiluted by anything better.

When I finished eating, Lucy suggested we show ourselves around some more. Since the ladies and Mr. Williston were leaving in the morning and would be staying at the inn this evening, we said our farewells. We offered our heartiest thanks for their assistance. Then, Lucy and I strolled down the steps and back into the crowd.

"I'm guessing we are not staying at the inn this evening?" I said.

Lucy gave me a naughty smile. "I've missed you too," she replied. "As I thought I demonstrated earlier. I think I will need to do a better job of convincing you. And, yes, we will stay in our bedroom tonight, despite the hole in the wall. Theo and the girls have all moved into their rooms on the third floor. Tom Collinwood and his uncle will be moving into rooms above the stable. So, the manor is once again becoming a home."

We ambled among the people for another hour until my thigh began to throb again. Lucy noticed my growing distress. She steered us back to where Bella and Andy were.

"Time to check your bandages, I think," she said. "Can you hoist yourself up, or should I get some help?"

"There's one of the armsmen," I noticed. "I'll ask him."

Ike Jones was one of the six former Rangers who were behind the first group by a few days. I explained that I needed his help. He was fairly tipsy but agreed to assist me.

After he shoved me up, he said with pretended awe, "Cor, I've touched His Lordship's ass. I may never wash my hands again."

Lucy and I both laughed. If Ike weren't wearing a helmet, I would have tried to rumple his hair. As it was, I wheeled Andy around and patted Ike on the shoulder.

"Have fun, Ike," I urged. "And thank you for shoving me up by my lordly butt."

As we rode to the manor, I asked Lucy about my sense of Andy feeling pleased and proud earlier. "Is that similar to the way Chauncey communicates with you?"

"Yes and no," she answered. "With Chauncey, I don't get only a sense of how he is feeling, I *know*. With Andy, and also with Bella, there is a link but not nearly as strong and solid. They are both quite sympathetic animals. Has Andy ever moved or changed pace at almost the same time as you had the thought?"

"Many times," I said. "Particularly in dangerous situations when quick action makes a huge difference."

"Bella and I haven't faced any danger the way you have, but I feel she would react as quickly. According to his aura Carl Stensland has no affinities, but he does have a knack for finding sympathetic animals. It's one of the reasons young Jerry was so upset with their leaving," she explained. "Jerry is very receptive and was able to perceive their feelings. I'm glad you felt Andy's sense of pride this morning. If you pay attention, you'll find he projects other feelings sometimes."

"But you say your connection with Chauncey is stronger?" I asked.

"Very much. It's complicated. To put it into words without sounding ridiculous is problematic. Finally, it's very personal, so discussing it makes me uncomfortable. Let me just say that if an animal decides to bond with you, you will know it without any doubt."

When we returned to the manor, Jon Sinchak was on duty. He seemed half-potted, swaying as he came to open the gate. As he swung it open, he seemed to be leaning on it to prevent falling down.

"Did you have a nice time at the festival, Jon?" Lucy asked sweetly.

"Oh, yes'm, Lady Lucy. It were a swell occasion," he replied, sounding as though his tongue and lips were unaccustomedly thick and sluggish.

"Mr. Sinchak, if you find sleep overtaking you," I said, "just make sure your boots stick out from the guardhouse. That way, a visitor can kick your feet to wake you up."

"Aye," he acknowledged. He lifted his hand as though to knuckle his forelock, but it seemed he forgot what he was doing, and it turned into a wave instead.

His appearance brought a smile to my face. Ordinarily, I would not tolerate a guard being drunk on duty but today was a unique circumstance. I doubted Sinchak or any of the guards would ever do that again.

When we rode up to the stable, no one was present. I slid off Andy's back carefully. When I reached the ground, my left leg gave way, and I hop-staggered backward a few times before recovering my balance. I tied Andy next to the water trough, and he began drinking immediately.

No one was present at the manor. Lucy ordered me to remain at the back steps while she retrieved fresh gauze. While she went inside, I began to undress. I destroyed enough clothes today and stripped to my underthings. When she returned, she was wearing only a thin slip.

"Neither of us wants to ruin more clothing, I see," she said.

Lucy unwrapped the bandage on my forearm first. As she reached the lower layers, she slowed and peeled the gauze away carefully. When she reached the end, the gash was only bleeding in a few small spots.

"I don't want to disturb the scab that's forming," she said.

She quickly wrapped it with fresh gauze and then looked at my thigh. After removing the gauze, she warned, "This might hurt."

She began trying to squeeze from the wound the brown paste she mashed into it earlier. It did hurt—a lot. When she felt there was no more to extract, she started to pack fresh goo into the hole. While it did not cause as much pain as the first time, that's a relative term. It still was agonizing. After she bound my thigh again, she turned to me and clasped my hands.

"This is a perfect time to practice the incantations I taught you," she said. "Before we do, we need to get you in bed. C'mon."

"Why?" I asked as I stood and followed her.

"As you repeat the verses, search within yourself as you were taught at the Temple of Bellona. In the same place, you should be able to sense a connection to Eir. Since Eir is not your dominant, you need to use the incantation to summon her. Pull a plume of that and try to fill your wound with it, if that makes sense."

"I understand," I said, "but why should I be in bed?"

"Because I doubt you will be able to control it, and you will drain all your energy, as you did before you learned how to control Bellona's gift. You will collapse," she explained.

"At least that will keep Fenwick from dragging me away so soon," I cracked, "even though I won't be able to enjoy being here with you if I'm asleep."

"Fenwick doesn't need you for another month," Lucy said. "It's not safe to sail right now."

"He told you what he wants?" I asked.

"Shh," was Lucy's response.

As we climbed the stairs, I realized that Lucy was becoming more comfortable sharing things with me. She could not have spoken with Fenwick since they were never alone without me. Lucy knew of the reason for his visit either as a result of her clairvoyance or from Queen Liliana. I did not want to bring that up since it might make Lucy less forthcoming.

When we reached the bedroom, Lucy shut and bolted the door. Then, after whisking her shift off, she scampered to the bed and forced me down on my back. Very quickly, I forgot all about being wounded.

Later, she said, "Start the invocation now."

I began the recitation Lucy taught me. After the seventh or eighth repetition of the verses, I sensed the presence of something in that place within myself that is not a place. I apologize for how that sounds, but I don't know how else to describe it. Continuing the chant, I became more sure of it and coaxed out a tendril of its unique energy. It possessed a different—well, flavor is the word that seems most apt—a different flavor from Bellona.

As though pulling a string, I mentally tugged it to the gash in my forearm. That tendril began to act on its own, pouring into the wound. Just as I sensed it was out of control, I lost consciousness.

When I woke, I was in total darkness. I briefly wondered where I was. Then, hearing Lucy's breathing next to me, I was able to piece things together. I knew Lucy was lying beside me because I leaned over and sniffed her hair. For some reason, that scent meant happiness to my soul.

Unfortunately, as I returned to wakefulness, other issues were clamoring for my attention. My thigh hurt. I was ravenously hungry. Finally, I needed to relieve myself. This last took precedence over the other two.

Trying to remember where the lavatory was, I attempted to slide gently to the edge of the bed. That required moving my left leg, and an involuntary grunt escaped me. Lucy woke.

"Caz, don't move," she whispered. "Let me help."

She lit a candle, which she could do without a flint, got out of bed, and came to my side. By now, I had managed to reach a sitting position, with my legs touching the floor. Lucy clasped my right hand and pulled me to a standing position. She then maneuvered herself under my left shoulder and helped me stagger to the lavatory, where she lit another candle. My urgent need overcame any reticence I might have felt about allowing her to watch me void my bladder. Of course, she chose that moment to embarrass me by giggling.

"I don't normally get to see him unless he's all puffed up, eager, and acting self-important," she explained.

I rolled my eyes in response, which made her laugh again.

"What day is it?" I asked.

"By now, it's Maniday," she answered, "in the wee hours of the morning."

"It can't be. The Feast of Andvar was Freyday," I said.

"And it is now early on Maniday," she responded calmly. "You have been asleep for more than two days. I suspected this would happen. I'll bet you're hungry as well."

"Starving," I stated.

"Let's get you back in bed, and I'll fetch you something. Wash your hands."

Lucy moved my hands over the pot, then wet them using a small pitcher. She handed me the soap, and I lathered them, then she rinsed the suds away with the pitcher. With that finished, she helped me hop back to bed.

She took a candle and left the room. While she was away, I inspected my left forearm since there was no longer a bandage on it. There was an ugly scar, but the edges of the cut seemed to have bonded together. Someone removed the stitches while I was unconscious, and there was no dried blood.

Lucy reappeared with a tray. It held two plates and a mug, in addition to the candle used to light her way. She brought it to me, placing it on the small table beside the bed. Whisking away the cloth covering the plates, I saw what appeared to be roast chicken between two thick slices of bread and (thank all the heavenly beings!) a large slice of raspberry pie. The mug held cider.

I seized the bread and meat in my hands and tore off with my teeth as big a chunk as my mouth could fit. It was only after swallowing the third mouthful that the pangs from my stomach eased, and I was able to slow down and behave in a more civilized manner. I paused briefly and took a sip of cider.

"Thank you," I said.

"You're welcome. I made sure that Laurie saved the last piece of pie for you. You would have been inconsolable if you missed it."

I leaned over to give her a kiss. "I would have been," I admitted.

It did not take long to devour the bread, meat, and pie. Oh, the pie! The tartness, the sweetness, the texture, the flavor... Lucy began to laugh uproariously. I wondered why, then realized I was making "nom, nom, nom," sounds as I was eating it. That also made me laugh, though I managed to keep my lips closed. I drained the last of the cider, then sighed deeply.

"Explain to me how you knew I would collapse," I asked.

"I knew it would happen because you have not learned to control Eir's energy," she answered. "Just as when you first accessed Bellona's energy. Think of their power as a keg of ale. How do you normally get the ale from the keg?"

"You tap a spigot into the top of the barrel, then put it on its side, and draw it off that way," I replied.

"Exactly. When you went on your pilgrimage, they taught you how to draw off Bellona's force in a controlled way, like using a spigot to control the flow," she explained. "Before that, you were getting to the ale by bashing the end of the keg with an ax."

"And I ended up collapsing, just like this," I said.

"Correct. You just bashed Eir's keg with an ax," she said. "Don't worry, the Goddess is not offended. It's just that her energy flooded out and left you empty. It did wonders for your arm, though."

The next thing I remember, it was light. Lucy was not in bed next to me. Looking around, I noticed the hole in the wall was now plastered over. The workers must have done it while I was asleep.

I managed to hop to the lavatory by myself. Lucy heard me and came upstairs. She found me washing my hands.

"Good," she said. "I'll bring your breakfast."

"Wait! Is it still Maniday?"

"Yes."

Lucy fed me four more times that day, with me dozing in between. I commented that I thought my stomach was like the Abyss of the Seven Hells. She agreed.

"This is nothing new," she reminded me that night. "You've done this before."

"I know, but this is the first time I initiated the process on purpose, if that's what one should call it," I said.

"Well, I think you should do it again," she warned. "This time, for your leg."

"Will I lose another two and a half days?"

"Probably not. I've been doing some things while you've been asleep," Lucy said. "You'll probably collapse again, just not as long. But, before you do, we need to move to the other bedroom. Mr. Pruitt's men need to finish ours."

In the new bed, I repeated the invocation process as I did before. This time I tugged the tendril to my thigh. As before, I lost consciousness.

This time, when I woke, it was the evening on Onsday. Lucy was correct. I only lost a day and a half.

When the morning of Freyday arrived, other than my seemingly unquenchable hunger, I realized I felt almost normal. My thigh still hurt, but only in the sense of having a deep bruise. I was able to walk on it with only a slight limp. Lucy brought me breakfast, and I asked if we could have a bath.

"You want a bath?"

"I want *us* to have a bath," I clarified.

She caught my meaning and winked. Not long after, Rose and Gladys began carrying buckets of hot water into the lavatory to fill the tub. When they announced the tub was full, Lucy and I thanked them. Then Lucy closed our bedroom door and threw the bolt. We did enjoy a bath, but only after we got a little dirtier.

14

Once we were dressed and I was able to leave the bedroom, we went to the study. I began to quiz Lucy on what I missed. She sat in my lap, on my good leg, before giving me the report.

"Mr. Pruitt is nearly finished," she said. "He will begin work on the ballroom today. He is caught up on payment and will require only a further few hundred ducats for the work remaining."

"How much did this end up requiring?" I asked.

"Including the furniture, and some rugs that have not yet arrived, it will come to just under sixteen thousand ducats," Lucy said. "We donated a thousand to the Temple. We will have nearly four thousand ducats remaining in the Easton bank, so all is well."

"What is happening in the outside world?"

"Edwin was taken away in chains to the capital," she said. "Your father returned to watch them take him away. I kept your father company. He left you a note."

"How is his mood?" I asked.

"Good," Lucy replied. "In a strange way, I believe this incident helped your father make a break with the past. Edwin is a wretched excuse for a man, especially compared to you. More than half the March saw that with their own eyes. Your father did too."

"I suppose I should return to Bannock Hill soon."

"Perhaps not," Lucy said. "As I said, your father left you a note and invited me to read it. He seems to have a rigorous program in mind for the armsmen. In addition, Fenwick is still here. He told me you will need to come to the capital as soon as you can travel and are expected in Aquileia on the first of Haustman. He said the king is buying you a new wardrobe, which I did not understand."

"For the last trip I took with Fenwick, the king provided me with clothing appropriate for 'Lord Compote.' It was mostly linen, so it was wonderful for the southern climate at that time of year but not durable. Then, when we were captured, I lost most of it. Where is Fenwick?"

"Now his comment makes sense. I invited him to stay here, but he chose to stay at the inn," Lucy said.

"What has been the reaction of the people to the festival?" I inquired.

"People enjoyed it, though some remain worried that Edwin's attack was an unshakeable bad omen," Lucy explained. "Aquileians are a superstitious bunch, so that is not a surprise. The people here have never had a celebration like this, so they had no expectations and didn't really know what to make of it. They have also never had a fair, which seems to me to be a crime against the Gods. After you speak with Fenwick, if you will return before the end of Haustman from whatever he is asking you to do, we should host a harvest fair."

"I think that's a wonderful idea," I agreed. "If I'm going away the burden of organizing will fall upon you again. I don't feel that's right."

"I would not have suggested it if I weren't prepared," she replied. "I realize a harvest fair will be much more work than the festival, but I watched how the fair at our wedding came together. So, rest assured, I know what I'm taking on."

"If you don't mind, I certainly won't stand in the way," I said. "Now, where is the note my father left?"

Lucy uncoiled herself from my lap. She went to the desk and opened the top drawer. When she pulled out the paper, she returned to me and resumed her position.

Dear Son,

You should know it gives me great pleasure to write that. You are everything a father could wish for—thank all the heavenly beings!

In speaking with the kersants, I shared with them that you have hardly been able to spend any time with your lovely wife since you were married. They agree with me that you should, as they are all a little bit in love with her, as I am. In other words, don't hurry back to Bannock Hill. I am considering dismissing the militia so they can return home in time for harvest. The kersants and I are working out a plan to post forward scouts who can alert us if the nomads return. I don't think they will.

Enjoy some time with your lovely bride and recover quickly.

Father

"That's a very pleasant note," I commented. "Your father thinks highly of you, as he should."

Suddenly, I heard the scrabble of paws and sensed a presence behind me. I craned my neck to see. There was Theo, looming in the doorway.

"Mr. Fenwick to see you," he intoned.

"Please ask him in, Theo," I replied.

"He already did," Fenwick said, sliding past Theo's huge bulk. "Thank you, Theo."

"You're welcome, Mr. Fenwick," Theo said as he faded away.

My jaw dropped. I couldn't believe Theo's behavior. Lucy saw my reaction and started laughing.

"I forget to mention," she said as she laughed, "Theo decided he likes Fenwick—because Toby likes Fenwick."

"What?"

"Toby, as you've seen, worships Theo," she explained. "Toby is indifferent to everyone else, except Laurie and Tom Collinwood. He likes Laurie when it's feeding time. Otherwise, he ignores her, like he does the rest of us. He allows Tom to pet him sometimes. He doesn't dislike anyone in the household—he simply doesn't care one way or the other. Remember, Mr. Joiner said he was raised to be a working dog, not a pet."

"When Toby first saw me," Fenwick said, taking up the narrative, "he came right to me, gave me a few sniffs, put his head in my lap, and let me scratch him behind the ears. Theo trusts Toby's judgment."

"So now Theo's list of people he likes has doubled," I said.

"I'm afraid to say he still doesn't care for you, Your Lordliness," Fenwick smirked, sprawling sideways in the armchair opposite where Lucy and I were sitting. "He is quite happy with his new position, though he credits Lady Lucy for it."

"It was actually Lord Rawlinsford who seized the opportunity to be rid of him," I said.

"I know," Fenwick said smugly.

"Won't you stay for lunch, Aloysius?" I asked, trying to wipe the superior expression from his face.

"Why, thank you. If it's acceptable to you, milady," he said.

"You two!" Lucy said, giggling. "I've only ever seen Caz like this with Freddy."

"You remember Freddy, of course," I said. "You kidnapped him."

"Yes. That didn't end so well—for either you or me," he smirked. "Lord Rawlinsford bashed me in the head, and then the king gave me a limited amount of freedom. That didn't bother you at all, did it, chum?"

I couldn't maintain my façade any longer and started to laugh. In truth, I liked Fenwick. I just didn't want him to be too comfortable. In this, I was probably doomed to fail.

"You've teased me long enough, you scallywag," I pretended to scold him. "What unpleasantness has His Majesty dreamed up for us?"

"Milady?" Fenwick asked, looking at Lucy. "You're keeping score, correct? Please mark that down—he cracked first."

"What are you talking about?" I asked.

"We were having a contest, didn't you know? The challenge was whether you would ask for the specific reason for my visit, or you would wait me out, and I would collapse and tell you without being asked. Regardless, I won this round. One point, milady," he stated.

Lucy licked her finger and drew an imaginary tally mark in the air. "Duly noted, Mr. Fenwick," she confirmed drolly.

"Wait? Whose side are you on?" I demanded.

"Come now, dear," Lucy responded. "He clearly won that round."

"Unfair! I wasn't even aware we were playing!" I protested. "I need an official ruling. Who is the umpire?"

"Theo," they both replied at once.

"I see how it is," I complained through my laughter.

"Even though he tried to kill you twice and kidnapped my cousin, I do like him," Lucy commented to me.

"I bask in your approval, Your Loveliness," Fenwick quipped, rolling his shoulders as if absorbing it. "Now, to business."

"Yes, please," I sighed.

"You may recall that I was to accompany Albert to negotiate a trade agreement with the new sub-vizier in Alygien," Fenwick stated. "Thanks to the queen, our negotiations expanded."

"The queen? What?" I asked.

"Yes, the queen," Fenwick replied. "She must like either you or me an awful lot. I think it's me."

I waved my hand at him to continue.

"Somewhere in her books and scrolls, she learned that the Grand Vizier has several examples of tan-zyan among the royal jewels of Scaramanga," he said. "What the Grand Vizier does *not* have and desperately desires is electrum. Buried in the vaults below the castle are many large pieces of electrum. She informed me of this before Albert and I departed. While we were meeting with the new sub-vizier in Alygien, I casually mentioned that our kingdom's collection of gems lacked any pieces of tan-zyan, and we would be willing to trade valuable jewels in exchange in order to complete our collection. The new sub-vizier, being sharper than his predecessor, asked what we would be willing to trade. 'Oh,' I responded, 'diamonds, emeralds, rubies, sapphires, and perhaps even electrum for particularly fine examples of tan-zyan.' At this, the sub-vizier nearly lost control of his bowels."

"Was Albert a part of this other negotiation?" I asked.

"No, but we agreed beforehand it might better come from me as an underling rather than the Crown Prince," Fenwick explained. "I needed to make the approach. It would have been unseemly for Albert to do so—due to his position, not his personality. By the way, he is a very different man from what I remember a few years ago. I heard you might have something to do with that?"

"I don't have the foggiest idea what you're talking about, Aloysius," I responded, "and even if I did, I could not tell you, however much I might wish to. If there was anything to that story, which there is not, and I shared that information, the king would probably send the royal assassin after me and anyone with whom I discussed it."

"Ah," Fenwick responded, understanding my meaning. "Anyway, the sub-vizier asked us to wait until he received a reply from the Grand Vizier. We stayed in the sub-vizier's residence for an additional four days. Finally, the sub-vizier breathlessly informed us that the Grand Vizier was extremely interested. He humbly begged us to return home, collect some electrum and return to visit the Grand Vizier in the royal palace in Sablanca to trade two pieces of electrum for two tan-zyan stones. Where, presumably, we would try to cheat one another as best we are able."

"This actually sounds fun, Fenwick," I commented.

"Aha! Now I know you're interested," he claimed.

"How?"

"Because you called me Fenwick and not Aloysius," he said. "You only call me Aloysius to upset me."

"It *is* your name," I responded.

"Which my parents gave me, without my having any say in the matter," he complained. "And which you know I detest. But when you are being serious and genuine, you call me Fenwick, as I prefer."

"You're really making far too much of this, Aloysius," I said.

"Arrghh!"

Lucy, still in my lap, seemed amused at our badinage.

"Also, doesn't it bother you that Lucy is listening to these secret plans?" I suggested.

"You cannot possibly be that stupid," Fenwick commented.

"Excuse me?" I retorted, implying I was offended.

"Queen Liliana undoubtedly discussed the entire scheme with your lovely wife before Albert and I even knew we were going to sail to Scaramouche the first time," he asserted.

"Is this true, dear?" I asked with false naiveté.

Lucy merely looked at me and laughed.

"Well, I'll be," I said in wonderment.

Even Fenwick laughed at this. "Hoo," he breathed as he recovered himself. "Now, back to the plan. You and I will accompany Albert and Lord Rawlinsford—"

"Wait!" I almost shouted. "Freddy is part of this?"

"Yes," Fenwick answered. "While I found your version of 'Lord Compote' quite amusing, I understand that Lord Rawlinsford's rendition is the standard by which all others are measured and inevitably fall short. His version is a necessity on this venture."

"And he agreed to this?"

"What do you think?"

"He has probably had his trunk packed for weeks," I admitted.

"Exactly. Not only was Lord Rawlinsford excited to take part, but he also volunteered a clever wrinkle," Fenwick said. "He has been practicing his legerdemain vigorously in anticipation."

"You have Freddy learning sleight of hand tricks?" I asked incredulously.

"He already knew the basics," Fenwick stated. "He said he taught himself so he would learn to spot cheats at the card table. It's why he knew he had been cheated when he lost the ring that reunited the two of you."

"He never told me that!"

"Of course not!" Fenwick retorted. "Lord Rawlinsford, unlike you and me, is a gentleman. It simply would not do for anyone to know he possessed such a skill, or he might be accused himself."

"Freddy does *not* cheat!" I thundered.

Raising his hands and lowering them slowly in a calming gesture, Fenwick stated, "I never said he did. All I said was he learned some of the tricks so he could spot them if others used them."

"Then that's rather clever," I admitted. "Did you know this?" I asked Lucy.

She nodded. "I used to help Freddy practice," she said. "Back when we were practicing other things."

"What other things?" Fenwick inquired.

"Kissing," Lucy responded. "I was curious what all the fuss was about. So Freddy and I taught ourselves and practiced for a week or two until our lips were chapped. By then, I learned enough, and that was the end of it."

"Oh, where was I when you needed a practice partner?" Fenwick sighed.

"I still need practice on transforming humans into newts," she replied calmly. "Sometimes they don't come out quite right and are missing bits. Are you volunteering?"

I burst into laughter. As I recovered, I licked my finger and drew an imaginary tally mark in the air. Lucy grinned.

"Fine, so Freddy is coming as Lord Compote and is practicing legerdemain. Please explain," I requested.

"This part is really clever," Fenwick declared, "and I wish I could take credit for it, but Albert developed it. He did cite you as a source of inspiration, you'll be happy to know—something to do with Lord Compote and switching lead for gold. Anyway, because neither Albert nor I trust the Grand Vizier any further than we could throw him—and he is rumored to weigh nearly twenty-five stone—Albert reckoned we would need to outsmart him. Lord Compote is the curator of the royal gem collection, didn't you know?"

All I could do was laugh, picturing Freddy in that role.

"I anticipate they will allow us to choose stones first," Fenwick said. "Then we will adjourn to haggle, during which process, Lord Compote will demonstrate his near-complete lack of knowledge regarding tan-zyan and his severely limited expertise with other gemstones. This will convince the Grand Vizier and his people that their hope of swindling us will be easier than they possibly imagined. Then, when it comes time to trade stones, they will have switched the tan-zyan for sapphires and we will ride away, none the wiser. Except Freddy will already have switched sapphires for tan-zyan before that, so they will be swapping sapphires for sapphires. According to what Queen Liliana has read, they look nearly identical unless one uses a magnifier."

"This all sounds very clever," I admitted, "but Freddy still wouldn't know tan-zyan from blue bottleglass."

"Aha!" Fenwick almost shouted. "We finally get to the kernel at the very center of the matter. That is why the Royal Assassin and Your Lordliness are coming on this journey. According to the queen, you and I will know when Freddy has tan-zyan in front of him and can signal him."

I looked at Lucy skeptically. "Dear?" I asked.

"You should," she stated. "Have either of you used your power in a manner similar to trying to extend your range of, say, hearing or eyesight?"

"Yes," I responded.

Fenwick shook his head.

"Well, practice," I told him.

"Yes, Your Lordliness," he said as though chastened.

Ignoring our byplay, Lucy continued. "If you can extend your power in that way, you will 'feel' the stone. Not only will you be able to recognize the presence of the stone, but you will also be able to judge its quality. Flaws in the stone make it feel 'dirty.' That's the only way I know how to describe it. You will know it when you feel it."

"So, we trade sapphires for sapphires," I reviewed. "Theirs will probably be of lesser quality since we are supposed to believe they are tan-zyan. Then we ride away, blissfully unaware that the Grand Vizier has just bamboozled us."

"Exactly," Fenwick confirmed. "And here is the official missive."

He handed me a letter with the royal seal.

15

With Lucy still a pleasant weight in my lap, with her arm around my neck and her head close to mine, we read the letter.

Lord Oritur,

We read your recap of recent events with great interest. It pleases us that our trust in you has been so quickly repaid. In our opinion, nomads will likely not return this year. We suggest dismissing the militia in time for the harvest and then have them return to their posts for further training until their year of service is complete.

Mr. Fenwick has, by now, shared information about his upcoming assignment. With the threat to the March eliminated, for now, we would like you to join him and the others on this undertaking. You will depart from Aquileia on or about the first of Haustman, by which time the late summer storms that plague the Surrounded Sea should be finished.

Before you go, you will need to return to our tailor in the capital to obtain clothing suitable for your role in this escapade. When you do, we hope you and your lovely wife will join us for dinner. Let Mr. Fenwick know when you will be coming back, and he will inform us in turn.

M

"When would you like to go, dear?" I asked Lucy.

"I know you feel better," she said, "but traveling immediately would not be a good idea. In addition, I would like to stay until Mr. Pruitt is finished. That should be before the end of the week. If we leave a week from today, we will arrive on the following Maniday."

"That will give me just under two weeks," I said, "since I need to sail on the first of Haustman. You certainly may stay longer if you wish. I also need to make an arrangement with Carl to board Andy. I do not think he will mind being in Jerry's care while I am on this adventure."

"Now, if we are successful," Fenwick stated, "the queen wishes for us to waste no time in having the tan-zyan set into rings. She also wants both of us to have a diamond set into the pommel of our swords. Both these expenses will be our personal responsibility. Further, upon our deaths, ownership of the tan-zyan in the rings will revert to the crown—unless we have offspring who share our link to Bellona," Fenwick explained.

"That makes sense," I said with a shrug.

"You should also have a ring with an emerald and a sapphire," Lucy suggested to me. "And you, Fenwick, should have one with a green tourmaline and a red jasper."

"Why?" he asked.

"Did the queen not tell you of your other affinities?" Lucy asked.

"No. I have not met with the queen alone," Fenwick said, "and I sense she is reluctant to speak of our special talents in front of the king. He is aware of why the tan-zyan will be useful, but I doubt she has gone into great detail with him about it."

"Oh," Lucy said, clearly disappointed. She had been extremely reluctant to share any information with me about my affinities. Queen Liliana was the person who informed me without any reservations. Lucy was affected by her upbringing and by the warnings her grandmother had drilled into her as a girl. As a result, she was extremely reluctant to share information regarding magical affinities or her glimpses of the future.

"You might as well tell him, dear," I said, patting her hand. "Fenwick will just find out the deities to whom green tourmaline and red jasper are linked."

"I suppose you're right," she sighed. "In addition to Bellona, your other affinities are with Mielvanir and Myngvi."

Mielvanir is the god of travel and commerce. Myngvi is the male god of fertility—both in terms of male potency and agriculture—and, to a lesser extent, love. It was an interesting combination, but then, Fenwick was unlike anyone else I ever met.

"That helps explain one thing," I said.

"What?" Lucy asked.

"Why Fenwick is so good with languages. How many do you know?" I asked.

"Aquileian, Rhetian, Scaramanga, Garoth, Vandas, Mooren, Hier, and some Nagahny," he replied.

"That does explain it," Lucy confirmed. "Have you ever been to a country where they don't speak those languages?"

Fenwick thought for a moment. "No," he answered. "Though I didn't know any of them when I first arrived in those countries."

"How long did it take you to learn?" Lucy inquired.

"A day or two," he answered with a shrug, as though that was normal.

"Fenwick, haven't you noticed that most people struggle to learn foreign languages?" I asked.

"Sure, but most people are stupid. I thought that was the reason."

Lucy laughed. "No, Fenwick. Your affinity with Mielvanir makes it easy for you. Majors and Minors! With your blessings, if you were a pirate instead of an assassin, you would be lord of the pirates!"

"Well, for now, I'm an indentured servant," he replied. "The king agreed to allow me to live if I pledged myself to him for twenty years. I can't complain, though. He pays well and promptly and has given me some fun assignments, like this one. By the way, were either of you aware that there are already three different songs I've heard being sung in the taverns about your recent victory?"

"Really?" I replied with amazement. Gus Polever had told the men it was the type of thing they wrote songs about, but I thought he was exaggerating.

"Yes, really," Fenwick replied. "One is quite heroic and features the exploits of Your Lordliness. Another is quite humorous. The third is humorous and scatological, on the edge of being obscene. Can you guess which is the most favorite and which the least?"

"The last one is the favorite, of course," Lucy said. "The first song is clearly the least popular."

Fenwick licked his finger and drew another imaginary tally mark in the air. "That's two points for you today, Your Loveliness."

Our conversation was interrupted by Theo announcing lunch was served. We gathered in the dining room. The difference between my last meal here and now was immense. There were now thirty-six matching chairs at the huge table. The table itself was covered by an enormous piece of brilliantly white linen. At each of the nine places set were matching silver utensils and a linen napkin. The napkins were embroidered with the initials L A F. As Lucy took her seat, I pointed to the embroidery.

"Lucille Austermain FitzDuncan," she said. "Susannah gave them to us."

After lunch, Fenwick departed. I began to feel woozy with fatigue. I jotted a quick note to my father. In it, I shared that the king also suggested dismissing the militia for the harvest, then recalling them to finish out their year. I also informed my father of my upcoming travel at the king's request.

That finished, I went to the stable and gave the note to Tom Collinwood and asked him to carry it to Bannock Hill. Returning to the house, I asked Lucy into which bedroom we were moving, and she took my hand and led me to our room, now finished. I fell asleep while my head was still on the way to the pillow.

Over the remainder of the week, my energy returned. Since there was not much for me to do, I spent time recalling the things I learned during my visit to the Temple of Bellona to see if I could use them with Eir. I began with the breathing exercises that would bring me to a state of utter calm and intense inward focus. Then I started repeating in my mind the incantation Lucy taught me.

At first, that would cause me to lose my concentration, and I would need to begin again. After two days, I was able to accomplish this. I then was able to sense the node of Eir's power in addition to the one containing Bellona's. Once could do that, I attempted to pluck the tiniest tendril of energy from Eir, just as they taught me to do with Bellona at her Temple. This was the reason I needed that unwavering inner concentration. Without it, the power would surge beyond my control as it did before.

Having learned how to manage Bellona's power, this came more quickly the second time. On Tirsday, I asked Lucy to be present when I endeavored to try to apply Eir's energy to my still-healing wounds, in case I lost control. We sat on the bed, and I took my time to achieve the proper state. When I was ready, I fastened onto the tiniest tendril I could manage and drew it over to my forearm, hoping to lessen the scar. I sensed I could reduce its thickness slightly and then stuffed the wisp of power back in its place.

When I returned my attention to the world, I looked at Lucy, who was grinning. "Look what you did!" she whispered excitedly.

She pointed to my forearm. The scar was reduced just as I "saw" it. Even better, I felt no more fatigued than when I began.

"I still need to practice," I said. "With Bellona, I no longer need to focus so intensely. I can find her and access her without needing to withdraw from the world around me."

"That is because she is your dominant," Lucy explained. "Eir is not, so you will always need to block out other influences. Your practice should center on achieving that inner sense more quickly. Once you can do that, you can try to use the power on someone other than yourself."

"As you have done for me," I remarked.

Mr. Pruitt declared the work complete later that day. We walked through every room in the manor and the stable, and he described the extent of repairs in every room. At the end of the inspection, Lucy declared she was satisfied. When I inquired if we owed him any further payments, Mr. Pruitt admitted he slightly overcharged us by a total of seventeen ducats, six florins. I suggested he keep half and donate the rest to the Temple, asking for blessings upon the manor.

We left the next morning, Freyday. Lucy's saddlebags were more voluminous than mine. She already wrote to the woman living in our house, Roberta, to warn her of our arrival. She also informed Freddy and Greta we were coming.

Our three-day journey to the capital was uneventful. The weather was pleasant, we encountered no difficulties, and Bella and Andy seemed to enjoy the exercise and change of scenery. We arrived at our house in the late afternoon of Maniday. Roberta greeted us effusively, happy to have company.

I had not been in the house since Lucy began to furnish it. When we bought the house, it was dusty, and the furniture was dated. Now, if there was a spot of dust anywhere, it was too small for my eyes to see. The furniture and rugs Lucy chose established a sense of elegant and cozy comfort. I really liked it and told her so.

Once I carried our bags up to our bedroom, I excused myself. Lucy asked where I was going, and I told her we would board the horses at the Foaming Boar. We could have kept them in the backyard—there was a shed where we could store their tack—but I knew Jerry would be thrilled to see them.

The Foaming Boar was an inn owned by a former sergeant in the Rangers named Carl Stensland. When the king named me Lord Oritur and I left for the March, Carl was the one I asked to find former Rangers who might enjoy returning to military life. Jerry was an orphan Carl found hiding in the stable a couple of years earlier. Carl gave Jerry the job of taking care of the guests' horses and his own, in return for room and board, plus a small wage. My horse Andy originally belonged to Carl, as did Lucy's horse, Bella. When I needed to leave for the March, Jerry was quite upset with me since he loved both animals.

Riding Andy, I held Bella's reins. I could sense Andy knew where we were. As we neared the inn, Andy projected a feeling of excitement. When we rounded the corner of the building to the stable, both Andy and Bella began to neigh. I had not even come to a stop when Jerry came dashing out. Andy nuzzled him on one side and Bella the other. Jerry clasped both their heads with his arms and pulled them close. The two animals began to nicker softly.

Jerry looked up at me with tears in his eyes. Seeing that, my eyes welled up in response. I slid to the ground and tried to control my emotions. Jerry was murmuring to both horses, and I could hear the tears in his voice. I went inside to inform Carl that I was boarding the horses for the next two weeks.

Carl was bustling in preparation for the dinner hour. He caught sight of me and nodded to indicate he would return quickly. In less than a minute, he strode in wearing a grin, extending his hand.

"Aren't you a sight for sore eyes!" he exclaimed. "What brings you back?"

"Some things to which I need to attend," I replied, shaking his hand. "Thank you for sending so many men. We needed all of them. Together we achieved an unprecedented victory."

"I want to hear all about it," he said, "but I don't have time now. Will you and Lady Lucy stop in some other time?"

"You can depend on it," I said.

"Have you seen Jerry?" he asked.

"I left him with Andy and Bella. Neither of us was capable of talking right then," I said.

"I'm not surprised," Carl admitted. "He loves my new horse—Davy—but he still misses Andy and Bella."

"They missed him too, from what I could see."

"Caz, I'd love to chat, but you caught me—"

"I know, Carl. I needed to compose myself since Jerry's reunion had me on the verge of tears. Lucy and I will be here in the next few days, I promise."

I returned to the stable and found Jerry in the process of unsaddling Andy. Sneaking up behind him, I rumpled his hair. He nearly jumped out of his shoes before squirming away.

"Cor, Mr. Caz, taking advantage of me in my distressed state," he complained, but his smile put the lie to it. "Here I am all weepy at seeing these two again, and you decide to attack me."

"Majors and Minors, Jerry! How much have you grown lately?" I asked. "You have to be four inches taller than when we left."

"Eh, that might be right. I don't keep track myself. I just know none of my clothes fit, and Mr. Carl like to pitches a fit about it."

"Jerry, I'll have you know that Andy shared with me that he knew where we were, and he got very excited when he turned in," I shared. "If I'd been touching Bella, I bet I would have sensed the same from her."

"They already let me know they're happy to see me," Jerry said with some smugness.

"I know they are," I agreed. "I don't have the time to tell the story right now, but Andy helped us win a huge victory recently. I promise I'll tell you all about it when we both have more time. Also, if you would check, I have a feeling both of them need to visit the farrier. Would you be willing to take them?"

"Sure, Mr. Caz."

"Good. Here's a ducat. I know it won't cost half of that, so I want you to use the rest on yourself."

16

I walked back to our house to find Lucy gone. In the kitchen, Roberta told me she had just stepped out for a minute, so I knew she went to Freddy and Greta's. I smelled dinner cooking.

"How soon until dinner is ready, Roberta?" I asked.

"Another forty minutes," she replied.

"I'll go find Lucy," I said.

Across the street and three doors down was Freddy's house. His family bought it for him while we were both still in school since it might be years before another property in this section of the city came up for sale. That lack of availability is one of the compelling reasons I bought our house. Then our lives changed dramatically when the king proclaimed me Lord Oritur and commanded my father to adopt me and name me as heir.

Knocking on Freddy's door without encountering the obstacle that Theo represented would be a treat. One of the benefits of having Theo as the manager of the manor is that he could not deny me access. Roger came to the door. Roger had been with Freddy before Theo. Freddy's parents sent Theo to replace Roger since they could no longer tolerate having Theo around their home.

Upon seeing me, Roger bellowed, "Milord, Mr. FitzDuncan to see you."

"Damme, Roger," Freddy hollered back. "He's Lord Oritur now. I know I told you that."

"Sorry, milord," Roger shouted. "I forgot. Won't you come in, milord?"

"Thank you, Roger."

Unlike Theo, Roger offered to take my jacket and sword, then hung them carefully in the hall. Fortunately, at the manor, Theo would not be answering the door. We delegated that task to whichever of the girls was closest.

I walked back to the salon. Freddy unfolded himself from the sofa where he was sprawling, displacing Greta in the process. She was using him as a backrest.

"It's good to see you, Caz," he said effusively, taking my hand in both of his. "We have so much to tell you."

"Likewise," I said, leaning forward to kiss Greta's cheek.

"Lucy has been entertaining us," she said. "Telling us all about Theo and his dog."

"Did she reach the Fenwick part yet?" I asked.

"No," Lucy responded. "I'm almost there."

"Fenwick?" Freddy said. "The assassin?"

"Yes," I confirmed.

"The number of people Theo professes to like has doubled," Lucy said.

"He used to say you were the only person he liked," Freddy said.

"Well, he likes Fenwick now as well. Apparently, when Fenwick first arrived at the manor, Toby, the dog, trotted right to him and allowed Fenwick to scratch him behind the ears. Toby ignores the rest of us. He's not hostile—just indifferent. Theo decided Toby was a good judge of character, so he decided he likes Fenwick," Lucy explained.

"Oh, my," Greta said.

"What else?" Freddy inquired.

"Since Toby jumped into Theo's arms, twice in my hearing, Theo has put together sentences of four words," I added.

"Humph," Greta grunted. "I don't believe it."

"With my very own ears," I affirmed.

"Actually, when Caz has been away, it's not unusual to hear him string together six or seven words occasionally," Lucy commented.

"Now I know you're fibbing," Freddy stated.

"All the Gods, Major and Minor, and all the heavenly beings," Lucy said, holding her hand up as if swearing an oath.

Lucy and I departed shortly afterward. Greta invited us for breakfast in the morning. We told her we wouldn't miss it.

The morning of Onsday, a day and a half after our arrival, Lucy and I were eating breakfast when there was a knock at the door, followed quickly by Freddy, calling, "Hullo?"

"Come in, Freddy," I shouted.

Freddy appeared in the doorway with Fenwick right behind.

"Good morning, Freddy. Good morning, Aloysius," I said.

"Aloysius?" Freddy asked, then began to laugh.

"That was my parents' choice," Fenwick started to answer.

"If my parents saddled me with a name like that, I might have turned into an assassin also," Freddy joked.

"Freddy, you'd be a terrible assassin," I remarked. "Would either of you like something to eat?"

"Lord Rawlinsford already fed me," Fenwick admitted.

"Good," I responded, "because I would hate to ask Roberta to make breakfast all over again."

"What do you have planned today, Your Lordliness?" Fenwick asked.

"Somehow, I don't think it matters, does it?"

"Not really," Fenwick stated. "We are expected at the tailor."

"When?"

"As soon as you finish eating," Fenwick replied.

Lucy laughed.

"Why is this funny?" I asked.

"Because Fenwick just has a certain way about him," she replied. "I would find it rude for another person to make a demand like that, potentially disrupting the entire day. But with Fenwick, it's to be expected. It doesn't seem to bother you either."

"The likes of a creature such as this?" Freddy responded. "What good does it do to take offense? The lower classes have no concept of priorities. No offense, Mr. Fenwick. I'm sure you're one of the better examples. But everything they do is entirely in pursuit of immediate gratification of their animalistic needs, don't you see."

I began roaring with laughter. Fenwick and Lucy looked puzzled. Freddy simply sat there waiting for someone to agree with him.

"Lucy, Fenwick, meet Lord Compote," I said once I caught my breath.

Their perplexed expressions faded into smiles as they understood.

"Pleased to meet you, milord," Fenwick said to Freddy.

Freddy rolled his eyes in response.

"He's much better at Lord Compote than you," Fenwick told me.

"I already told you that," I said.

"Majors and Minors," Lucy exclaimed. "I'd forgotten how funny that is. So, who is it again, Freddy?"

"Freddy will tell you it's Lord Compote," I said. "I can share that he is based on a former schoolmate named Louis Fresnel. Fresnel is dim-witted, pompous, obscene, opinionated, vain, arrogant in his stupidity, insensitive, and completely unaware of how others perceive him. The two of you have something in common, Fenwick."

Fenwick lowered his eyebrows at me.

"Fresnel insists people call him by his last name," I said.

Lucy licked her finger and drew an imaginary tally mark in the air. "All even," she announced.

"Actually, I think you still have us both by one," Fenwick suggested.

"Oh, I'm only playing for fun," she replied glibly. "Not like the two of you."

"Oh, this is for you, Your Loveliness," Fenwick said, producing a piece of paper embossed with the royal seal.

"We are invited to dine this evening with Their Majesties," she said upon opening it.

"As are we," Freddy added.

"I'm not," Fenwick said glumly.

"As I was saying," Freddy said, "the lower classes no longer have a sense of their proper place in the social orders. Look at Ashe, here. It has taken me *years* to train him to the point where I don't cringe in potential embarrassment every time we are in public. Mr. Fenwick, dinner this evening is obviously an occasion for titled nobility, not tradesmen. I doubt Their Majesties would ever stoop so low."

"Thank you for simplifying that for me, Lord Compote," Fenwick replied, knuckling his forelock. "Who is Ashe?"

Freddy sniffed with obvious disdain for such a dull question. "He is, imbecile," he said, jerking his head to indicate me. "Reg Ashe, my factotum."

Freddy and I walked to the nearby market square and hired a hackney to take us to the tailor. Fenwick gave us the address before we left the house. In the coach, Freddy was squirming with excitement.

"I've been dying to be involved with another one of your adventures since the Parkinson thing," he said. "To be summoned by the king and asked to take part—that was even more than I hoped."

"How did that transpire?" I asked.

"A couple of weeks ago, I received a note from the king. In it, he asked very politely if I would call on him at my convenience," Freddy explained. "You and I know there is no such thing as 'our convenience' when the king issues such an invitation. I dropped everything and went to the castle immediately. The king and Albert met with me. After thanking me for coming so promptly, the king disappeared, and Albert explained what our task would be. He got very excited when I mentioned to him I knew some sleight-of-hand tricks.

"When Fenwick told me, I was surprised as well, old friend," I said. "I never knew."

"It is not the sort of thing one casts about," Freddy replied. "If people knew…"

"Yes, it would be taken the wrong way," I agreed.

"I have been practicing since being asked to participate," Freddy said. 'With all due modesty, my skill is up to the task."

"It does not bother Greta that you are putting yourself at risk like this?" I asked.

He looked at me quizzically. "Greta is coming, too. Didn't you know?"

I tried to keep my feeling of alarm out of my expression and response. "Are you sure that is a good idea, Freddy? There is the possibility that we are discovered, and it may become quite dangerous."

"I explained that to her," he said with a hint of defeat on his face. "She refused to take 'no' for an answer. 'Lord Compote would never travel without one of his saucy maids,' she said. She has even engaged a seamstress who made three different scandalous costumes for her. I tried and tried to talk her out of it but made no progress. However, once I bowed to the inevitable, I was able to see how she will be useful."

"How?" I asked, not understanding.

"All sleight-of-hand tricks depend upon distraction," Freddy explained. "Greta will be an irresistible distraction. Further, you yourself told me the secret to ventures of this type was to display what your audience expects to see. In this case, they will see Lord Compote, an imbecile who is not even qualified to be a curator of burnt matches, let alone the royal jewels. His dimwittedness and his naughty dalliance with his lovely maid will convince the Grand Vizier and his people that I could not possibly be a threat to their scheme to cheat us."

"Are you sure they plan to cheat us?"

"I have no idea," Freddy admitted. "Fenwick, on the other hand, is absolutely certain. I trust his judgment."

"As do I," I said, then sighed heavily. "Lucy will be jealous."

"Lucy *is* a bit jealous," Freddy confirmed. "At least, from what I saw before you arrived yesterday afternoon. She has other things to do—namely, organizing the harvest festival she mentioned that she wants to have in Easton. Greta and I plan to attend, by the way."

When we arrived at the tailor, we asked the hackney to wait. Our visit to the tailor was brief. They measured us in every conceivable way. The cobbler was there also and confirmed that the lasts he made of my feet were still the proper size. Freddy had already sent him lasts of his feet from his regular cobbler.

When we returned to the hackney, Freddy decided to go to his club, the Equestrian Club. He had a card game scheduled with Greta's brother Ratty, Linc Ellsworth, and Quint Pompeo. He asked if I wanted to play two days hence, and I accepted. After dropping Freddy at the club, the hackney took me to our house, where I paid the fare.

I found Lucy chatting with Roberta in the kitchen. As soon as there was a break in the conversation, I asked Lucy to join me in the parlor. She followed me in and sat on my lap. I must say, feeling her pleasant weight and holding her that close was one of the things I missed most when we were separated.

"Lucy, I'm sorry," I said.

She gave me a puzzled look.

"I just learned that Greta is going with us to Scaramouche. I had no idea. If I had known, I would have asked if you wanted to be included."

"You're sweet," she replied, kissing me softly. "There isn't a part for me to play. Besides, I have something more important."

"The harvest fair," I said.

"Exactly. I will admit I was jealous at first, but having a night to sleep on it, I know I will reap much greater happiness from the fair," she said. "You have been on the border most of the time since you arrived, so you have not seen what I have. Growing up, the examples of lordship I observed from my father and uncle differed from what has happened in the March during your father and grandfather's tenure. The principal difference is involvement. Because of his marriage, your father distanced himself—"

"He hid," I said. "You won't offend me by speaking plainly, dear heart."

"Fine. Your father hid," Lucy agreed. "From what I have learned in speaking with people, even before that, your grandfather was not especially fond of supporting things like fairs and festivals. I suspect that is because he looked only at the cost and did not consider the benefits."

"Keep going," I asked. "I'm curious."

"Something my family, and Freddy's family, have always understood is that these public events should not be measured solely in terms of expense," she continued. "A fair, where people gather and exchange goods and produce, makes those transactions easier to arrange and complete. This increases overall prosperity. My father reckoned that each ducat he spent in sponsoring a fair would then be spent six more times. A festival, like the one we just held, also had a beneficial effect, though not as much as a fair."

"How do you figure?"

"Let's say a thousand people from outside Easton came to the Feast of Andvar, attracted by the prospect of a free meal and a bit of fun. I think it was many more than a thousand but let's use that number."

I nodded in agreement.

"How many of those thousand rode in that morning and departed that evening?"

I shrugged my shoulders. "Half?"

"Even if it was three-quarters that means over two hundred people came to Easton for more than just the day. Where did they spend the night? How did they feed themselves the rest of the time? Did they buy anything while they were in the city?" Lucy asked. "I can see from your face that you are beginning to understand. The amount of money they spent was probably much more than the thousand ducats we contributed. All of which helped make local merchants a little more prosperous than before."

I pondered for a minute.

"So, sponsoring an event like this increases prosperity," I said,

"And goodwill, which I have not mentioned," she added.

"And goodwill. The merchants who reaped a profit due to the festival now have more to spend on the things they need or want. As a result, everyone's circumstances improve over time. Is that correct?" I asked.

"That's how my father and uncle have always viewed it," she said. "Increased prosperity for all eventually brings increased tax revenue, though it is hard to trace exactly how it happened."

"So, instead of viewing fairs and festivals as expenses, we should view them as investments?"

"Yes. And because there have been no events of this type for so long, the first few times we conduct them people will notice the gains more easily," she said. "As a result, while it might be fun to indulge in some play-acting in Sablanca, my time is better spent in Easton."

"Plus, I don't think I would be allowed to play slap and tickle with Lord Compote's maid on this venture," I added.

"That's another compelling reason to stay behind," she joked.

17

Lucy pulled my gray suit of clothes from the armoire for our dinner at the castle that night. She also selected a pair of black court shoes for me instead of boots. For herself, she selected an attractive dress the color of honey. It went marvelously with her hair, which Lucy arranged in a simple twist. Greta earlier booked a carriage for all four of us, so we walked to their house when we were ready.

The carriage was waiting out front. As we neared, Greta and Freddy appeared. Freddy and I assisted the ladies up, then climbed in ourselves.

"I'm trying to think of the last time the four of us shared a carriage," I said. "And whether the evening turned out well or ill."

"It was a fun night," Lucy said. "We went to Linc Ellsworth's party at winter solstice last year."

Majors and Minors! I thought. *Was that only nine months ago? So much has happened since then!*

I kept that to myself. I let the others talk about the things they'd done since then. There were some things I couldn't discuss, even with such close friends.

We arrived at the guard post, and a page was waiting to escort us across the bridge to the castle. The seneschal met us and guided us to the dining room. I gave the guard outside the door my sword before entering.

Once inside, the seneschal instructed me to sit on the king's right and Lucy on the queen's left. Albert was on my other side, and Freddy and Greta were next to Lucy. Queen Liliana was already seated. The rest of us needed to wait until King Mark sat down. When he did, Freddy assisted Greta and then Lucy with their chairs. Once Lucy sat, Albert did, then Freddy and me. That always seemed the most complicated part of the meal.

Over the first course, the king wanted me to describe the skirmishes with the nomads in more detail. In particular, he wished to know how we achieved success despite being severely short-handed at the outset. While I understood this was a topic of keen interest to him, I knew the other five at the table were far less interested. I credited my experience on the Rhetian border and the importance of instigating action. This, at least, brought Albert into the discussion, and even though he was a horrible commander back then, he was able to show he did learn some things from his experience.

During the second course, the king questioned me about my father's state of mind. Though I responded initially, Lucy soon took over. The queen then asked Lucy about the repairs to the manor and our sponsorship of the Feast of Andvar.

"I understand your half-brother tried to kill you?" the king inquired.

"He was not very successful, Your Majesty," I replied. "In fact, the Feast was only slightly disrupted."

"Well, Edwin was a failure in all things, except his last," the king remarked.

Seeing my look of puzzlement, Albert said quietly, "He succeeded in hanging himself in his cell."

The little I knew of Edwin did not suggest that a gutless worm like him would ever be able to muster the courage to take his own life. That meant Fenwick did it. I said nothing.

When the third course arrived, the queen asked about our weddings. This was by far the most pleasant topic of the evening and one to which all the guests, and Albert, could contribute. However, the king's interest waned quickly. Just before dessert arrived, the king pushed himself back from the table. All of us, except the queen, jumped to our feet.

"I apologize," King Mark said, "but I will not partake of dessert this evening. I am feeling a bit gouty lately and don't wish to make it worse. So please stay and enjoy, and do not allow my departure to spoil or end your evening."

After he departed, Albert took his father's seat. Once we were all in our chairs again, the queen said, "That is Mark's way of saying he is uncomfortable with the most important topic of discussion, which we have not yet touched."

The door opened, and Fenwick entered. He took the seat on the end next to Greta. He was just in time since they served dessert immediately after he sat down. They even served Fenwick a portion.

"I don't wish to discuss the details of what you plan to do," Liliana said. "Albert has explained it to me in broad strokes. My only desire is to determine whether you are all willing to assume the risk inherent in the venture."

"If there is a risk, it will come after we leave Sablanca," Fenwick said. "My most grave concern is that they discover our substitution before we reach the coast. Should that happen, there is the potential for armed conflict."

"Armed conflict?" I asked.

"The crown prince would not travel to a foreign capital without a *full* retinue of the Castle Shield," Albert stated. "When we traveled to Alygien, I brought only one troop of forty men. Visiting the capital of Scaramouche, diplomatic protocol demands I arrive with no less than a full company of one hundred and twenty. There will also be some foofaraw where I inspect the Grand Vizier's soldiers, and he inspects mine. That will take place after our first meeting."

Albert paused to take a bite of his dessert, an unbelievably delicious hemispherical chocolate creation.

"An armed confrontation is potentially highly embarrassing for the Grand Vizier," Albert continued. "Since the entire exercise is to trade electrum for tanzyan, he can hardly fault us for doing just that. The only recourse he might have is to claim that, unbeknownst to him, his people cheated us and substituted sapphires. In which case, we reassure him that we spotted the deception and rectified the problem before leaving. So, while a confrontation is possible, I doubt it will come to actually exchanging blows, so to speak."

"With that in mind, are all of you still willing to participate in this?" the queen asked.

Fenwick, Albert, and I did not really have a choice—the king, my liege lord, requested that I take part, so I would. Freddy was nearly foaming at the mouth since he wanted to do this so much. That left Greta, and all eyes turned to her—by far the smallest person at the table.

"All of you have engaged in audacious exploits," she said. "I have not and have envied you the excitement. This might be my last opportunity. I understand the risk and I still wish to play my role."

Queen Liliana smiled and complimented Greta. "Well-said, my dear. Well-said. Now, Lucy, you are not a part of this. Would you like to be?"

Lucy shook her head and explained to the table what she had discussed with me earlier. "Besides," she said, "this is Greta's chance to shine."

When it came time to depart, I was ready. Since our arrival, we met with everyone we wanted or needed to. We caught up with our friends, heard all the latest gossip, and enjoyed some fabulous meals. In addition, Lucy and I met with Pierre Luin, my financier, and Graham Throckmorton, my solicitor. Between those two, we smoothed out any difficulties caused by my rapid departure to the March.

Lucy prepared some ginger oil and licorice root to help us stave off seasickness. She did not come to the dock for a farewell since we needed to play our parts. Any sailor or soldier would only know we were who we said. I was back in my Reg Ashe persona, in the role of Lord Compote's factotum. Greta was his saucy maid. Thankfully, in front of the soldiers, she wore one of her two more demure outfits. According to Lucy, Greta had three others made that would have caused a riot.

I was dressed in burgundy. The cloth was of a decent weave, as one would expect for a servant of a wealthy noble like Lord Compote. As Albert's factotum, Fenwick wore a similar outfit in a muted gold. Freddy's clothing was the height of current fashion, though the jacket and breeches were of a lesser thickness to accommodate the heat we would encounter in Scaramouche. Instead of a cravat, he sported a small ruff. The buttons and cuffs of his shirt sprouted decorative frills of lace. Fop is the word that immediately sprang to my mind regarding his appearance.

There were three large ships, each one holding forty horses and men. Ours had forty-one horses since Albert was bringing his. When we landed, Lord Compote, his maid, and I would engage a carriage, though Fenwick and I would be relegated to sit next to the coachman on top.

It was my task to bring Lord Compote's baggage aboard, as well as his maid's. Both brought large trunks. His maid would share his quarters, which raised eyebrows among the ship's officers. Fenwick and I were each allowed a "serpentin" below deck with the crew. A serpentin was a piece of sturdy cloth suspended on either end. Having slept in one before, it did not trouble me.

I daubed some ginger oil on my upper lip when we set sail. On my last trip across the Surrounded Sea, I was horribly seasick both coming and going. The ginger oil made an enormous difference. It did not eliminate the nausea entirely, but made it bearable, particularly with the help of licorice root to settle my stomach. As a result, I endured three miserable days but stayed on my feet the entire time. Freddy seemed to suffer the same as I did. Greta, Albert, and Fenwick were unaffected.

During the trip, Freddy, Fenwick, and I worked out a system for how we would identify the best pieces of tan-zyan for Freddy.

"They will likely dump a small cloth bag of gemstones on a soft cloth," I said. "It will probably be a dozen or less."

"They will probably have a couple of pieces of tan-zyan, but most will be sapphires," Fenwick added. "They will do this to see if you can spot the difference. Arrange the stones in a grid, as though organizing them will help you decide. Caz and I will identify the two best examples of tan-zyan. I will signal rows, starting at the top. Caz will signal files, starting from the left."

"What sort of signal?" Freddy asked.

"I might sneeze," Fenwick replied. "If I sneeze twice—achoo, achoo—that means?"

"Second row down," Freddy responded.

"What if I comment that a button has gone missing?" Fenwick said. "And I point to it?"

"I count the number of buttons down from your collar," Freddy said.

"Then I might tap my finger three times as though I am bored," I added.

"Third from the left," Freddy stated.

"Or I might comment that it has been four nights since I slept well?" I suggested.

"Fourth from the left," Freddy replied.

"It would be best if Caz and I identify both the stones we want before you pick any of them up," Fenwick said. "Then, you can pick up any stones you wish."

"You should probably begin with one we did not identify," I suggested. "If you plan to use your magnifier to assist with the transfer, use it for other stones as well."

"There will probably be two stones that are just a bit larger than the rest, possibly with a deeper blue color," Fenwick advised. "They will also likely have flaws within them that cannot be seen by the naked eye. So, though they look to be the biggest and best, they will be among the least valuable."

"So, those are the two I should pick," Freddy surmised.

"Exactly," I said. "If you appear to swallow the bait, we hope the Vizier's people move to conclude the negotiations quickly. On the other hand, if you pick stones that are really valuable as being your choice, they will drag things out and distract you so they can switch those for less valuable ones."

"What they won't know," Freddy said triumphantly, "is that I have already taken the two stones we want and switched them for sapphires of similar size."

"There is a possibility that they do not include any tan-zyan in the first set of stones," Fenwick said. "If that is the case, Caz will stretch his arm over his head and scratch above his ear. If that happens, Lord Compote, you can point out that they must have made a mistake by not including any tan-zyan, but you will forgive it, as an error like this is to be expected from such an uncivilized people."

When we arrived, Fenwick left the ship immediately. He returned with three broad-brimmed straw hats. He gave one to me and another to Albert.

"You'll want to wear these," he instructed. "Otherwise, the sun will burn your skin to the color of cooked lobster. Your Highness, the men should consider wearing them instead of their helmets for the same reason, plus they will be much cooler."

"Take the supply officer and buy enough for the men," Albert ordered. "They can wear their helmets when it is time to show off."

It was too late to start our journey when all the horses were finally unloaded. Fenwick returned with hats for the soldiers and then met with the captain of the company. There was an area just outside the city of Alygien where the soldiers could bivouac. Using a map, Fenwick showed the captain how to reach it.

The soldiers set off. Not long after, a carriage rolled up. Unlike the one Fenwick hired when we visited, this was enclosed rather than open to the air. The driver was the same—Ari. Fenwick and I secured Albert, Freddy, and Greta's trunks to the rear and roof. We drove up to the same marvelous inn where Fenwick and I stayed on our earlier adventure in Scaramouche.

Fenwick handled the negotiations and secured rooms for Prince Albert and Lord Compote. The desk clerk wrinkled his nose upon hearing the second name. He squinted at Freddy. Fenwick quickly explained that Freddy was the brother, and they bore given the title. The clerk did not recognize me at all since I was clearly a servant and unimportant.

Fenwick would stay in the spare room attached to Albert's. Since Greta, as Freddy's maid, was assumed to be staying in his attached room, I was given a bunk in the staff dormitory. Fenwick shrugged his shoulders apologetically but then ruined the gesture by licking his finger and making a tally mark in the air.

At least I was allowed to eat that night, unlike before when I had to pretend to be horrified by the prospect of eating with my fingers. Fenwick, Greta, and I were seated separately from Albert and Freddy. Freddy's version of Lord Compote had no qualms about using his fingers.

"You see, Your Highness," I overheard Freddy say, "one must make allowances. These people are clearly untamed by the refinements of civilization, and therefore, it would not do to upset them. Indeed, their base nature would undoubtedly lead them to react in a barbaric manner if we were to violate any of their mores. So, we must eat like animals. The food is damnably good, though— damnably good."

Albert assayed a bite. "Mhm," he agreed, "surprisingly good. Your sleeve is entirely covered with sauce, though, Lord Compote."

"Seven hells!" Freddy exclaimed. "Well, since we're eating like animals, it must be acceptable to do this."

With a loud slurping noise, he began to suck the gravy from the lace of his shirt cuffs. When he finished, they were still stained. He tried to fold the cuffs back to keep them out of the way. Unfortunately, as soon as he moved his hand, the lace flopped back.

"There's simply nothing for it. Bunny," he called out to Greta, "something else for you to scrub tonight besides me."

Albert gave Lord Compote a horrified look. Seeing it, Lord Compote responded.

"No sense having a maid who looks like that and not taking full advantage of the situation, eh? No sense at all. A saucy young filly like her needs to be ridden hard and put up wet, eh? She's not a very good maid, to tell the truth, but she makes up for it, eh? She makes up for it," he said to Albert with a broad wink.

Greta, playing her part, lowered her head and blushed prettily. The other patrons of the dining room who understood Aquileian were appalled. They began to whisper to one another while keeping their eyes riveted on Lord Compote.

"See, poppet," Lord Compote called over to Greta later, "I'm eating like an animal. An animal!"

He made a growling sound and then flicked his tongue between his two fingers. Greta again looked down and turned pink with embarrassment.

"I told you he was much better at this," I whispered to Fenwick.

"This is like watching an artist paint a masterpiece," Fenwick whispered back. "Words fail me."

"Stop it, boys," Greta hissed quietly. "It's taking every bit of my willpower to keep from rolling on the floor with laughter."

18

We set off in the morning. Fenwick and I loaded the trunks back on the carriage. Freddy and Greta climbed in, and Fenwick and I took our perches atop, wearing our straw hats. When we reached the encampment where the soldiers spent the night, they were mounted and waiting. They, too, were wearing straw hats. They looked slightly ridiculous, but if what Fenwick said was true, that was a small price to pay instead of being burnt by the sun.

The road was dusty and hot. There was little in the way of vegetation we could see on either side. We stopped three times for water in what could scarcely be called towns. They were gatherings of perhaps a dozen huts around a well. The residents poured out of the huts on our arrival, clamoring for our attention, trying to sell us things.

"Good luck charms," Fenwick explained, pointing at the various people, "a supposedly ancient relic of the old empire, a tonic to make a man irresistible to women, a potion to regrow hair—oh, here's a new one, a curse tablet."

Fenwick called that man over and spoke with him. After the man provided what seemed to be a lengthy explanation, haggling began. Fenwick reached into his purse and withdrew a two-florin piece. The man shook his head violently, and negotiations resumed. Fenwick finally pulled out another one-florin coin, and the man grudgingly accepted it and handed over a thin piece of metal.

"This is a piece of lead," Fenwick explained. "Lead being one of the Lord of the Seven Hells' favorite substances, as everyone knows."

"I did not know that," I replied. "I was taught that the Lord of the Seven Hells liked gold, silver, and jewels."

"As was the rest of the world," Fenwick commented, "but it's part of the man's explanation. No matter. As the owner of this curse tablet, I scratch into the lead the name of my victim and what I want to happen to him. Then I squeeze the lead in my hands and reduce it to the smallest size I can without melting it—this is apparently important, no melting. Once I have compressed it as much as possible, I bury it underground near where the victim lives. Then, recognizing the hunk of metal as a curse tablet, the Lord of the Seven Hells will draw it to himself and fulfill the curse in exchange for the gift of one of his favorite substances."

"Sounds marvelous," I commented. "You'll have to let me know if it works."

"Perhaps you will learn first-hand," he commented with a wink.

The rest of that day and the next two were the same—hot, dusty, and long. The road climbed steadily the further we went. The two nights on our journey were spent in ordinary travelers' inns that were not nearly as luxurious as the first one. Fenwick and I spent the nights sleeping on top of the coach with Ari. It grew surprisingly chilly as the night wore on. Finally, late in the afternoon of the third day, we reached Sablanca.

Even from the outskirts, we could see the Grand Vizier's palace. Gleaming white, it stood on the highest ground in the city. Fenwick guided us on the most direct path.

Just before we reached the palace, Albert ordered the soldiers to put on their helmets (but to keep their straw hats for the ride back to the coast). When we arrived, the Grand Vizier's people were ready for us. They threw open the gates, and Albert and the men of the Castle Shield entered in style.

Fenwick jumped down and trotted over to stand next to Albert's horse. As Albert's factotum, he would also serve as his translator. The Grand Vizier himself came out to greet Prince Albert. Without Fenwick to translate for me, I assumed the usual flowery greetings were exchanged.

When they finished, Albert dismounted and handed the reins of his horse to the captain of the company. He gestured for us, and Freddy exited the carriage. Greta and I followed at a respectful distance. After introductions were made,

Albert, Freddy, and Fenwick were led inside. A member of the Grand Vizier's staff approached Greta and me.

"You," he said, pointing at me, "Take." He pointed at the trunks.

Ari, bless his heart, helped me get the two trunks from the roof. With the first of the trunks, the staff member then took me inside. He pointed to a room.

"Prince," he said, then pointed to the next room down the corridor. "Other."

After I took Albert's and Freddy's trunks to the proper rooms, the staff member pointed at Greta. "Prince?" he asked.

I shook my head. The man nodded. I hoisted her trunk with my small bag on top of it and told her to follow me. We reached the room, and I took her trunk inside. Greta followed and sat on the small sofa.

The room was almost as big as the rooms in the first inn. Like them, one wall was open to the breeze. It seemed cool and comfortable. I left Greta there as the staff member tugged me away. He took me down the corridor and around a corner.

"You. Here," the man said. "Stay."

It was a tiny room. It might almost be better described as a cell. There was no door in the doorway and only a tiny window set up high. The only furniture was a low cot. I set my bag on the floor and sat down on the cot to wait.

A few hours later, another member of the household staff brought me a plate of food. By the time it reached me, it was cold. It would have tasted much better warm, but I was hungry enough that I ate it all. I wondered if Greta were still in the room where I left her and if she was, whether her food was served cold. I hoped not. Even further, I hoped she was invited to dinner. She was hoping to wear one of her naughty dresses.

After it grew dark outside, someone came and collected my empty plate. I undressed to my underclothes and stretched out on the cot. At least it was better than sleeping on the roof of the carriage. Fenwick came in later and woke me.

"The transaction will occur first thing in the morning after we eat," he said. "We arranged it that way since Albert claimed he had urgent business waiting for him at home, and we needed to begin our return immediately. Your friend Lord Compote is a marvel. It's a miracle neither Albert nor I gave away the ruse by laughing. By the time they served dinner, he had managed to insult everyone in the room except Albert. Though they claim not to understand Aquileian, some members of the household knew enough to figure out what a dolt Lord Compote is. I think part of the reason they tolerated it was because of the dress Greta was falling out of. Tomorrow will be interesting."

Fenwick disappeared into the darkness. I resumed sleeping. The morning light came through the window just enough that my unconscious mind recognized it. I woke and dressed.

Shortly afterward, a staff member delivered a plate with a piece of egg pie. This time it was warm. It was more heavily spiced than the last time I ate a similar dish in Alygien, but it was still tasty. Not long after I finished, the same person who showed me to the room the day before came.

"Come."

I buckled on my sword, lifted my bag, and followed. We collected Greta from the room she shared with Freddy. This morning she was wearing another one of the scandalous maid costumes.

Though petite and slender, Greta still possessed an attractive figure. Her attire showed every one of her assets to its full potential. The bodice of the dress was low and compressed her chest to display an enticing bit of décolletage. The front of the skirt reached only to mid-thigh, showing off her trim legs encased in sheer black stockings. Her shoes had a tall, slender heel, which further accentuated the shapeliness of her legs and added an extra sway to her hips as she walked. She wore her hair up, with soft tendrils of curls framing her pretty face, topped with a frilly lace cap.

I tapped the man on the arm, pointed to the trunks, and then to myself. He shook his head.

"We take," he said.

The man took us to a room where Albert, Freddy, and Fenwick were finishing breakfast.

"There you are, Ashe!" Freddy, as Lord Compote, exclaimed. "Where in blazes have you been? What if I needed you, eh?"

Adopting my obsequious Reg Ashe manner, I replied, "I am sorry, milord. They took me to a room and ordered me to stay. I thought it best to follow their instructions so I would not cause any difficulty."

"Hmmph," Lord Compote grunted. "You should only concern yourself with *my* instructions, Ashe, eh? You do not serve them. You serve *me*. You *do* understand that, don't you?"

"Yes, milord. Perfectly. Still, I was afraid—"

"I've told you this a thousand times, Ashe," Lord Compote stated. "The only person you need fear is me."

"Now that we are all here," Fenwick interrupted, "I believe they are ready for us."

A more elegantly dressed member of the Grand Vizier's staff directed us to a room that was quite starkly furnished. There was a table covered with a thick cotton cloth. One side of the room consisted of windows open to the air.

When we entered, I withdrew a wisp of Bellona's power and then tried to extend it to fill the room. A different staff member, also dressed lavishly, entered carrying a small blue bag of what appeared to be velvet. He emptied the bag on the white cloth and spread out a half dozen stones. None of them were tan-zyan, according to what I sensed of my power.

I reached and scratched my head. Freddy made a show of leaning over and peering at them. After he looked at each stone, he began laughing.

"Is something wrong, Lord Compote?" Albert asked.

"These people are every bit as uncouth as I was telling you, Your Highness," Lord Compote said. "They cannot even tell tan-zyan from sapphire."

Before Albert could ask Fenwick to translate, the staff member pretended to have just noticed he made a mistake. He began scooping up the stones and putting them in the bag. He bowed low. He spoke in Scaramanga to Fenwick.

"A thousand pardons, Your Highness and Your Lordship. He brought the wrong bag," Fenwick translated.

A different person appeared with another small bag. He was even more decoratively dressed. He bowed low. As he did, his eyes fixed upon Greta—particularly her exposed upper chest. He turned his head in the direction of Fenwick as he started to speak, but his eyes remained fastened to Greta's bosom.

Fenwick translated what the man said. "My ignorant servant cannot follow the simplest instructions. It is extremely difficult to find good servants these days. It was better when they were slaves, and we could beat them properly. That is the only way these wretches ever learn. I apologize. Here are the correct stones."

The man poured them from the bag and arranged them in two rows of six. I could tell five of the dozen were tan-zyan. As Lucy had counseled, three of the five felt "dirty" in varying degrees. The two that felt "clean" were not the largest. I looked to Fenwick to see if he could sense them. He gave me the slightest hint of a nod in return.

Meanwhile, Freddy was leaning over the table, staring intently at the stones. When he straightened, Fenwick sneezed. I coughed twice as though clearing my throat. Fenwick sneezed twice more, as often happens. I yawned and stretched, then used three fingers on each hand to rub my eyes.

Freddy leaned forward over the table again. He started murmuring to himself. Using his index finger, Freddy pushed one stone away, then another. He pulled one of the three largest stones toward himself, then the first of the tan-zyan gems Fenwick and I identified.

Freddy pushed three more stones away and pulled two more forward—one of the tan-zyan gems and a larger sapphire. After another minute, he pulled the other large sapphire toward himself. He shoved the rest away.

Freddy then began to arrange the five gems he selected in a line. He pointed to one and asked, "Would you like to see, my pet?"

He left it on the table but moved aside slightly. Greta leaned far forward to see it properly. This caused her bodice to gape open further. I must admit, I could not help stealing a glance. Greta is damned attractive, after all. The vizier's man was goggle-eyed.

"No," Freddy said, pulling the stone away from Greta, then pushed it into the group he had already ruled out.

The stone he pushed away had been in the same place as one of the two tan-zyan gems. The one he moved was not tan-zyan, though it was of similar size and shape. I used my ability and sensed that one of the two tan-zyan gems was now in Freddy's pocket. How Freddy switched the two had escaped my eyes. It must have happened in the brief second I was distracted by Greta. I wanted to smile but maintained a bored expression. The vizier's man noticed which stone Freddy discarded, and I could see a hint of satisfaction on his face.

Freddy then reached into his other jacket pocket and withdrew a magnifying eyepiece. He fussed a bit as though trying to get it seated properly in his eye socket. When he finished, Freddy picked up one of the larger sapphires and examined it using the magnifier. He hemmed and hawed, then returned it to the group he was still considering.

Freddy then picked up the second of the two tan-zyan stones. As he brought it up to examine it, the eyepiece fell. It landed, nestled in the middle of Greta's upthrust bosom.

Freddy laughed uproariously. "Well," he said, "if that isn't simply the softest place for it to fall."

Freddy thrust his fingers rudely into Greta's bodice, saying, "Be still, poppet."

He was not at all subtle about taking his time to fish the eyepiece out. In fact, it seemed he pushed it deeper in order to fondle her bosom more thoroughly. Greta, of course, blushed furiously, looking to the side, as she suffered the groping by her employer.

"Don't squirm, mopsy, or it may slide down further," Freddy said with an indecent grin.

Freddy finally retrieved the eyepiece after manipulating both of her breasts thoroughly and reinserted it. He held the stone up and examined it. When he put it down, Freddy pushed it into the group of those he rejected. But, again, the stone he pushed away was no longer one of tan-zyan. Both of those gems were now in Freddy's pocket.

For the next few minutes, Freddy made a show of examining the three remaining jewels. He studied them with his eyepiece, turning them to show every angle. Freddy murmured to himself and even hummed. Finally, he pushed one of the remaining three stones away, leaving two in front of him.

The vizier's man asked a question. "Are these the two you want?" Fenwick translated.

Freddy nodded. Albert then withdrew a small wooden box from his jacket pocket. He handed it to the vizier's man. Nestled inside the box were two pieces of electrum.

At this point, Fenwick predicted haggling would take place if the vizier's man felt it was necessary. Instead, it seemed as though he wanted us to leave immediately. Through Fenwick, the vizier's man let us know that he hoped we were as delighted by the transaction as the Grand Vizier would be. He hollered, and one of his servants came to lead us outside. Then, with one last lingering look at Greta's chest, he left the room.

When we arrived outside, another member of the household staff approached. Through Fenwick, he apologized profusely.

"The Grand Vizier sorrowfully regrets to say he is feeling unwell. As a result, the planned inspection of each other's soldiers will unfortunately not occur. Nevertheless, he wishes you well upon your journey home and looks forward to a future visit."

Albert spoke to the captain of the company about the change of plans. The men doffed their helmets and put their straw hats on. Fenwick and I retrieved our hats from inside the carriage. After assisting Lord Compote and his maid inside and shutting the small door, I joined Fenwick and Ari up above.

Albert waved his arm, and the soldiers began to move out. We followed. The whole way through the city of Sablanca, I expected the Grand Vizier's soldiers to come after us. They did not.

At the first water stop after we left the city behind, Fenwick warned us again we could not speak openly. People were watching us, and in Scaramouche information was a valuable commodity. Nonetheless, Fenwick, Albert, and I managed to whisper our congratulations to Freddy and Greta for their magnificent performances.

For the remainder of our journey to Alygien, my ears strained to hear the sound of approaching hoofbeats. In this, I was disappointed. I wondered whether the Grand Vizier knew of our deception.

"Undoubtedly," Fenwick assured me.

"Then why is he allowing us to leave?" I asked.

Fenwick paused before answering. "I only spent a few hours in his presence," he said. "So I cannot be absolutely certain of this. My feeling is that he will not send soldiers after us. If he did, it is as Albert predicted. It would be an admission that we outsmarted him."

"Out-cheated him," I corrected.

"To these people, it's the same thing," Fenwick said. "In order to stop us, many people would then know something was wrong. If word spread that foreigners outsmarted him, his reputation would suffer. As things are now, there are only two people who might know. The Grand Vizier has probably already threatened them and their families with death if word trickles out further."

"Will this jeopardize the trade arrangements you and Albert negotiated?" I asked.

"That was one of Albert's chief concerns," Fenwick shared. "I don't believe it will."

"I would think they would be angry with us and might cancel the measures," I said.

"Or they might believe we just proved we are worthy of respect," Fenwick countered. "By hoodwinking the Grand Vizier himself in his palace, we showed that Aquileians are not to be taken lightly."

19

It was only after we were back aboard the ship and sailing away from the coast of Scaramouche that we dared to talk about what happened. Freddy, of course, was brilliant. We praised him until he was nearly sick of it. To this day, there are moments I remember of Freddy in the guise of Lord Compote that make me laugh out loud. We praised Greta as well. She played her role to perfection. Albert and Fenwick told me of Freddy's performance at the dinner with Grand Vizier, saying it far outshone the first evening at the inn.

We arrived in the city of Aquileia in the morning on the twenty-first of Haustman. After wishing Freddy and Greta the fondest of farewells, our first order of business—Albert instructed us—was to return to the castle with him. Now that we had the tan-zyan jewels, Fenwick and I would sign contracts agreeing to return them to the crown upon our deaths, unless we had a son or daughter with a link to Bellona.

Queen Liliana presided over this. She also summoned the royal jeweler to set the stones into rings and to add a diamond to the pommel of our swords. Following Lucy's advice, I asked the jeweler to design a ring that included an emerald for Eir and a sapphire for Njörun. Fenwick requested one with a green tourmaline and a red jasper.

Because I needed to return to Easton as quickly as possible to assist Lucy in preparing for the harvest festival, I asked the queen if she would select the other stones for my ring and the diamond for my sword. She agreed and would have Fenwick deliver them to me when they were finished. The queen also reminded me she would be sending the bill with Fenwick.

Once the jeweler measured my finger, I departed. It bothered me to leave my sword behind, but it was unavoidable. I took my bag and had one of the guards on the city side of the bridge whistle up a hackney for me.

The hackney delivered me to my house. Though I would have relished a bath, I felt an urgent need to return to Easton. I unloaded my bag, then packed what I needed for the journey in my saddlebags. I took the best of my two other swords and slid it into my scabbard.

Saying farewell to Roberta (and asking her to wash the dirty clothing I left behind), I walked to the Foaming Boar with my saddlebags over my shoulder. Jerry was a bit morose that I would be taking Andy away again. His mood brightened only slightly when I paid him for taking care of my horse.

"Mr. Caz, you already paid Mr. Carl for Andy's board," he protested. "And you let me keep the money I didn't need for the farrier."

"Yes, but you and I have a separate arrangement," I said. "Two florins a week. It's been three weeks, so here are six florins."

"Well, thankee, I guess," he replied. "When are you coming back?"

"Sometime before the winter solstice, I think. There is at least one wedding we will attend," I told him.

"That's not so long," he admitted.

"Is Mr. Forteney still allowing you to borrow books?" I asked.

"Aye," Jerry replied. "My reading is getting faster.

"Good boy," I commented. "Keep doing that as much as you can. Do you have a favorite book so far?"

"Aye. It's about a king a long time ago, and his knights, and a quest to save a fair maiden from a demon," he answered.

"I like that story, too," I agreed.

Jerry then hugged Andy and whispered in his ear. I heard him say in a quiet snarl, something to the effect of, "Throw mean old Mr. Caz and break his neck, then come back here to me." That comment irked me.

"Jerry, that's not funny in any possible way. You and I have teased each other back and forth, but what you just said was not teasing. It was mean-spirited, and I take great offense," I scolded. "If that is how you feel, that you want me dead, then I think you, Carl, and I need to have a serious talk."

Jerry went red in the face. He started to protest but swallowed his words before they came out when he saw how angry I was. It was then that he realized exactly what he'd said and how ugly it was.

"I'm sorry, Mr. Caz," he said sincerely. "I was trying to be funny, but it came out all wrong."

"I accept your apology, Jerry," I said. "We'll see you again in a few weeks."

The journey to Easton was made pleasant by the vibrant colors of the leaves changing color. There was a bite to the air in the morning and evening. Autumn was painting the Aquileian landscape.

Late in the afternoon of the third day, Andy and I arrived at the gate of Easton. There was a large sign proclaiming a harvest fair to be starting on the twenty-eighth of Hausman and running through the first of Gorman. Anyone interested in displaying his wares or produce could sign up with the guard at the manor.

Jon Sinchak was the guard on duty when I reached the manor. He welcomed me back. I asked him how many people signed up for the fair.

"It's nearing a hundred, milord," he said. "Not so many lately, as I think most have already put their names in. Lady Oritur also feels there will be another twenty or so who show up from further away without telling us in advance. People are looking forward to it."

As I rode to the stable, I began to feel as though I was returning *home*. The idea made me stop for a moment. Though I lived above the bookseller's shop for nine years, it never felt like home. Our house in the city did not quite feel that way—perhaps it would someday. Here, this big, ancient, drafty pile of stones, did.

I wondered whether it was because I spent part of my boyhood here, or something else. The days of my youth were far enough away in time, and my life had taken such twists since then that it was almost as though the memories belonged to someone else. Lucy is what made this feel like home, I decided.

Thinking not too far back, I always felt extremely comfortable when I visited the rooms above her shop. My rooms always seemed more pleasant whenever she was there. Lucy's presence here had a similar effect. Even better, in a short period of time, she created a household. Rose, Hazel, Gladys, Tom and his uncle Ted, Laurie the cook, and even Theo and Toby were already forming into a group that I thought of as *ours*.

Ted Collinwood took Andy from me when we came to a halt. I slid from the saddle and threw my bags over my shoulders. When I reached the kitchen door, I made sure to stomp my feet and rattle the knob so Laurie would not be surprised.

When I opened the door, the most marvelous smell greeted my nose. I smelled dinner, of course—some sort of mutton dish—but the other scent was of baked apples, cinnamon, and something else. Looking at the stove, I saw two big pots on top. I hoped they might be water heating for a bath.

Sticking my nose forward and taking deep sniffs, I pretended to be entranced as I crept closer to the oven. The handle on the door was almost within reach. Then, suddenly, a wooden spoon cracked me smartly in the back of the head.

"Milord, don't you dare," she scolded as I rubbed the back of my head. "Lady Lucy had a feeling you was coming home, and she asks me this morning, 'Oh, Laurie, won't you please bake an apple and cranberry pie. I think my husband is coming home and it would be such a nice surprise.' I told her you always sneaks through the kitchen and tries to steal a peek, and there weren't gonna be no surprise. And here you are, a-tip-toeing in my kitchen. Another step and you'd have opened the oven door and ruined your fine surprise."

"Hello, Miss Laurie," I replied. "It's nice to see you, too, after so many weeks away. I didn't even need to open the oven to know there's an apple and cranberry pie in there, probably just starting to bubble. Did you put a crust on top or no?"

"I did," she said, her hands on her hips. "How did you know it's apple and cranberry? I didn't think you could smell the cranberries."

"I know because you told me, Laurie. Right after you tried to beat me senseless."

Her hands flew to her mouth as she realized she had let it slip while she was scolding me. I laughed as I strolled away.

"Everything smells wonderful, Miss Laurie," I called over my shoulder. "I'm already looking forward to it."

When I reached the hall, I heard voices from the study. So I ambled down that way. Lucy and my father were examining a large piece of paper spread over the desk. I dropped my bags with a thump.

Lucy saw me first and dashed to me. She threw her arms around my neck. We exchanged a passionate kiss. When we broke apart, I caught my father smiling.

"I asked Theo to have the girls prepare your bath," she said. "Knowing you would want one, I got them started as soon as I saw you at the gate. It should be ready soon. Your father and I are looking over plans for the fair. We are having difficulty trying to fit everything in the main square."

"Must the fair be held in town?" I asked. "What about the land just outside the walls? Some fields should already be clear or were lying fallow already. Surely one of the owners would be willing to host the fair in exchange for some compensation?"

My father cleared his throat. "Actually, we own the land surrounding Easton," he said. "We let it out to tenant farmers."

"Then it should not be a problem," I said, "as long as we are not heavy-handed about it. If you are worried about how the tenants might react, perhaps we allow Lucy to negotiate on our behalf? I'm willing to wager her powers of persuasion are far greater than ours."

With that idea in mind, they returned to the map, studying the best place outside the walls for the fair. I picked up my bags and trudged upstairs to find Tom Collinwood carrying two large buckets of steaming water from the hoist. He was accompanied by Rose and Gladys. I suspected the job was initially assigned to the girls, but they took advantage of Tom's innocence, batted their eyes at him, and convinced him to do the heavy lifting.

In our bedroom, I dropped my bags and sat heavily on the bed. The thought of a hot bath was damned attractive. I last washed while on the ship, returning from Scaramouche. The men of the Castle Shield found it amusing to see me caper in the stream of cold seawater spewing from the pump. The sailors manning the pump found it even funnier, trying to blast me in my most sensitive areas.

I was just thinking of removing my boots when Lucy flew into the room, slamming the door behind her. She launched herself at me, forcing me down to the bed. After a long and heated kiss, she leaned up with her hands on my chest.

"I missed you," she said.

She snaked her hands up under my shoulders and lay atop me. Her head was resting on my chest and tucked just under my right ear. My arms were around her, and I held her gently, breathing in the marvelous smell of her hair. We stayed like this, just being together, until there was a soft knock at the door.

"Milady, the bath is ready," I heard Rose announce.

Lucy uncoiled herself from me. She tugged off my boots quickly and then began to shed her clothes. I was not as quick.

"Hurry up!" she called over her shoulder and skipped to the lavatory in her thin shift.

Dinner that evening saw just Lucy and my father join me. I asked how plans for the fair were coming together. Lucy wanted to know what happened in Scaramouche first.

I shared the whole story with them. In describing Freddy's genius in his portrayal of "Lord Compote," Lucy had to explain to my father that Freddy had always been a gifted mimic. Remembering how Freddy behaved during the whole enterprise had me laughing all over again. I also shared how Greta provided a helpful distraction at critical moments.

"For the life of me," I stated, "I did not see how he switched the jewels. I was trying to pay attention, but he did it so quickly and so smoothly that I missed it. The first time was when Greta bent forward to take a look. I flicked my eyes away from Freddy for the briefest fraction of a second. That was all it took. The second time was when he bobbled the magnifier into Greta's cleavage, and I missed it again. He was simply marvelous."

Lucy and my father then brought me up-to-date on the fair. They confirmed that ninety-three people signed up requesting a space to showcase their goods or produce. When I saw Lucy and my father examining the map, they were trying to determine how many others who did not request space in advance would appear.

"The square would hold the ninety-three, my father said, "but not many more. Lucy expects at least twenty more to show up."

"Word will have spread," Lucy explained. "Some of the most entertaining parts of the fair will arrive from outside of the March."

"The mummers, the puppeteers, the soothsayers, and so on?" I asked

"Exactly," Lucy confirmed. "While the real business of the fair is to provide an easier exchange of goods, the entertainment is what draws many."

"And the food," I said.

"Ah, yes. The food," my father said with a sigh. Like me, he must enjoy the different edibles only found in this type of setting.

"Have you determined a suitable place?" I asked.

"Yes," my father replied. "Your lady wife will call on the tenants tomorrow. Of course, they have no choice in the matter, since we own the land, but I certainly don't want to present it that way."

"How will you organize the site?" I asked. "Someone will need to plot out the aisles and locations. We will need to provide water and dig latrines. Disposal of refuse—"

"We have over a hundred armsmen who are getting bored with training," my father interjected. "They will provide all the manpower we need."

"That reminds me, father... have you found quarters for all the new men?" I inquired.

"That is what brought me to Easton this trip," he responded. "Happily, I found places for all of them at reasonable rates. Six of the new men are single and will have rooms above the stable, along with the Collinwoods. After the fair, we will return to Bannock Hill until the first snow. They will all enjoy leave after that until the new year."

"That's when they begin traveling to the different towns and training the new draft of militia—right?"

My father nodded.

"And this year's militia?"

"I gave them leave to assist with the harvest as we discussed," my father said. "They are due to return to their posts on the fifteenth of Gorman. There are repair projects in every border town to which they need to attend. Once those are complete, they will be free to go. I think they will finish all of them before the first of Ylir—a few weeks earlier than the usual dismissal. I worry that they will expect this every year."

"Well, we will have to do our best to make it happen," I said with a grin. "What is the news regarding the harvest?"

"Excellent yield throughout the March," he reported. "Combined with dry conditions in much of the kingdom, this will be a good year. We will not have a record crop, though. The three towns that were sacked are still unoccupied, and the land was untilled. Finding new residents is another task we must accomplish this winter. Still, things could be better."

"In what way?" I asked.

"Long before I was born, Port Charles became unusable because of silt. With the harbor clogged, keeping the Pheas River passable was no longer important. If we could clear the river and dredge the harbor, we could ship our grain to Newcastle, Aquileia, and Aurora more quickly and cheaply. Then a good crop like this and poor conditions in the rest of the kingdom would mean prosperity for nearly everyone in the March."

"How much would it cost the dredge the harbor?" I asked.

"Your grandfather was the last to consider it seriously," my father said. "I seem to remember him mentioning a figure of twenty thousand, with another five to clear the river and make it navigable as far north as it used to be."

20

Two days later, Lucy received a letter from Greta. She and Freddy were coming to visit for the fair. They were also bringing Linc Ellsworth and Nellie Fassbender, Quint Pompeo and Siobhan Harper, and Greta's brother Ratty with Inger Fairchild, who was Siobhan Harper's cousin. Ratty and Inger met at our wedding, so Lucy and I were pleased to see they were still seeing one another.

"We will be full," Lucy commented. "All the guest rooms will be used. I will need to alert Laurie."

"And Fenwick will probably be here as well," I added.

"Do you think he will mind taking one of the stable rooms?" Lucy asked.

"I think he will have no issues with that," I said. "He usually likes to stay at one of the inns so he can come and go, but I think they will be full. The stable will give him the freedom he likes."

Lucy was successful in obtaining permission from our tenants to use the land. The particular field where Lucy wanted to set up the fair was recently harvested, and only coarse stubble remained. My father gathered Paulie Florio's unit of armsmen, and they designated the aisles with posts and ropes. They dug latrines and established a temporary corral for the horses belonging to guests.

One of the biggest concerns was water, but the tenants agreed to allow the use of the well in exchange for two ducats. I was happy to give them the money. Realizing the water needed to be carried in something, I then bought forty wooden buckets.

Vendors began arriving on the twenty-sixth of Haustman. We put Theo in charge of the map with the assigned locations. We used the town constable's deputies and the kersants to guide people to their particular spots. We thought having Theo in that role would eliminate complaints about where we placed people, and it did.

From just before noon that day until darkness fell, I was busy running back and forth and assisting wherever I could. I showed people where the well was and where to find a bucket, helped with unhitching animals from wagons, and even had to chase down some chickens that escaped. Gladys brought me dinner that night, which I ate standing up. Then, when it was too dark to see beyond the glow from the torches here and there, I asked the kersants to post guards and headed for the town gate in the darkness.

"You owe me sixty-five hundred ducats, Your Lordliness," came a voice from right next to me.

I nearly jumped out of my shoes. It was Fenwick, of course. My mind was thinking of dozens of things, so it was no miracle he snuck up on me.

"Ah, Aloysius," I said when I recovered from my start. "I would say it's nice to see you, but I can't see a damned thing. Nice to hear your voice…suddenly…in the dark."

"Did I frighten you?" he asked, twitting me since he knew he did. "Is that why you're using that name?"

"Why, yes, it is, Aloysius," I replied as I continued to walk. "How clever of you to put that together. We have a room over the stable for you if you would like it."

"I already spoke with Her Loveliness," he said. "And thanked her. The inns are full."

"Which is why we saved a room for you, where you could slip in and out as you wish. When would you like your money?"

"I'm in no hurry," he replied. "The wolf is far from my door. Tell me… what do you do with yours?"

"My what?"

"Your money," he stated.

"I have it invested in a number of buildings and businesses in the capital," I replied. "There is a man who manages it for me."

"If I'm not breaking some social taboo, what sort of returns are you getting?" he asked.

"It is probably terribly unrefined of you to inquire," I commented, "but I've come to expect that—it's part of your charm. It varies, but between twelve and fifteen percent per annum."

"Majors and Minors!" he gasped. "I get nowhere near that. The bank implies that I should feel fortunate that they pay *almost* two percent. Would you consider giving me the name of your person?"

"My turn to be vulgar," I said. "Have you accumulated six figures?"

"Yes," he replied dismissively, waving his hand. "Years ago."

We passed through the gate, nodding to the guards. The two of us turned onto the street that would take us to the manor. I looked over at Fenwick and saw a ring with the blue tan-zyan gem, a green tourmaline, and a red jasper. It was tasteful and not gaudy.

"Nice ring," I commented. "You should talk to Pierre Luin in the capital. Feel free to use my name. Best not to tell him how you heaped up such a pile."

"Spell the last name," he requested.

I did.

"Your ring is just as nice," Fenwick said. "Maybe even prettier. The red jasper in mine doesn't really match the other two."

"Have you tried it?" I asked.

"With the tan-zyan and the diamond? Yes," he stated. "Queen Liliana talked me through it the first time. You need to be careful. She chose near-flawless gems for us. The diamond could drain you completely if you don't keep tight control. I've been trying to feed it a small amount every day. The queen said that it is an enormous reservoir. We could drain ourselves completely five or six times and only then reach the limit."

Thinking back on some of the more dangerous encounters I had in the past, having that amount of Bellona's energy stored away and accessible would have been amazingly useful.

"Have you tried it the other way? Pulling it out?" I asked.

"I did," he said with a grin. "It feels amazing, and that was only a smidgeon."

We reached the manor. Lewiston was at the gate. He greeted us both. I headed to the front door. Fenwick broke away.

"Let me get your things," he said.

I found Lucy in the study, reading by candlelight. She waved me to one of the armchairs. When I sat, she curled into my lap.

"Fenwick is here," she said.

"I know," I chuckled. "He's bringing me my ring and my sword."

"Brought," he said from the doorway.

Lucy craned her neck around. "Let's see," she said.

Fenwick hammed it up. He dropped to one knee in front of me. He pulled out a small blue box and opened it, presenting it to me.

"Oh, Your Lordliness," he sighed, "will you accept this ring and make me the happiest man alive?"

Lucy laughed. "He's already taken, Fenwick. Nice form, though. At least when your time comes, you'll know what to do."

I took the ring from the box and put it on the ring finger of my right hand. The awareness of the gem I felt when we were identifying them for Freddy was immensely increased. Fenwick caught me staring at it.

"Much stronger, isn't it?" he said.

"Yes," I agreed, still looking at it.

Fenwick then handed me my sword. It was in a scabbard, attached to a sword belt, studded with small sapphires and diamonds. It looked exactly like the one he gave me before the two of us went to Alygien the first time—which his associate Bebo appropriated as compensation for rescuing us from the sub-vizier's residence.

"Is this…?"

"Yes, he replied. "On the way back to Alygien, Bebo ran into the same folks who attacked us. Since we killed their extra numbers, he was able to run them down and take their ship—and its cargo. Bebo never told me what it was. I'm guessing it was pretty damned valuable since he returned this to me. So, again, peace offering. My apology for almost killing you and my appreciation for you not killing me when you had the chance."

I offered Fenwick my hand. "Peace, brother. Thank you," I said.

He took it and repeated, "Peace."

"Aww," Lucy sighed. "That's so sweet."

"I'm still going to call him Aloysius," I said.

"He's still His Lordliness," Fenwick quipped.

"Boys," Lucy scolded, though with a smile on her face.

A moment later, she said, "I wonder what you will look like?"

"What do you mean?" Fenwick and I asked, almost in unison.

"Do you remember when we were in the Temple in Eatonford, and you saw the queen's appearance change?" Lucy asked.

I nodded and explained to Fenwick, "We were—well, the queen was—trying to destroy a grimoire. Suddenly, there was a projection of the queen's form, twice her size and glowing with light. I could see the queen through it, but the apparition demanded my attention and seemed to be the *real* entity in that moment. In contrast, the queen's actual body was motionless. It was... *incredible.*"

"That was when the queen drew as much power as she could from her diamond, through her topaz, and into herself," Lucy explained. "She needed it to obliterate that thing."

"Have you ever done anything similar?" I asked.

"Only a little bit. Nothing as strong as what Lily did," was her coy response.

I thought back. "At our wedding?" I answered uncertainly.

"Yes," she admitted, "but, again, that was only a small fraction."

"If that was only a small amount, I don't know if I could handle anything more."

"What do you mean?" Fenwick asked.

"From the moment she walked out of the house to where the ceremony would take place," I explained, "Lucy's beauty seemed... *transcendent.* Sorry, that's the only word I can think of. This will sound soppy, Fenwick, but I thought my heart would swell and burst with love, and I also, uh, never mind."

"You can't stop there," he complained.

"But I will," I stated flatly.

Lucy laughed at my discomfort.

"Your Loveliness, will you tell me?" Fenwick asked Lucy.

She shook her head, smirking.

The next day was even more chaotic. I was delayed getting to the grounds because I stopped by the bank to prepare a draft for Fenwick. Fortunately (for me, perhaps not so for him), my father wandered over in mid-afternoon. I immediately turned everything over to him since I was expecting guests. In the process of attending to a hundred different things, I had become filthy and needed to wash before anyone arrived. I will admit to feeling a twinge of guilt over dumping it all on my father, but the feeling passed quickly.

While trying to leave the grounds, I was stopped three times. By the time I reached the manor, there was no time remaining for a hot bath. I dragooned Tom Collinwood into working the pump and aiming the hose while I stripped and endured the cold stream of water, washing as best I could.

I marched upstairs without a stitch on, carrying my dirty clothing. Gladys and Hazel saw me and gasped, then giggled once they thought I was out of earshot. I found something suitable to wear, combed my hair, and checked my fingernails.

On my way down the stairs, I heard Rose call out, "Guests coming, milady!"

Lucy's voice called out from the receiving room in the front of the house, "Hazel! Gladys! Front door, please!"

Moments later, there was a knock. I went to the door and opened it to see Freddy. I stood there, looking past him at nothing. He looked at me, puzzled.

"Where's Theo?" he asked.

I shut the door in his face, as Theo had done to me so often. It took a moment for Freddy to understand. He began laughing. I opened the door again.

"Either the ladies can dismount and come in while you gentlemen take the horses to the stable in back, or you can all head back, and I'll meet you there," I offered.

The ladies, Greta, Nellie, Siobhan, and Inger, all slid off their horses. They handed the reins over to the men and climbed the steps. When they reached the door, I kissed their cheeks in welcome and ushered them into the receiving room where Lucy was waiting. Once they were inside, I shut the door and trotted through the manor to the rear entrance, and bade the maids come with me.

I threw open the rear entrance. Freddy, Linc, Quint, and Ratty were in the process of tying the horses to a post and pulling off the saddlebags. With that accomplished, they marched to where I was waiting, each carrying a saddlebag on both shoulders. I assigned Rose to guide Linc, Hazel to Quint, and Gladys to Ratty. I myself escorted Freddy to the room we had prepared for him.

We brought everyone to the receiving room. Next to the ballroom, it was the largest room in the whole manor. Dinner was still a couple of hours away, so we offered everyone some refreshments, which the maids quickly retrieved. I also submitted that all our guests would have the opportunity to have a hot bath.

"Sadly, we can only heat so much water so quickly, so you will need to take turns," I stated. "And while ordinarily I would never presume that any of you, beyond Freddy and Greta, are on intimate terms, I must point out that it will speed the process considerably if you are willing to share your bath with another."

This was not entirely the truth. Each of the guest rooms only had one bed. To be sure, the beds were large, but the couples would sleep together unless they made other arrangements among themselves. Lucy earlier assured me this was not a cause for concern from what she learned while we were in the capital.

While waiting for the baths to be readied, we sat and caught up on everyone's life. As Freddy and Greta did with Lucy and me, Linc and Nellie would share their wedding ceremony with Quint Pompeo and Siobhan Harper. It would take place in the evening of the first full day following the actual moment of the winter solstice, which would occur late in the evening the night before. Ratty Hawkins and Inger Fairchild were not yet betrothed. Still, their parents were discussing it, and no one knew of any potential impediments to their eventual union.

Rose announced that the first bath was ready. It was in the lavatory between Lord Rawlinsford and Mr. Ellsworth's rooms. After several glances between the two couples, Linc and Nellie rose and headed up the stairs.

Eventually, all four couples had the opportunity to wash the dust off from the three-day journey to Easton. Ratty and Inger were the last to return downstairs. Just after they arrived, dinner was served.

It was one of the most lively and humorous meals I can remember. I could tell Freddy wished he could talk about our recent trip to Sablanca, but he knew he could not. So, instead, he regaled us with the story of this year's Queen's Cup.

A year earlier, the night before the race, Freddy gave a lengthy exposition to Lucy and me on how to place bets in order to maximize one's chances of success. Lucy then teased him, saying he always ignored this detailed analysis and ended up betting on a gray horse, regardless of the odds. Because of Lucy's teasing, at the race Freddy placed his bet on the favorite. Lucy and I placed bets of twenty ducats on the gray, who faced odds of two hundred to one at the start of the race. Lucy and I won four thousand ducats each.

"Having learned my lesson from last year's debacle," Freddy explained, "this year, I resolved that I would split my bet. Half my wager would be placed on the favorite, half on a gray horse if there was one. There was a gray, a handsome lad indeed. Having made my choices, I clutched my betting slips triumphantly, sure I would not lose. Climbing the stands to our family box, I crowed to my lovely wife, boasting of my future victory."

He paused for dramatic effect, taking a sip of wine.

"As I was rubbing my hands together in glee at my cleverness, I happened to glance at sweet Greta. She looked troubled. 'Oh,' she said. 'I didn't bet on either of those. The piebald horse is the cutest I've ever seen, and his rider's colors are my favorite shade of blue.' I quickly checked the tote board and saw Greta's poor horse was currently listed at odds of two hundred and fifty to one. 'Not to worry, my pet,' I assured her, 'it was only a ten-ducat wager. Nothing to worry about.' My sweet, darling wife looked up at me with her beautiful blue eyes, smiled and brought the dimples to her cheeks, and said, 'Ten? I put fifty down on him to win.' That announcement gave me pause, I must admit," Freddy said. "Losing ten ducats is acceptable. I consider myself lucky if I only lose ten ducats at cards when Ratty is my partner."

That brought laughs from all of us, including Ratty, who freely admitted he was a wretched card player.

"Losing fifty ducats is a more serious sting to the purse, however," Freddy continued. "I consulted the tote board again. If the favorite won, we would not recover our losses. Fortunately, if the gray ended up the winner, we would return home better off than when we departed that morning. I patted my dear wife's hand and assured her all would be well. She gazed at me with a look that was exceedingly unfamiliar to me—one of complete and utter disbelief. 'The race has not yet been run,' she stated firmly, 'and such a beautiful animal, wearing my favorite color, would never let me down.' I clasped her hands tenderly, looked deep into her eyes, and said gently, 'You might as well have thrown fifty ducats into the pond for all the good it will do.' Well, you would think a good wife, a sweet wife, would accept her chastisement in good spirit. Sadly, that was not the case here. Remind me, dear heart, how did you respond?"

"I believe, love of my life, I called you an arrogant prick," Greta responded sweetly. "Yes, 'arrogant prick' is exactly what I said."

Ratty furnished the conclusion. "The piebald led the race from start to finish. The closest competitor was six lengths behind. The gray finished in eighth place, the favorite in twelfth. Greta returned home with a bank draft for twelve thousand five hundred ducats. Freddy returned home with nothing, including his dignity. Greta, out of the kindness of her heart, did not lock him out that night."

21

The fair opened the next day at ten o'clock. It was a perfect fall day. The sky was blue, the air crisp and cool. On the horizon, you could see trees still clad in their autumnal finery.

Lucy, my father, and I presided over a brief opening ceremony. Lucy and I then began to stroll through. She paused now and then when she found particular plants and herbs she was seeking. Using paper and a sliver of graphite, she made careful notes, learning where the farmer was located, anything else he grew that interested her, and when the different plants were ready. She was especially pleased to find a maker of small glass bottles and vials and placed an order with him.

When we heard the bell in the center of Easton ring noon, we looked for food carts. Lucy shared my enthusiasm for the types of treats that seemed to be available only at large gatherings of this type—dough fried in bubbling fat and drizzled with honey, grilled meat and vegetables on a stick, thinly sliced potatoes cooked in boiling oil, and, of course, fudge. After nibbling away to our hearts' content, we continued our wandering.

We turned the corner, and I saw the wagon with the moon, stars, and lightning bolts painted on the canvas that belonged to "The Amazing Dr. Flamel." This smelly old man was present at the fair that took place at our wedding. The day after our wedding on a lark, I went in to have him tell me my future.

"You have had adventures," he said then, "but your greatest are yet to come. You will travel to a far-off foreign land and return with a priceless treasure.

Something you have hoped for will be yours sooner than you expect. And your birthright will be bestowed upon you."

I wanted not to believe him, but his comment about my birthright caught me off guard. He had wheedled another two florins out of me before telling me my father would adopt me and name me his heir within a year. For someone born a bastard, that was something I wished for as a boy. As I grew older, that dream seemed to become more impossible to attain, but it never lost its potency.

After that initial visit, Lucy and I then discussed the malodorous doctor. When she went in and visited him, he told her something that disquieted her. We decided that in her case, it must have been a lucky guess. Regarding my situation, he learned who I was because of the wedding. He figured that, as a bastard, my fondest wish would be to have my father recognize me formally.

Now, months later, I reconsidered what he told me. When he mentioned traveling far away and returning with something priceless, I thought it was simply a vague generalization. However, in light of our trip to Sablanca and return with two pieces of tan-zyan, I viewed this pronouncement differently. His prediction about my birthright proved true almost immediately, explaining my current circumstances.

Turning to Lucy, I asked, "What do you think?"

"Go ahead," she urged. "See what Flamel has to say this time."

I pushed aside the flap covering his wagon and climbed aboard. Dr. Flamel again was wearing the blue robes decorated similarly to the cover of his wagon. His beard was still long and gray, his eyebrows bushy, and his odor filled the air. He looked at me when I sat on the stool opposite him.

"Ah. The disbeliever," he commented snidely. "What do you think now?"

"I'm intrigued," I admitted.

"If you want a reading, it will be three florins," he said, holding out his bony hand.

"Your sign says one florin," I responded.

"That's for the bumpkins," he sneered. "For you, four florins."

"You said three a moment ago," I argued.

"Now it's five," he cackled, "because you're annoying me."

I fished three two-florin pieces from my money pouch, figuring he would bump the rate again. When I handed them to him, he nodded. "You learn. That's good."

He waved his hands over the crystal sphere, muttering some argle-bargle. Twice, he paused his mumbling, saying "mmm" the first time and "ah" the second. Finished, he leaned back with a smug expression.

"Six florins," he demanded.

I had developed a sense of Dr. Flamel. If I protested, he would increase the fee. At the same time, he would not demand so much for something vague. There must have been something meaningful he saw in the crystal. He was a charlatan, but he did have his own strange ethics. I handed over six florins.

"Good boy," he commented, as though I were a pet dog. "The first time she was abducted, you were blamed but saved her. Only you can save her now. A former enemy will beg, a former enemy will lend his support, and former enemies surround her. The crystal does not say whether you live or die."

"Anything else?" I asked.

"Some people will call you witch-lord. What a crock! Your wife is the witch. You're merely blessed. That's all I saw. Get out."

When I opened the flap, I blinked in the bright daylight. Lucy saw my troubled expression and came over and clasped my hand. She led me away from Flamel's wagon. When we were far enough away, I repeated what Flamel said.

"What do you think it means?" she asked.

"At the time I met you, Julienne Traval was kidnapped by Bergeron duPais. As you recall, they tried to blame me for her disappearance," I said.

"I remember," Lucy replied. "Her father was convinced you were behind it."

"I need to think about it more," I said. "The only thing I am reasonably sure of is that Julienne Traval has been, or will be, kidnapped."

"Is there a clue in the second part?" Lucy inquired.

"I don't think so," I answered. "It seems unrelated. I can't think of anyone who would think I'm some sort of witch-lord, whatever that is. Flamel was certain about you, though."

"Give me some money," Lucy demanded. "I want to hear what he has to tell me now."

I gave Lucy a handful of coins. She stormed back to Dr. Flamel's wagon and climbed up. As soon as she pulled the flap aside, I heard his querulous voice.

"Get out!" he screeched. "I have nothing for you, and I wouldn't tell you even if I did. Get out!"

Lucy backed down carefully and rejoined me. She handed the coins back. "I don't think he wants to talk to me," she smirked.

She clasped my hand and began to pull me forward. I followed, reluctantly at first. We reached a farmer's wagon, and he had something that caught Lucy's eye. She let me be while she spoke with him.

"As before, Flamel has no aura indicating any sort of affinity or ability," she reminded me when she returned to my side. "The crystal emitted no magical resonance, and I was straining to sense anything I could. All the things he told our friends at the wedding were nonsense. Much of what he told you has been eerily accurate. He mentioned one thing to me that might be true, but it is still in the future."

Lucy shrugged her shoulders in resignation. We continued our wandering course through the fair. By now, it was becoming crowded. People recognized us, and a few thanked us. We ran into our friends who were moving in the opposite direction. I took little enjoyment from it. Despite the pleasant surroundings and good wishes, Flamel's soothsaying troubled me.

Our last stop was the wagon that was serving as the "office' for the fair. My father was sitting on the bench of the wagon with Colin Rissolo. Theo was on the back, with Toby sitting underneath him on the ground.

"Now that it's underway," my father said, "it's calm as can be. The only worry is the stalls where the brewers are, but there are plenty of armsmen and deputies wandering about. I doubt anything bad will happen that we can't snuff out quickly."

"If you see Fenwick," I requested, "will you please tell him I'm looking for him?"

"Hey Fenwick," my father replied instantly, looking just past me. "Caz is looking for you."

I turned around to see Fenwick grinning at me. I shook my head.

"One of these days, you need to tell me how you do that," I said.

"Do what?"

I rolled my eyes in reply. "Come walk with us," I asked.

Lucy and I turned our steps back toward town. Before I forgot, I gave Fenwick the bank draft I'd been carrying around. As we walked, I tried to explain what happened with Dr. Flamel. At first, Fenwick looked at me as though he was worried for my grip on sanity. But the more I explained, Fenwick's expression grew less concerned.

When I finished, I said, "Fenwick, you know I'm not one who goes in for a lot of hocus-pocus."

"Which seems a bit strange," he said, "considering you are married to the most skilled witch in Aquileia, at least, in my limited experience."

"Thank you, Fenwick," Lucy remarked. "Maybe a squirrel instead of a newt."

"Thank you, Your Loveliness. I shall appreciate it, I'm sure," Fenwick said. "Plus, Caz, you have some abracadabra of your own. Is there any other way to interpret what Flamel said?"

"The first part can only refer to Julienne Traval. I can explain the whole thing but in the interest of not wasting your time, just accept that," I suggested. "After that, there is a former enemy who begs, one who helps me and others who hold the woman. Believe it or not, Fenwick, I don't have that many former enemies."

"Neither do I," Fenwick retorted.

"That's because you kill them all," Lucy pointed out.

"I didn't kill your husband," he retorted.

"Not for lack of trying," she snickered.

"Fine," Fenwick huffed. "I did tell you I was having bad feelings about it, even before I kidnapped your cousin, didn't I? It's just—well, I had my reputation to uphold. If I let you go, I would have been pressured to drop my fee, and it would have been nothing but work, work, work from that point on."

"If it makes you feel better, some of my former enemies are dead," I offered.

"Who?" Fenwick asked.

"Bergeron duPais, Prince Wim, Edwin—"

"You're welcome," Fenwick stated.

"Edwin?"

Fenwick nodded. "Who else?"

"Is Paul Jacques still alive—Lord Barrowton?"

"No. You're welcome."

"You move fast," I commented.

Fenwick tilted his head in acknowledgment.

"Um, Parkinson… I think his real name was Stuart Malley. Um…"

"What about former enemies still alive?" Fenwick inquired.

"Albert, but he's a friend now."

"And I'm not?" Fenwick complained.

"Not until Lucy says. After Albert, Herbert Traval, Nils Pedersen—"

"That's not a good former enemy to leave alive," Fenwick remarked.

"No, but we showed up at his place with the Castle Shield. Albert and Ollie threatened to burn him alive if he didn't leave me alone, so I think that made me a lower priority," I said. "After Nils Pedersen, there's you, a guy named Laurence Depew, but trust me, he's no threat. After that… I think that's all."

"What about the nomads?" Fenwick asked.

"They have no idea who I am. Same with the Rhetians from when I was a Ranger," I replied. "So, from the fact that the kidnapped woman is Julienne Traval, it's only logical that her father, a former enemy, begs me to save her or something. A former enemy is supposed to help me. It could be Albert or Mr. Traval. I doubt it will be Nils Pedersen."

"I doubt that too," Fenwick agreed.

"That leaves you or Laurence Depew. If it's Depew, I'm in trouble, so I'm hoping it's you."

"That might be the nicest thing you've ever said to me, Your Lordliness," Fenwick quipped.

"Don't let it go to your head," Lucy counseled.

"I don't think it's Albert," I said. "I don't see him getting involved in a kidnapping—not now, at least. Herbert Traval could help with transportation or financially, but I have him as the beggar. The last part is that she is surrounded by former enemies. That's where I figure Nils Pedersen comes in. Kidnapping for ransom is part of his repertoire."

"It's also something pirates do," Lucy offered. "At least it always was in the books I read as a girl."

"She's right," Fenwick affirmed. "Rhetian pirates would qualify as former enemies."

"Isn't that a bit of a stretch?" I complained.

"No," Lucy and Fenwick answered in unison.

I blew out an exasperated breath. "I suppose I'll find out if and when it happens."

"You've been acting as though you're certain it will," Fenwick remarked.

"The last time we encountered this Dr. Flamel, we went to see him for a chuckle," I explained. "He told Lucy something that disturbed her. Then he saw something regarding me and demanded more money before he would share it. When he did, he told me my birthright would be restored. Immediately after the wedding, the king summoned me and did exactly that."

"Your wedding was lovely, by the way," Fenwick commented. "Except for Lord Barrowton's ridiculousness."

"You were there?" I asked.

"Certainly," Fenwick replied with a slight shrug and tilt of his head.

"I would have given you an invitation," Lucy said.

"Thank you, Your Loveliness, but the way you conducted it, I did not need one."

"True," she conceded. "There is a big double wedding the day after Winter Solstice. Would you like an invitation to that? I can arrange it."

"And how would you introduce me to your friends, Your Loveliness?" Fenwick asked. "I'd like you to meet Aloysius Fenwick. He's an assassin."

"You don't need to be Fenwick," I suggested. "You could be Lord Compote, an important member of the king's staff."

My quip lightened the mood. Everyone laughed.

"Even better, it's a masque," Lucy added.

"A what?" Fenwick asked.

"A masque," Lucy repeated. "All the guests will wear masks."

Nellie Fassbender and Siobhan Harper shared this information with us during their visit. I had only attended one masque before and enjoyed it. The relative anonymity provided by the masks encouraged a more carefree and flirtatious attitude in the guests. The most visual evidence of that was in the attire worn by the ladies. They dressed in dramatically more daring attire for a masque than they would anywhere else.

"I might just do that," Fenwick said. "Please, Your Loveliness, if it's not too much, 'Lord Compote' would appreciate an invitation."

"For one or two?" Lucy asked.

Fenwick's eyes sparkled. "Oh! Make it two," he urged. "I need to find a 'Lady Compote' who can help me put Aquileian society on its ear. I doubt I will be as good as Lord Rawlinsford at playing Lord Compote, but with the right lady wife, I might hold my own."

I turned the conversation back to Dr. Flamel and his original prognostications.

"In my case, Flamel was eerily accurate in what he told me at the wedding," I stated. "This morning, he gouged me on the cost of his 'reading' then again before he would tell me. From his behavior, I was convinced he saw something."

"The only way to know for sure is to allow things to play out," Fenwick commented. "If what you suspect is true, the woman has already been kidnapped or will be quite soon."

"Will you help me if it comes to that?" I asked.

"That depends on two things," Fenwick replied. "The first is whether the king has any tasks for me. At the moment, I don't think so. There's his idiot cousin Braintree and some of that family, who are sitting in cells below the castle, but I believe the king will conduct a trial. That way, he exposes and discredits them and, at the same time, demonstrates his reach and power. Having them simply disappear does not suit His Majesty's purpose."

"And the other thing?" I asked.

"Are we friends?"

I looked to Lucy. She nodded. The expression on her face indicated she thought I was being absurd.

"Fine," I sighed, pretending reluctance. Fenwick cocked an eyebrow. "We have been for a while now," I admitted, "though I was reaping a perverse sense of pleasure from denying it."

"That's what I thought," he said.

22

Throughout the three days of the fair, the weather stayed pleasant. There were healthy crowds all three days, and people enjoyed themselves. Our guests departed on the last day. Our friends enjoyed themselves and expressed hope that we would invite them again. We had taken great pleasure in their visit, so we were able to assure them that we would have them back as soon as was practical. Before they left, Lucy had them add "Lord and Lady Compote" to the guest list for the wedding. That intrigued them. Lucy assured them it would be something humorous. Fenwick departed on the same day but without saying farewell. Like the other guests, he was returning to the capital.

The following day, my father and I stood on the back of the wagon, watching the last few attendees leaving. Once they were gone, our armsmen began restoring the area, removing any traces of the gathering just ended. Within hours, one could not tell anything took place except for the well-trampled stubble.

"What next?" I asked my father as we climbed down from the wagon.

He scratched his head, then responded, "In an ordinary year, the armsmen and I would still be fending off the last few attacks. They would be granted leave once the nomads departed. Then, after the Winter Solstice, I would visit every town in the March and hear their complaints and requests. When I finished that, I would summon the armsmen, and we would begin training the new draft of militia and, as the weather improved later, work on repairs to the fortifications. I suppose we can move the 'circuit of the March' forward if you would like."

"Not just yet," I replied.

As we walked back to the town gate, I started to tell my father about Dr. Flamel. My father's expression was doubtful until I shared with him the earlier prediction Flamel made about my adoption. At that juncture, my father's face softened.

This conversation was, of course, more prolonged and not as direct as I am recounting here. It lasted until we reached the manor. My father was still somewhat skeptical.

"So, you're expecting someone to come and tell you about this woman being kidnapped, and you're supposed to rescue her? Why?"

"Why me?" I asked, "or why should I do it?"

"Yes, to both," my father answered.

"I don't have a good answer," I admitted. "Perhaps it is because I rescued Miss Traval before. No one has arrived seeking my help yet, but when or if someone does, I imagine I will respond. I don't understand why I feel obligated—I just do."

When we returned to the manor, I asked my father to help me draft my report to the king. I felt he would be interested in the information my father shared regarding the harvest. Before I closed the letter, I included our plan to repopulate the three towns that were wiped out the year before. We would need more people than the March could provide.

Dinner that evening seemed strange with no guests. Lucy and I included the staff to thank them for their work while the house was full. All of them enjoyed the fair and shared their favorite things about it with us.

After dinner, Lucy and I retired to the study. She curled up in my lap after I kindled a blaze in the fireplace to ward off the autumn chill. Both of us sighed at the same time, which made us laugh.

"I know we are returning to the city for the holiday," Lucy started, "and for the weddings, but I don't think we should stay long."

"Why?" I asked.

"There is a reason why the dining table has thirty-six places," she said, "and the ballroom is the biggest room in the manor. Your father never entertained, and I have a feeling your grandfather did not do much. I think we should. Do you remember the dinner at the castle last year for the solstice? That was King

Mark and Queen Liliana doing for the kingdom what we should do for the March. Inviting some of the leading citizens to share a celebration."

"Would you like to do something like that this winter?" I asked.

Lucy laughed. "No. I'm not ready to take on another project right now. However, we should consider this in the future. The earliest event I would consider is the fertility festival near the end of Thorri. In the future, though, we should consider remaining here for Winter Solstice."

"Just curious," I asked, "when will we use the house in the capital that we just bought, repaired, and furnished?"

"The house will see plenty of use over the years," Lucy assured me, reinforcing her statement with a small kiss. "Please don't press me for specifics, but you may rest easy on that question. I have a question for you—have you begun to use your ring?"

"To store energy?" I asked.

She nodded.

"A little. Why?"

"I think you will need more than you have stored so far," she said, "if what Dr. Flamel told you comes about."

"Do you know something?" I asked.

Lucy's pained expression told me what her lips would not.

"How much more?" I asked.

"I have something planned for the two of us in a short while," Lucy replied with a smirk. "But after that, you should drain yourself into the diamond."

"But then I'll sleep for a week," I countered.

"No," she said. "I think there is a way to avoid that. Trust me?"

Lucy led me upstairs then. We spent a delightful hour. She then made me place my ring against the diamond in the pommel of my sword.

"Don't try to control it," she advised. "Let it flow as it will."

Sitting on the edge of our bed, I grasped my sword in my left hand. I touched my ring to the diamond, then went inside myself, finding the wellspring of Bellona's energy. Pulling a strand free, I directed it through my finger, into the ring, and then into the diamond, which seemed to me a welcoming empty space. Bellona's power flooded through me in a way I had not felt since I learned to control it.

When I woke, Lucy was still asleep, half on top of me, her head on my chest. I buried my nose in her hair and breathed deeply. It was not yet dawn. She sensed I was awake and squirmed slightly.

"How do you feel?" she asked.

I had not yet reached the stage of wakefulness where I knew. Considering myself, I felt normal—well, better than normal. I was expecting to be mired in the exhausted state I'd experienced before, but that was not the case. In fact, I felt suffused with health and well-being.

"I feel magnificent," I said with wonderment.

She was now awake, propping herself on my chest and looking in my eyes. "Good," she said. "Drain yourself again. Trust me."

I moved to the edge of the mattress. My sword was where I dropped it. I picked it up, repeated the process from the night before and felt the same, almost joyous, torrent of energy flow through me.

This time when I woke, it was daylight but a gray, rainy day. I guessed it was near midday. Lucy was not there. With the exception of a ferocious hunger, I felt every bit as good as I had in the morning.

I found clothes and put them on, then went in search of Lucy. Rose was the first person I saw, and she directed me to the kitchen. When I arrived, Lucy and Laurie were chatting.

"Oh good," Lucy greeted me. "There you are. Hungry?"

"Starving," I answered.

Lucy laughed, seemingly expecting that answer. I was still a bit befuddled from sleep, but I knew I should not feel as vibrant and peppy as I did, especially after draining myself twice. Along with Lucy's laugh, it made me feel like there was a joke I simply didn't understand.

"Go sit," she instructed.

She followed almost on my heels, carrying a plate of rolls and slices of cold roast from dinner. Having put that in front of me, she left, then reappeared a moment later with a large piece of apple-cranberry pie, butter for the rolls, and a cup of cider. She sat to my right and looked at me fondly.

"Aren't you eating?" I asked.

"Already did," she answered. "Go ahead and begin. How do you feel, other than hungry?"

"Goob," I mumbled, my mouth already full.

I tore into the meat like a wild beast, albeit one that uses a knife and fork. Lucy watched me eat with a loving smile on her face. When I finished the meat and began on the rolls, she disappeared.

When she returned, she had piled as many slices from last night's roast beef as before on a fresh plate. She placed it in front of me and took away the other. I immediately took up knife and fork and dispatched this helping almost as speedily as the first. She smiled at me and raised a questioning eyebrow.

I shook my head slightly. After plowing through the other roll and the slice of pie, I finally paused to drink the cider. Considering how much and how rapidly I ate, I should have felt uncomfortable. But, instead, I felt satisfied. She rose, taking the dirty plates with her.

"What did you do to me?" I asked when she returned. "I should still be asleep, not awake and feeling wonderful."

"Well, I had a hunch, so I went digging through my books," she said. "I thought it was possible to do it, and there was a description in an old volume that described it. While you were asleep, I restored your asomatous energy."

"My what?"

"Asomatous energy," she repeated. "It's hard to communicate in Aquileian exactly what it is without taking a lot of time and needing a lot of words. Think of it as your spiritual energy or force."

"I think I understand," I said with a smile.

"When you connect with Bellona or Eir, their numen binds with your asomatous energy and transforms it into what you feel and use," she said.

"What's numen?"

"Again, there isn't a simple explanation," Lucy said. "The term 'divine essence' is as close as I can come in a simple explanation."

"So their divinity combines with my whatever, and that's what I feel," I reiterated. "When I let their divine power rush out, it binds with my stuff and wooshes away. That's why I feel exhausted when I allow them to drain me. Is that the idea?"

"Correct. It uses up all your spiritual energy very quickly," Lucy agreed. "Mind and body are linked, so you collapse and are exhausted."

"Is that also why I get so hungry afterward?" I asked.

"Yes, but please don't ask me to explain that, or I would confuse you completely," Lucy said.

"How were you able to restore my asymmetric energy?" I asked.

"Asomatous," she corrected. "It is only possible because we have affinity with Eir in common. Since you gave me my betrothal ring and my wedding necklace, I have been storing bound energy in them little by little."

"Bound energy?" I asked.

"Your stuff linked to the divine essence," she said. "The diamonds can only store bound energy."

I nodded, showing I understood.

"I pulled the Eir-bonded energy I stored in the diamonds out through my emerald into your emerald. Then, your emerald unbound Eir's divinity from the 'stuff' and then filled your reservoir with unbound asomatous energy."

"Did it have any effect on you?" I asked. "You didn't drain yourself, did you?"

"No," she smiled. "It was all from what I had stored. That used up almost everything, though. It's not a perfect transfer. About half of it is lost. When you pull bound energy from your diamond, none is lost. If you were in battle and used your link to Bellona and drained your energy, you could restore it from what you stored in your ring."

"You know, you could have just told me, 'I took care of it, it's complicated, don't ask,' and I would have been perfectly happy with that explanation," I admitted. "Thank you for explaining it and for doing it."

I tried to adopt my most innocent expression so she wouldn't hit me. She shook her head. "I'm trying to teach you more about these gifts you've been granted…"

"And I do appreciate it," I answered hastily. "I do. Everything you tell me I take to heart. It's just…"

"You're cheeky, and you can't help yourself," she sighed. "I know. Come with me. I have a list of things for you to attend to," she said over her shoulder. "Meet me in the study."

I went and waited for her. She glided in, went to the desk, and retrieved a piece of paper. After she gave it to me, I scanned it.

"Item one," I read aloud. "Bank draft of four hundred and fifty-one ducats to Schumacher. What's this for?"

"Filling out the sets of dishes, plates, and glassware, plus a few serving pieces that are missing," she explained. "If we are ever going to put someone at every seat at that table, we need to replace the breakage that has happened over the years."

"Item two—fifteen ducats, seven florins to Birdsall."

"Pots and pans they delivered while we were at the fair."

"Item three—stationery, five ducats, two florins. Lucas Stationer."

"We need stationery," Lucy explained. "We need some that is ours, some that is yours, and some that is mine. I ordered it a few weeks ago. They just finished it.

"Item four—bank draft of seventy-two ducats to Rosa Thistlewaite."

"She's making curtains for us. It has probably escaped your notice, but this big old place has no curtains—at all!"

"You're right," I said.

"Of course, I'm right. We need curtains."

"Not what I meant," I retorted. "You're right—I never noticed."

"Go on, you," she said, pretending to snarl.

I skittered out of the room, clutching her paper. As I headed to the rear entrance, I called back, "I love you, Lucy! Thank you! Be back soon."

When I reached the end of the hall, I turned around. Lucy was standing outside the study with her hands on her hips. Even though she was trying to fight it, I could see her smiling.

23

D r. Flamel's prediction made it seem like the crisis involving Julienne Traval was already underway. Yet a week passed without any news, and I was beginning to doubt the aromatic doctor's veracity. My skepticism evaporated late in the afternoon on Freyday, a week after his pronouncement.

I was in the study, reviewing the account books Mr. Williston set up for the household. With quill in hand, I was entering the information from the accumulated receipts. Accompanied by the clacking of small paws on the wood floor, Theo appeared. Without a word, he dropped a letter on the account book in front of me. Flipping it over, I recognized the seal—a duplicate of the emblem displayed on Traval & Company signs.

Dear Lord Oritur,

I find myself in the uncomfortable position of needing to ask for your assistance. This morning, I learned my daughter Julienne was captured by Rhetian pirates while returning from Nagah. The blackguards have demanded payment of twenty-four thousand ducats for her safe release. From previous dealings with brigands of this stripe, I cannot trust them. The only thing I can think of that gives me any peace of mind would be to ask you to deliver the money to them and ensure my daughter is set free.

Before you were ennobled, you charged your clients half the value of items you recovered for them. I cannot put a price on my daughter's life. If you are still interested in financial compensation, I will pay whatever you ask. I do not mean to insult you if that no longer interests you.

All the resources of my company will be at your disposal. If you need to hire others, I will pay their wages. I will reimburse you for any expenses you encounter. Whatever you need to be successful, I will gladly provide if it is in my power to do so.

Please know that if you agree to assist me, whatever the compensation, I will always be in your debt.

Herbert Traval

When I undertook to win back Lord Tulley's gold a year before, Traval was of great assistance. I thought our differences were long since patched up. However, the tone of his letter indicated he felt uncomfortable asking for my help. I suppose the irony of the situation contributed to that. After all, the first time we crossed paths, he believed *I* was the one who kidnapped Julienne.

From the time Flamel uttered his prophecy, there was no doubt in my mind *whether* I would help Traval—of course I would. Lucy was in agreement. It was too late in the day to leave, though—I would depart for the capital in the morning.

I arrived in the capital in the late afternoon of Maniday, the eighth of Gorman, in a light rain. Rather than stopping at our house, I rode directly to the office of Traval & Company. The same thin-faced querulous old man was at the desk in the small outer vestibule, wearing the green eyeshade I remembered from earlier visits.

"Lord Oritur to see Mr. Traval," I told him.

While I still was not comfortable using my title, in this case, it amused me. I knew I would get a reaction. The old man did not disappoint me.

"Who?" he replied, squinting at me.

"Lord Oritur," I repeated. "I've come up a bit in the world since I last saw you."

"Majors and Minors!" he complained. "What in the Seven Hells is the world coming to? The likes of you? Why, the first time you showed up here, I had you thrown out on your ear!"

"Please tell Mr. Traval I am here," I requested. "Not only does he *want* to see me, but he also begged me to come."

"I don't believe it," the old man muttered. He did get up from his tall stool and headed inside, though.

Moments later, the door swept open to reveal Herbert Traval. "Thank all the heavenly beings you are here!" he gushed. "Please, come in!"

On my way past, I smirked at the old man. He scowled in reply. Mr. Traval took me to his office. He took my oilskin and cloak and offered me a seat.

"Tell me everything," I requested.

The words spilled out of him. "Just after that business in Newcastle, Julienne asked if she could join the firm. I admit I was skeptical about what a woman could do, but she proved to be more than capable. Julienne demonstrated her ability to find opportunities and negotiate arrangements for mutual benefit and steady profits. Her most recent idea was to travel to Nagah. Julienne heard that significant deposits of copper and tin were discovered and wanted Traval & Company to be the first merchant to establish a presence and gain an advantage over our competition."

"Isn't the route to Nagah dangerous?" I asked.

"It can be," Traval admitted. "That's why I gave her our fastest ship and a hand-picked crew. She left Aquileia in early Heyannir with instructions to wait out the late-summer storm season. I did not want her to leave Nagah until the middle of Haustman. We were expecting her return when we received this instead."

He withdrew a letter from his desk and handed it to me. It was the ransom demand. The author's command of Aquileian was limited, but the intent was clear.

We have Julian Trabal, daughter yours. We kill except you give viginty cat mill ducts by your viginty groman. Bring auric manaway. Viginty cat mill ducts viginty groman or die.

I looked up from the paper. "Viginty?" I asked.

"In Rhetian, twenty," Traval said, "though he misspells the word. Cat is Rhetian for the number four, also misspelled."

"Pirates don't have much need for a refined education," I remarked. "Mill?"

"Rhetian for thousand, again, misspelled. Auric is gold," Traval answered. "Manaway is the Rhetian name for the easternmost of what we call the Persimmon Islands. It's usually a six-day sail from here. Only a few sheep farmers live there, the last I knew. There's no good anchorage because it's surrounded by reefs. Ships need to drop anchor outside the reefs and row inshore."

"So, someone needs to deliver twenty-four thousand ducats to these people before the twentieth of Gorman," I said. "As I recall, that would be two chests of twelve ingots each. The chests would weigh ten stone."

"Yes," Traval confirmed. "Funny that you and I were having a similar discussion not quite a year ago."

He paused, staring at his desk. "Lord Oritur, will you help me? I am full well aware of how the fates mock me, forcing me to beg a man I accused of kidnapping my daughter to rescue her from a kidnapping. Please?"

"Mr. Traval, I thought we put that behind us a year ago," I said. "Rest easy. I would not be here except to help."

"Thank you," he said sincerely. "Whatever you need, I will provide if I can."

"I don't even know what I need," I admitted. "I am hoping to meet with a friend and associate later. Between the two of us, we should be able to give you a list soon. If you'll excuse me now, Mr. Traval. I rode directly here and would like to go to my house and rest from the journey."

"Absolutely," Traval said as he rose from his seat. "By all means. Meet with your friend, figure out what you need, and return. But you must sail soon."

I left the office and rode to my house, leaving Andy tied out front. Gathering my saddlebags, I made as much noise as possible, stomping on the porch and rattling the door. Then, using my key, I opened the door and immediately hollered, "Roberta!"

She was already halfway from the kitchen. "Oh! Milord! I did not expect you," she said as she wrung her hands.

"I apologize, Roberta. Unfortunately, there was no time to warn you. Any note I sent would arrive after I did."

"Will you require dinner, milord?" she asked anxiously.

"It is not likely you have enough food for both our dinners, and I think I smell yours already," I replied with a smile. "I need to take Andy to the Foaming Boar, so I will get dinner there. If I could trouble you for one thing, it would be a bath, but please finish your dinner first. I don't know how long I will be, and if the water is cold when I return, that will not be your fault. Regarding future meals, we can discuss those in the morning."

"Certainly, milord," she replied.

I dropped my saddlebags at the foot of the stairs and locked the door on my way out. Andy knew where he was and turned to the inn without my direction. He was looking forward to seeing Jerry.

As we rounded the rear corner of the inn and entered the stable area, Andy blew out his cheeks and let his lips flap. A moment later, Jerry slid down the ladder from the loft and came trotting to us. Jerry drew Andy's head to his and stroked it.

"Andy will be here at least two weeks," I said. "Make sure he gets exercise."

With that, I left. I made my way through the kitchen and into the common room. The dining room was nearly full, but I spied one small table open. Carl Stensland saw me and crossed over immediately.

"I'm here for dinner, Carl," I said. "I just rode in. Is that table saved for anyone?"

"Saved for you, I suppose," he replied with a wink. "Go sit. I'll come by as I'm able."

No sooner did my butt hit the chair when I heard in my ear, "That seat taken?"

"Majors and Minors, Fenwick!" I hissed. "You got me again!"

"You simply don't pay enough attention," he replied, sliding into the seat opposite me.

"How did you know I would be here?" I asked.

"Pretty simple," he replied. "Big commotion at Traval & Company six days ago. Three days for an express letter to reach Easton. Then three days for you to arrive. I knew you would board your horse here. Since you could not warn your maid you were coming, there wouldn't be food, so you would eat here, too. If you were delayed, I would also have come tomorrow night."

"I suppose it wasn't that difficult," I admitted. "It's the way you creep up on me."

"Ah, that's the trick of it," he replied, wagging his finger at me. "So, where's the girl?"

"Rhetian pirates—"

"Another point for Her Loveliness," Fenwick interrupted, then licked his finger and drew a tally mark in the air.

"She did say that," I admitted. "That puts her two up on me. Anyway, Rhetian pirates took her, based on the note that Traval received. They want twenty-four thousand ducats delivered to the easternmost of the Persimmon Islands by the twentieth. Traval says he'll supply us with anything we need. So what do we need?"

"A boat," Fenwick listed, "the fastest Traval can lay hands on. Experienced crew—especially a sailing master familiar with that area and men who are strong swimmers. Some thugs—I'll find those. Detailed maps. The gold, of course, though we might not need it."

"I was thinking the same thing," I said.

"Oh, you were, were you?" Fenwick snorted. "What ideas do you have, Your Lordliness?"

"Well, some I might dismiss, depending on how you answer this: are all Rhetian pirates like the ones we encountered sailing back from Alygien?"

Fenwick waggled his hand from side to side.

"Fine—not terribly bright," I stated. "Would it be safe to say they are a dozen or so in number?"

Fenwick waggled again.

I started explaining one idea that came to me. Halfway through, Fenwick jumped in. Obviously, we were thinking alike. Fenwick began describing another plan. I added some refinements. We were in the middle of discussing a third alternative when Carl dragged a chair over.

"Carl, this is Fenwick," I said. "He tried to kill me twice. The first time he came damned close. The second time, he ended up in the prisoner wagon. Fenwick, this is Carl Stensland, a former sergeant in the Rangers and owner of this fine establishment. Carl also has a unique ability to find horses that can read your mind. Lucy and I bought Bella and Andy from Carl."

The two men shook hands, appraising one another. Fenwick was the first to smile.

"Pleased to meet you," he said.

"Likewise," Carl responded, returning the smile. "So, what were the two of you discussing so earnestly, with hands waving about and such?" he asked.

"Kidnapping," I answered.

"Actually, a kidnappee, I think," Fenwick countered.

Carl clearly did not understand.

"A girl was kidnapped," I explained. "Her father asked me to deliver the ransom and ensure she returns safely. Mr. Fenwick is an amazing person to have at your side in difficult circumstances like I suspect this will be. He has graciously offered his assistance."

"Who took her?" Carl asked.

With that, we jumped right back into our discussion. We talked through the three ideas we were developing. Carl added some valuable suggestions to each. Suddenly, we noticed we were the last people in the dining room.

"Damme!" I exclaimed. "So much for my hot bath."

Then, of course, I needed to explain. Neither Carl nor Fenwick gave me any sympathy. As I stood to leave, Fenwick asked to meet for breakfast.

"If we show up at Freddy's around seven o'clock, he will probably feed us," I suggested.

"Will Greta be wearing one of her saucy maid costumes?" Fenwick inquired.

"Probably not, but you could ask her to change when we arrive," I suggested.

"That would be such a feast for the eyes, I might not even need breakfast," Fenwick quipped.

"You know the first time she wore a costume like that, Lucy dressed up as well," I remarked.

"Her Loveliness? Dressed as a naughty maid? Along with Lady Rawlinsford?" Fenwick queried. "Oh, my."

"Oh, my, indeed.," I agreed.

24

Fenwick and I met at Freddy's door as the clock was ringing seven. Roger opened it upon our knock. He tried not to act surprised.

"Lord Oritur and…" he asked, looking at Fenwick.

"Mr. Fenwick," I offered.

"Lord Oritur and Mr. Fenwick, milord," Roger hollered.

"My goodness!" I heard Freddy exclaim. "Send them in, Roger," he bellowed in response.

Roger took our jackets and swords, and Fenwick and I proceeded to the drawing room. Freddy, as usual, was sprawled on the sofa. Greta was curled inside of him, her head propped on her hand, with her elbow on Freddy's ribs. Both of them were in dressing gowns.

"You'll have breakfast with us, I presume?" Freddy asked.

"Why, thank you, Freddy," I responded.

"Two more for breakfast, Roger," Freddy shouted.

He started to rise, but I waved him back down. I shook his hand, then kissed Greta on the cheek. Fenwick also shook Freddy's hand and then kissed the back of Greta's hand. That took all of us by surprise. Including, I think, Fenwick. I saw a trace of a blush on his cheeks.

They wanted to know what brought me to the city, so we told them as succinctly as possible. I could tell Freddy was hoping we might need him for this adventure. I quickly informed him this was likely something that would be resolved by swordplay and violence rather than guile and deception. My explanation satisfied him. The rest of our conversation turned on the fun they had during their visit to the March, and the upcoming weddings at the Winter Solstice.

"Since it will be a masque," Fenwick asked, "is there any chance I might see you dressed in one of your saucy maid outfits, Lady Rawlinsford?"

"That might be fun," she remarked eagerly. "I never wore the spiciest one."

When we left, Fenwick suggested walking to Traval's office, as he wanted to discuss a few things. He first thanked me for putting him in contact with Pierre Luin. Pierre was now handling Fenwick's finances. However, the second item Fenwick mentioned stunned me.

"If there was another woman like Lady Rawlinsford, who could tolerate my lack of standing in the world," he said, "I would be hooked like the dumbest fish that ever swam the ocean."

"Fenwick!" I gasped quietly, openly surprised. "What brought that on?" My tone and interest were sincere. This was the first genuinely personal thought he ever shared with me.

He shrugged in response. I sensed he felt uncomfortable revealing even that much. If he wanted to share more, he would in his own time, so I left the subject alone.

I broke the silence two blocks later. "Of the ideas we discussed," I said, "the one I like best is us simply marching in and killing them all. My only concern is the crossbows they will have."

"Let's hold off on a final decision," he suggested. "We don't know what vegetation there is on the island. If there are trees that could provide cover, that might sway our thinking. Without that, I might agree with you."

"What are we needing from Traval?" I asked.

"The swiftest boat he has or can obtain," Fenwick responded. "We need enough crew to man that ship and just as many for the pirate vessel, which is probably the ship Miss Traval was on. It is probably a more sound vessel than the one they had. We'll capture it and bring it back once we kill them all. We should also bring some bully boys, armed with crossbows."

"How many?" I asked.

"Our best guess is that the Rhetians will number a dozen or so," Fenwick said. "If we are near equal in numbers, that will make them more cautious. Bringing fewer will give them a false sense of security. I think four will be the right number. I'll hire them." Fenwick grinned broadly. "They have no idea of what they have invited to their island… You know, I'm actually looking forward to this."

I gave him a quizzical look.

"The last time I used my power in a meaningful way was against you," he said. "I know what you're going to say—the arrival of the City Watchman distracted you, along with the goon I hired for the night—but up to that point, weren't you having fun?"

Part of me wanted to issue a snappy response, but I held my tongue briefly. Thinking back on that rainy night, fun wasn't the first word that came to my mind. I understood what he meant, though. It was challenging, terrifying…

"Exhilarating," I responded, "not fun."

Fenwick rolled his eyes. "Fine," he conceded, "but didn't it make you feel *alive?*"

I didn't say anything, but I had to admit to myself that Fenwick's point was valid.

When we arrived at Traval & Company, the cranky old man showed us in without bandying words. We presented the list of things we needed to Traval. He wrote them down.

"None of these will be a problem. As far as the island," he said, "it is mostly open. There are some trees on the lee side… I mean, the west end of the island. Nothing like a forest, though. Just enough to provide some shade and a bit of shelter."

"We will be ready to sail on the tide two days from now," Fenwick told him. "Will you have everything ready?"

"Yes." Traval then consulted a chart. "High tide will be just before half-past six in the morning."

"We will be there," I said.

After we left, Fenwick excused himself. "I have some people I need to see," he said.

"Would you like to join me for dinner?" I asked. "I need to let the housekeeper know how many to expect."

Fenwick shook his head. "I'll fend for myself," he said. "See you on the docks the morning after tomorrow."

As I headed for our house, it occurred to me that I probably owed the king a letter. I let Roberta know it would probably be just the two of us for dinner and thanked her for drawing my bath the night before (even though it was quite cool by the time I dipped myself in the water). Then I went looking for paper and quill.

In the letter, I informed him of my intention to assist Herbert Traval, Fenwick's involvement, the harvest fair we held, and the report that crop yield in the March was good. Then I worded our desire to repopulate the three towns that were sacked the previous year and begged his assistance in sending us people looking for a new start.

That led me to think about what my father told me about Port Charles. I knew nothing whatsoever about the process of dredging a harbor or clearing a river. It seemed to me those were specialized skills that only a few people would have. So I added this to my epistle.

The favorable harvest in the March, and our hope to return land to cultivation when we repopulate the three towns, along with news of poorer results elsewhere in the kingdom, brought Port Charles and the Pheas River to my attention. Many years ago, I understand that the March used to be able to send grain by ship to other markets. At some point, the harbor filled with silt. Afterward, the river was neglected, except for small stretches where neighboring communities kept it clear for their own uses.

It occurs to me that reopening the harbor and river would benefit the March and the kingdom. Transporting grain overland by wagonload limits the quantity, increases the cost, and takes more time compared to shipping by sea. However, I know nothing about what would be required to clear the harbor and river. Are there experts who could examine Port Charles and the Pheas River in order to determine whether such a project is feasible and whether it would be profitable?

I await your response and remain, as ever, your humble servant.

I sealed the letter and, since I had nothing more pressing, I decided I would deliver it to the castle myself. It would be easier to hire a hackney than to go and get Andy. I walked over to the market square and found two coaches waiting for a fare. After that, it was a simple matter to drive to the guardhouse at the castle bridge, deliver my letter and return.

When I returned to the house, having nothing better to do, I decided to try to siphon more energy into the diamond on my sword. Accessing my connection to Bellona was easy by now, and I diverted as much of that force as I felt I could spare. However, reaching for my connection to Eir required achieving a deeper mental state and reciting the incantation. I made a few attempts before I succeeded in blocking out all distractions. It was in vain, however, since as soon as I began, I felt that to continue I would drain myself more than I wanted.

As it was, I think I overdid it. The next thing I remember was a knocking on the door. Before I could drag myself from my chair, Roberta answered it.

"Milord?" she called.

"Yes, Roberta."

"A note arrived for you."

The royal seal was on the back. I slid my finger under the flap and opened it. "Please dine with us this evening. Six o'clock. M"

A quick riffle through my armoire yielded acceptable clothing to wear to dinner with the king. The temperature dropped in the later afternoon, so I also wore my cloak and carried my oilskin if it decided to rain. I headed to the Foaming Boar to get Andy. With the king, dinner could be short or long. I suspected it might be long tonight, so I wanted Andy nearby since hackneys were scarce after dark. When I arrived at the stable, I whistled for Jerry. He came down the ladder from the loft and began to saddle Andy.

"Thank you, Jerry," I replied when he finished. "We might be returning late this evening. I am having dinner at the castle. I apologize in advance if I need to wake you."

They were expecting me at the guardhouse at the castle bridge. A page was there to take Andy and another to guide me across to the castle. On the far side of the bridge, another page was waiting who took me inside and brought me to one of the dining rooms. I unbuckled my sword and left it with one of the two guards at the door. The page knocked.

Hearing the command, "Enter!" the page opened the door and announced me. The king and queen sat at the head of the table, with Albert to his mother's left. The king gestured for me to sit on his right.

"Your Majesties, Your Highness," I said, bowing, then took my seat.

"Tell us about this Traval business," the king asked.

I explained the situation with Julienne Traval briefly. Albert's ears turned red, as he was heavily involved when she was kidnapped over a year earlier by Bergeron duPais. I moved as quickly as I could to the plan Fenwick and I developed.

"Yes, Fenwick asked our leave to assist you in this matter," the king remarked. "We have no pressing need for him right now, and he assured us this would be a simple affair."

"I certainly hope so, Your Majesty," I replied.

Our soup arrived, and Queen Liliana took over the questioning. In particular, she wanted to know about the harvest fair and whether we judged it a success. She also asked after Lucy.

Over the second course, Albert spoke about the upcoming weddings between Linc Ellsworth and Nellie Fassbender, and Quint Pompeo and Siobhan Harper. Albert was serving as one of Quint's bridesmen, as he did for me. He apologized for being unable to come to the fair we held, as he was needed elsewhere.

When the third course was served, the king revealed the reason I was there.

"The information you shared about crop yields was most welcome," he said. "It would even have been cause for joy, except for the difficulty of shipping the grain to the rest of the kingdom, which you pointed out. We wish to discuss this in greater detail after we finish the meal."

Through the rest of dinner, Albert and Liliana carried the burden of conversation. The king was little interested in the gossip they shared with me. Instead, he clearly was eager for dinner to be over.

After dessert, the queen excused herself. The king waited for the table to be cleared, then unfurled a large map. The map included only the Eastern March and included a level of detail more thorough than any I had seen before.

"Records show that Port Charles was last used nearly a hundred and fifty years ago," the king said. "At the time, it was not a profitable operation, and the earl of the March ceased maintaining the harbor with our approval. Maintenance of the port and the river has always been the responsibility of the March."

"The population of the capital, and indeed, all the cities in the realm, was smaller. The grain from the March was not necessary to sustain them," Albert added. "Things have changed since then."

"If you look at this map," the king said, "you see a network of roads from most communities in the March to landings on the River Pheas. I imagine those roads are overgrown now, though the road beds should still exist. Similarly, the landings, if they were constructed of wood, are probably gone. There should still be some stonework, though."

"According to the records," Albert said, "the river was navigable up to this point, just south of Quinn's Ford. If we can restore the river and the harbor, then grain and produce from this entire area," he swept his hand over the map to indicate, "could be shipped economically to the capital, Newcastle, and Aurora, then upriver from there. The March would certainly benefit. So would the rest of the kingdom."

"We are sending the royal engineers to assess the harbor and the river," the king said. "They will prepare a report for us, which we will share with you once it is ready."

"Though maintenance of the port and river is the responsibility of the March," Albert said, "we have a suggestion that may provide assistance. It involves Mr. Traval and his current problem."

Though that pronouncement took me by surprise, I was able to mask my reaction. The king was watching me when Albert said it. He snorted in response.

"Lord Oritur, how you manage to conceal your reactions is one of the more impressive things we have ever seen," he commented, shaking his head. "Mr. Traval is prepared to pay a ransom of twenty-four thousand ducats. If you and Mr. Fenwick are able to return his daughter without requiring that money, we should like you to propose to Mr. Traval that he consider contributing that sum to the restoration of the harbor at Port Charles. In return, we are prepared to grant him certain concessions with respect to customs duties, and you will allow Traval & Company first choice of location for dock space and warehouse location in Port Charles."

"You will still need to cover the balance of the cost," Albert pointed out. "Without the report from the engineers, we have no idea of the total amount. Our hope is that the remainder is small enough that you would be able to recover your investment in ten years or less. If that is not the case, we will consider alternatives."

"Once we learn more about the cost and how long it will take, we can look at the financial benefits of resuming trade through Port Charles," I said. "I am well aware that I owe much of my good fortune and strong financial position to your generosity, Your Majesty and Your Highness. Investing in the future of the March and the prosperity of its residents is something I see as an obligation—a happy one and not a burden. I am eager to learn what the engineers determine. And, if it's not too much trouble, may I have a duplicate of that map?"

"I will have the copyists prepare one," the king agreed as he rose and rolled the map up.

As the king left, Albert offered to see me out. That meant the guard at the door needed to follow us in order to return my sword after I was no longer in Albert's presence. The guard did not seem upset, so I didn't allow it to bother me.

"So far, Caz, you have done much more than my father hoped for," commented. "Since I know you better, I am not as astounded as he is. Mother is completely unsurprised at your success—though she sees Lucy's influence. For instance, it was Lucy's idea to hold the fair, wasn't it?"

"It was, but the festival on Andvar's feast day was all mine," I said.

"I meant to ask you about that," Albert said. "What brought that on?"

"Gratitude."

25

I met Fenwick at the dock as the sun was rising. Even though I wore my oilskin on top of my cloak, the wind was cold. It brought a warning of the winter about to arrive. I boarded the boat with a small bag in hand, containing some clothing, along with the seasickness medicine that Lucy gave me before I set out from the manor.

The boat was not much bigger than the one belonging to Fenwick's smuggler acquaintance, Bebo. I introduced myself to the sailing master, Mr. Turnbull, then stowed my bag. There were no cabins—we would all sleep using serpentins.

Fenwick pulled me aside and informed me that the two chests containing the gold were already aboard. He and the sailing master loaded them the night before and placed them in a place that was difficult to find. The crew did not know about them. Neither did the ruffians Fenwick brought along. As far as they knew, we had no intention of paying any ransom. Fenwick and I would only do that if we had no other options.

We untied immediately and shoved off from the pier. There was an onshore breeze, so we needed to wait for the tide to pull us out slightly before we unfurled the sails. The sailing master merely waved his hand, and the crew had the mainsail up in seconds. It caught the wind and billowed out as the boat heeled over. Once sure we were clear, the foresail went up.

We zigzagged through the harbor before reaching the open sea. The boundary between the two was evident. On one side, the water was relatively calm. On the other, we began to pitch and roll, with waves crashing over the bow and spraying everyone aboard. Fenwick's hooligans began complaining right away.

Fortunately, Lucy sent me off with plenty of ginger oil and licorice root. I was able to share with the rough trade Fenwick recruited. After all, they would be of little help if they were still ghastly pale and vomiting when we arrived.

During the voyage, we had the hooligans practice rowing in the jolly boat, even though it was on deck. We chocked it upright with coils of rope and had them practice deploying oars, rowing in unison, and bringing the oars back aboard. Though they showed progress, I expected them to fall apart when they were actually on the water, being tossed about.

We caught sight of an island on the morning of the eighth day, the nineteenth of Gorman. The sailing master confirmed that this was the easternmost of the Persimmon Islands. I was impressed with his navigational skill and told him so.

We were on what he called a "broad reach" with the wind mostly behind us. Though the seas were still rough, we were fairly skimming along. The island grew closer by the minute.

By midday, we could see a boat, similar in size to ours, that appeared to be anchored off the west end of the island. We headed directly for it. When we drew closer, the sailing master confirmed it was a Traval ship. He ordered most of his crew to remain below the gunwales and out of sight. We did not want the pirates to know how many men we had aboard.

We dropped the sail, and the master turned the boat into the wind. The maneuver killed our progress, and the sailing master ordered the anchor dropped. Looking over at the other ship, I could see a single man aboard. Two others appeared on the shore. We knew there must be more.

The other thing we trained the ruffians to do was to lower the jolly boat over the side. They managed to accomplish this without disaster, though there were some moments when I was concerned. Finally, the boat was floating, the ropes loose.

With the boat in the water, the hooligans climbed down to perform the second task we tried to teach them—row. The four of them took their seats. One member of the crew would act as the coxswain, and he followed. Fenwick and I climbed down last. We unhooked the ropes used to lower the boat. Once we took our seats, the coxswain used his boathook to push us away.

"Out oars," he commanded. With some fumbling, Fenwick's men managed to put the oars in the oarlocks, with the blades out of the water.

"Give way together," the coxswain instructed.

The men dropped the blades of the oars into the water and pulled. It was a raggedy-looking stroke. The small amount of coordination they achieved while still on the deck was fading.

"Pull," the coxswain called. The following stroke was smoother, but there was still some unevenness.

"Pull," he called again.

By the sixth stroke, the men were more accustomed to the motion of the jolly boat and started to look as though they knew what they were doing. The coxswain steered us directly toward shore. When we passed over the surrounding reef, the water was calmer. As we drew closer, he began looking over his shoulder, judging the surf.

"Remember, follow my cadence," he reminded them. "We're going to catch a wave and ride it in, but you need to be on the mark."

The coxswain timed things well. Now in the smoother water past the reef, Fenwick's men were rowing well. The jolly boat seemed to be lifted slightly by a wave. We only fell gradually as they continued to pull the oars as the coxswain directed.

"Ship oars!" the coxswain ordered, and the men untidily brought the oars aboard. Moments later, we felt the scrape of sand under the prow. The coxswain scampered up between the men and jumped to the beach, holding the rope attached to the bow.

"C'mon, you louts," he called. "Beach the boat."

In a disorganized manner, the men remembered to follow the coxswain and pull the boat up beyond the surf line. Fenwick and I stayed seated. It was by no means the most accomplished display of seamanship I ever saw, but it did the job. Fenwick and I stepped out of the boat onto the sand. The men then dragged it high enough to tie the bow rope around a tree trunk. Nearby I saw a near-identical jolly boat in which the Rhetians rowed ashore.

Traval's description of the island was accurate. There were trees, but they were scattered, stunted, and windblown, struggling against the elements. Eleven men were watching us. Four of them held crossbows. Fenwick's four thugs retrieved crossbows from the bottom of our boat. The tension increased dramatically.

One of the Rhetians stepped forward. Fenwick did the same. While they faced off, I reached within myself and pulled forth a strand of Bellona's energy. It was not time for battle if all went to plan, but I wished to be prepared for anything.

Fenwick and the Rhetian began arguing. I only knew a few words of Rhetian. The Rhetian was angry with Fenwick. I heard the word auric, which means gold.

Fenwick and I planned to leave the gold in the ship unless there was no other way to free Miss Traval. Our response to the Rhetians would be that we would not bring the gold until we knew the girl was safe and unharmed. If she was violated in any way, there would be trouble for the Rhetians.

After some more heated discussion, the Rhetian realized Fenwick would not budge from his demand to see Miss Traval. He ordered his men to surround us, then stalked off, leaving us to follow. We left the coxswain at the jolly boat to guard it. After traveling fifty yards, winding through the scattered trees, we could see a ramshackle hut ahead.

It seemed to be constructed of driftwood. None of the boards were the same length. There were gaps between all of them. As we drew closer, we could see it was not a hut but rather a sheepcote, a three-sided shelter for sheep in bad weather.

When we were almost upon it, I could see Julienne Traval huddled on the ground. Hearing men approach, she looked up fearfully. Then, seeing that some of us were not Rhetians, her eyes widened.

Meanwhile, back on the water, the next part of our plan was unfolding. Among the sailors Traval provided, we asked for at least a half dozen strong swimmers, and who could hold their own in a fight. While we were on the beach, presumably commanding the attention of the Rhetians on their vessel, those men would have slipped into the water on the side of our ship furthest from the Rhetian ship.

They would brave the chilly waters with cutlasses on lanyards around their necks. When they reached the Rhetian ship, they would board and gain control of it. With their ship under our control, we hoped to win Miss Traval's freedom without bloodshed. However, if they still wanted to fight, we would oblige.

Now almost at the sheepcote, Fenwick spoke to the chief Rhetian. He would be asking permission for me to advance and talk with her. After a moment, the Rhetian waved me forward.

As I crossed to her, a look of recognition flitted across her face, followed by one of puzzlement. 'You?" she mouthed.

I returned the warmest smile I could. "Your father asked for my help," I told her. "I'm aware of the irony. So is he. Have they hurt you?"

She shook her head. "My wrists and ankles are rubbed raw from where they have bound me, and they've been a little rough at times, but my virtue is still intact if that is what you are asking."

"That was what I was asking. If those pirates harmed you in that way, there would be no mercy for them," I explained. "Not that there will be in any case. What of your crew?"

"All dead," she replied glumly.

"As the Rhetians might be soon," I said.

"But they outnumber you," she whispered.

"They would need to double their numbers to make a difference," I replied. "It may not come to that. Now that I've made sure you are unharmed, we will leave you here for a short spell. Do not fret. Things could become very violent very soon, and by staying, here you will be safe."

By now, I expected our sailors would have taken control of the Rhetian vessel. Using my connection to Bellona, I tried to expand my senses as far as the boats. Whether my ability would stretch that far was uncertain, but I did not receive any indication of trouble. Perhaps when we drew closer to the beach, I would have a better feel.

I stood and turned to Fenwick. "She is untouched."

He nodded and spoke to the Rhetian leader. Together they began walking to the beach. The rest of us followed. We were reaching the critical moment. I went within myself and grasped a thicker strand of Bellona's power than I ordinarily would, wanting to be prepared. The unique energy was flooding my entire body.

Just as I did this, the Rhetian leader halted. His four men with crossbows faced off against our four. Both sides had their weapons up and ready. The Rhetian leader and two of his associates surrounded Fenwick. They drew their blades—the nasty Rhetian sword with a blade bent upward about twenty degrees, six inches from the tip. Fenwick took a step back and drew his sword.

There were four Rhetians near me, and they also drew their swords. Like Fenwick, I skittered backward to give myself some room and pulled my blade. It was almost exactly as we hoped.

I could see the two ships bobbing in the waves past the reef. Both now flew the Traval & Company banner from their masts. Our men had gained control of the Rhetian ship. Fenwick saw it too.

Fenwick simply said, "Now."

Fenwick's men fired their crossbows. The Rhetians fired at the same time. All eight fell to the ground with bolts sticking from the center of their chests. That left Fenwick and me to face seven Rhetians. It was not a fair fight.

Bellona's energy sang in my veins. I felt a sense of exultation and wanted to scream my joy to the sky. The four Rhetians tried to surround me, but I gave ground to prevent it. At the same time, my blade moved with uncanny speed.

I quickly disarmed the first to lunge at me. My sword flashed past his guard, and I sliced his wrist, causing him to drop his weapon. The second man was more controlled, but I sidestepped his thrust and trapped his right arm under my left. I bashed him in the head with the guard of my sword and shoved him toward the other two Rhetians.

As the three of them staggered backward, I quickly pierced the chest of the one I had clouted, then flicked my sword up and around, making the third Rhetian's blade dance away, spinning through the air. It was a simple matter to follow that with a flick to his throat. His face bore an expression of stunned disbelief as his hands flew to his throat. The blood spurted through his fingers as he pitched forward to wet the ground with gore.

The fourth man was in shock. For a moment, he stood frozen. Then, when I made the smallest movement toward him, it triggered his response. He came for me, screaming. I blocked his thrust with my left arm easily and let him run onto my blade. His shriek died in his throat. He fell to his knees with his mouth and eyes still wide open. When I tugged my sword free, he toppled forward.

The first man, whose wrist I cut, had been screeching in pain. That noise suddenly ceased. I turned around to see Fenwick pull his sword from the man's back.

"He was annoying," Fenwick said with a shrug.

Surveying the area, I saw all the Rhetians were dead, along with the four men Fenwick brought. Further away, I spied all the sailors on both vessels lined up along the sides, yelling and jeering. In the water, I saw a man's head as he flailed about. I suspected the sailors threw the Rhetian they surprised into the water. While I watched, the head disappeared under a wave and did not surface afterward. After watching for long enough to be certain of what happened, the sailors groaned in disappointment at the loss of their entertainment and moved away from the sides.

Shaking my head, I trotted back and collected Miss Traval. The expression on her face was one of horror. That puzzled me until I looked and saw I was drenched in blood. I then noticed it was dripping from my face as well. I sawed through cords binding her wrists and ankles, then helped her to her feet. She was a bit unsteady.

"My feet and hands are numb," she explained.

After looking to see which side of me was less blood-covered, I put my left arm around her waist and helped her walk as we slowly headed for the beach. She needed to stop halfway there when the restored circulation caused pain too great to continue. After a minute, she nodded, and we continued.

While we staggered to the beach, I could tell I used more of my power than usual. I now felt unusually weary. I handed Miss Traval to Fenwick.

Reaching over, I touched my ring to the diamond in the pommel of my sword. I searched within myself and tried to "feel" a connection between the source of Bellona's power and the ring. When I sensed I had linked the two, I then searched through the ring into the diamond to find the energy stored within it. No sooner had I completed this bond when I felt vigor flow into me. It happened rapidly, like placing a bucket under a waterfall. I broke the link as soon as I felt "full," which took only a second or two. Then I gathered the tendril I still sensed and pushed it back where it belonged. Turning my attention away from that inner plane, I felt rejuvenated.

Unfortunately, with Fenwick's hooligans lying dead, the task of rowing us back to the ship fell to Fenwick and me. The coxswain untied the boat from the tree and dragged it around. Then, he shoved it into the surf line, bow first. Fenwick assisted Miss Traval over the gunwale and instructed her where to sit. The coxswain helped us shove the boat further into the water, then climbed aboard. Fenwick and I followed him.

Our weight caused the keel of the boat to touch the sand in the stern. The coxswain called, "Out oars," but his command was unnecessary. Fenwick and I were already fumbling, trying to fit them in the oarlocks.

"Give way together," he said when we finished.

The coxswain timed it so we caught the receding wave with our stroke, and we tugged the stern free. "Pull away smartly!" he instructed.

Fenwick gave me a questioning glance. "Row hard," I explained.

We made good progress to the reef but then it became much more challenging. We bobbed up and down. Looking back at the shore, it seemed we were not moving forward at all. Then, just as I was nearing exhaustion and the blisters on my hands were stinging, the coxswain called, "Up oars, boat oars," as he reached with his long hook to snag a line hanging from the ship.

As Fenwick and I struggled to stow the oars properly, the jolly boat bumped into the side of the ship. One of the sailors tossed a rope ladder down. Fenwick assisted Miss Traval to the ladder and then stayed behind her as she climbed to prevent her from falling. When she reached the deck, Fenwick climbed back down. The sailing master leaned over, wondering why Fenwick did not come aboard.

"We need everyone you can spare," I called up to him. "There are fifteen bodies we must bury or burn."

We could not leave the bodies for scavengers or to rot since our Gods would be displeased. Not long after my request, four sailors climbed into the boat, and six bundles of clothing were tossed down after them. Fenwick and I moved to the bow. The coxswain issued his orders, and we pulled away smoothly and headed to the Traval ship we regained. The clothing bundles were handed up so the men could dress, having been naked since swimming over. Once clothed, four more sailors climbed down a rope ladder.

The boat moved much more smoothly and swiftly with experienced men at the oars (and six now rowing). We reached the shore quickly, and Fenwick and I jumped out and held the boat fast with the rope. The sailors followed as soon as the oars were stowed and hauled the boat onto the sand.

The decision of whether to burn the bodies or bury them was an easy one to make. Aquileia and the Rhetian Empire had been at war for centuries over religious differences. The Rhetians believed there was only one all-powerful god. We knew they were wrong, and we worshiped the three Major Gods and nine Minor Gods properly. At the same time, one aspect of the Rhetian religion was their belief that cremation damned one's soul to eternal torment.

We tore apart the sheepcote quickly, then fanned out looking for deadfall and driftwood. It took about two hours, but we accumulated enough for an effective pyre. When it was complete, we piled the bodies on top and lit the wood. We stayed long enough to make sure the fire spread to include the whole pyre.

When we reached the beach, the sailors who recaptured the Traval ship returned to it in the jolly boat the Rhetians brought ashore. For us, the journey back to our ship took only a fraction of the time Fenwick and I needed.

Fenwick and I climbed the rope ladder. The sailors quickly fastened the jolly boat to the ropes hanging from the mast boom. When they climbed aboard, in a matter of a few moments, the jolly boat was back on deck and secured. Both ships weighed anchor immediately. We shared the same sentiment that we wanted to put the island behind us.

26

"You have to admit," Fenwick said later, "that was fun."

"I confess," I said, "I did enjoy it. But didn't it bother you to lose all four of the men you brought?"

Fenwick looked at me as though I suddenly sprouted horns. "Not at all. If they were alive and we brought them back aboard, they would be planning on relieving Miss Traval of her honor. The they would tear the ship apart, searching for the ransom money. So, the Rhetians did us a favor by killing them."

"Did you plan on them being killed?"

"Plan? No. Hope? Yes," Fenwick responded. "I can see from your expression that you are bothered. Don't be. They were scum and deserved to die. Not for anything they did on this journey, but I'm certain many things in their past would justify it."

"How do you know such people?" I asked.

"I was not as fortunate as you," he replied. "You stumbled into your way of making a living through your association with Lord Rawlinsford. I had no friends or acquaintances like him. You became a retriever of lost or stolen items. I became a hired killer. I think my profession was more lucrative, but it did require regular association with the lower levels of Aquileian society. They helped me find work, just as Freddy helped you, at least at first."

I considered what Fenwick said. He had a valid point. Though I am a bastard and suffered due to it, he came from less. Even though my time at school was more like being in exile, it was an advantage Fenwick did not enjoy.

"I apologize for judging you," I said.

"You don't often," Fenwick replied. "One of the reasons I like you."

"So, people like that helped you find work?" I asked.

"I told you before, you were the first decent person I was ever hired to kill," Fenwick stated. "The rest were all varying degrees of filth. Bad people hired me to murder other bad people. There was no ethical or moral dilemma—by killing my targets, society would be better off, plus I would get paid."

I laughed. Then I asked, "How did you manage to avoid becoming part of Nils Pedersen or Donald Farquahr's operations?"

Fenwick responded with a low chuckle. "Oh, they tried," he said. "Their first approach was to try to woo me. When I rebuffed them, they tried to compel me. I returned their emissaries to them in pieces. Finally, they decided to let me be."

We stood in silence for a time, watching the ocean flow by. The wind shifted slightly, and the sound of Miss Traval speaking with the sailing master carried to my ears. I turned to look.

"Were you serious when you said that if there was someone like Greta who could tolerate your lack of standing, you'd be hooked like a big, dumb fish?" I asked.

Fenwick gave me a guarded look. "Why?"

"She might be one of our sailing companions," I said.

"Miss Traval?"

I nodded.

Fenwick shook his head.

"Hear me out, at least," I pleaded.

Fenwick turned to face me with a scowl.

"Already in her life, she has been exposed to more danger than any five women of her standing would face in their lifetimes," I said. "There was the whole thing with Bergeron duPais. When I rescued her, she was drugged, naked, lashed to an altar, and about to be raped. Just now, pirates kidnapped her after she sailed to Nagah without a chaperone for the family business—something she did on her own initiative. Her idiot mother wanted her to marry nobility, but Miss Traval would prefer to be involved in her father's trading company. Doesn't that indicate she might be more willing to accept your unusual background?"

"Caz," Fenwick hissed through clenched teeth so he would not be overheard, "I'm an assassin."

"I know that. You know that," I said. "I don't think it would be the end of things if Julienne were to know that. As far as her parents are concerned, you are a highly valued, irreplaceable, confidential assistant to His Royal Majesty."

"Who kills people when His Majesty orders," Fenwick countered.

"Who just rescued her from pirates," I retorted. "I know I joked about it when we spoke about the weddings coming up, but her parents need know nothing more than that you work for the king and cannot share the nature of your duties because of their sensitive nature. And you have five or six days to get to know one another while we are stuck on this ship. 'Faint heart never won fair maiden,' Fenwick."

He growled at me but found a reason to start a conversation with her later. Over the balance of our journey back to Aquileia, the two spent more and more time in each other's company. I kept my mouth sealed firmly shut.

We arrived on the morning tide on Freyday, the twenty-sixth of Gorman. Herbert Traval was waiting on the pier when we tied up. The reunion between father and daughter was a joyous thing to see. Fenwick and I stayed aboard since there were still twenty-four gold ingots on the ship. We explained that to Mr. Traval when he asked why we were lingering.

He crossed the gangway and seized my hand, pumping it up and down with both of his vigorously. "I can't thank you enough, Lord Oritur," he gushed. "If there is anything I can do—anything at all…"

I gave him a kindly smile. "The first thing you can do is to add Mr. Fenwick to your thanks," I said. "This would have been an impossible task without him."

"Thank you, sir," Traval said, giving Fenwick the same enthusiastic pumping of hands. "As I said, anything."

"As far as that 'anything,' Mr. Traval," I said. "I have a business proposition to discuss with you at your earliest convenience."

"Certainly, milord. Certainly," he said. "Would tomorrow be convenient? I'll come—"

"Tomorrow would be fine," I said calmly, "and I will come to your office. Is nine o'clock too early?"

"That will be fine, just fine," he replied.

"In that case, Mr. Traval, Mr. Fenwick and I will take our leave," I said. "The sailing master knows where the two chests are, and I urge you to have them removed to a place of safety."

"Of course, of course. Thank you again, Lord Oritur and Mr. Fenwick. May all the heavenly beings bless you and keep you."

Fenwick and I took our bags and strolled to the end of the pier. There were no hackneys about, so I resigned myself to the uphill walk to the nearest market square to find one. I would return to our house, ask Roberta to prepare a bath and then worry about the rest of the day.

"Share a hackney?" I asked Fenwick when we reached the square.

"I don't think we are heading in the same direction," he said with a faint smile.

"After I meet with Traval tomorrow," I said, "I will return to the March. Do you have any idea where you're heading?"

"Unless the king's business pulls me away," he said, "I think I will stay in the city for a time."

"Good luck, my friend," I said in parting.

Roberta did prepare a bath for me, and it was heavenly. For the first time since we left the island, I felt like I had finally washed all the blood away. Even better, a copy of the map the king showed me was already waiting in a leather scroll case.

For dinner, I went to the Foaming Boar. It allowed me to settle my account with Carl for boarding Andy while I was away. I advised him I would be collecting Andy in the morning.

"Don't be surprised if you see Jerry acting more like his old happy self," Carl said. "He took it real hard when Andy and Bella left. The problem was he treated Andy as his, then Bella, now Davy. You bought Andy and Bella, and now I'm fixing to sell Davy to your friend Mr. Fenwick."

"I didn't know that," I said.

"Ya, someone—meaning your lady wife—told Mr. Fenwick that I have a talent for spotting horses that can almost tell what you're thinking," Carl said with a smile. "I don't know about all that. I just get a feeling about a horse that they'll be able to learn what I can teach 'em. Anyway, your Mr. Fenwick mentioned he wanted Davy before you left, and since then, I started looking around, and there are two I liked, and I couldn't make up my mind. So I bought both."

"And you gave one to Jerry to be his own." I guessed.

"Aye," he acknowledged, scratching his head. "And now he has Thunder to be his very own. The other thing bothering Jerry is something we both went through—he's growing like a weed, his voice doesn't know whether it wants to go high or low, and he's getting hair in new places. He doesn't know from one minute to the next whether he's hot or cold."

"I understand completely, Carl," I said.

"Oh, good. You saved my seat," I heard behind me.

"Damme, Fenwick! Why in the Seven Hells do you keep doing that to me?"

"Innate skill and years of practice, Your Lordliness," Fenwick replied.

"I didn't ask how—I asked why?" I protested.

"Because I can," he smirked, sliding into the chair opposite me. "Hello, Carl. Here's the bank draft. Is it acceptable if I come in the morning to collect Davy?"

"That'll be fine, Mr. Fenwick."

"It's just Fenwick, Carl. My parents cursed me with the first name of Aloysius, so I've only used my last name since I was old enough to make it stand."

"You don't say," Carl remarked. "My first name is really Euler. Once I got big enough to hold my own in a fight, I demanded everyone call me Carl."

I wanted to laugh, but not only was Carl a friend, but he also had been an enormous help. He could tell I had a smart-ass crack about ready to leap out of my mouth and gave me a stern look. Instead, I raised my hands in a gesture of peace.

"Your secret is safe with me, Sarn't," I stated.

The following day, after Roberta fixed breakfast, I slung the map case over my shoulder, hoisted my saddlebags, and headed off to get Andy. My horse was groomed, saddled, and ready to ride. Jerry saw me and came out from the back of the inn. He sported the grin I enjoyed seeing on his face.

As I was attaching the saddlebags, I said, "Thank you, Jerry. Andy looks well-cared for—I appreciate your good work. I understand you own a horse now. Can you tell me about him?"

Jerry grabbed my forearm and almost dragged me over to the stall. Thunder was huge—at least sixteen hands high—and black as a moonless night. Jerry's affection for the horse seemed to be returned. Thunder nudged Jerry's head with his own. Jerry gushed about how brilliant Thunder was, how quickly he was learning, how fast he could run—you get the idea.

"Jerry, Andy, Lady Oritur, Bella, and I will be returning in a few weeks. When I come back, I would like to tell you about the battles Andy and I fought this summer. But we don't have to, if you would prefer not," I said.

"I'd like that, Mr. Caz," he said. "I saw where Andy has a scar. Arrow?"

I nodded as I handed him six florins.

"Mr. Caz—" he started to say.

"Thunder will need to visit the farrier eventually. Set this aside for him. See you soon, Jerry," I said as I swung up on Andy's back, "and thank you."

Andy and I made our way to the waterfront and Traval's office. The usually miserable old man actually gave me a genuine smile when he saw me. He hopped off his stool and opened the door.

"Right this way, milord," he chirped.

Both Traval and his daughter were in his office. He shook my hand. Julienne kissed my cheek.

"Thank you for saving me again," she said as she blushed prettily.

"This time, Mr. Fenwick had as much to do with it as I did. So you need to thank him as well," I suggested.

"I plan to," she replied with a slight smirk that I hope her father did not see.

"So, milord, what is the business proposition you wish to discuss," Traval asked.

"If I may," I replied, brandishing the map.

After spreading the map over his desk, I began to share the idea of dredging Port Charles and clearing the River Pheas. Both of them listened intently. Then, when I mentioned our crop yields in reference to the poor harvest elsewhere in the kingdom, they both nodded.

"His Majesty has asked me to present the following proposal," I said. "Since Mr. Fenwick and I were able to rescue Julienne without paying the ransom of twenty-four thousand ducats, His Majesty would like you to consider investing that money to pay for dredging the harbor and clearing the river. The March will pay all costs above that for making the river and port usable again. In return, His Majesty offers relief from certain customs duties, to be determined. I offer you the first choice of location for dock space and warehousing in Port Charles. We do not expect an immediate answer. The royal engineers need to provide their assessment of what work needs to be done. I will return to the capital just before the solstice, and we can meet again."

"This is damned interesting, Lord Oritur," Traval stated. "All of us need to know a lot more before moving forward, but I do sense potential. So let's meet again when you return."

27

It snowed all three days of my journey home. The ground was not yet frozen, so the snow did not stick until the third day. By the time Andy and I arrived at Easton, it was six inches deep. It was near dark by the time we reached the gate of the manor.

"Welcome back, milord," Jon Sinchak said as he pushed the gate open.

"Is my father in?"

"He returned this afternoon," Sinchak said. "With the snow, he sent the armsmen home on leave early. The six unmarried men are now in the rooms above the stable."

"Then I better hurry, or there won't be any dinner left for me," I cracked.

"Plenty of time, milord," Sinchak advised. "It hasn't rung six o'clock yet."

"I forgot that it grows dark earlier in the east. Thank you for reminding me," I said.

When I arrived at the stable, I whistled, and Tom Collinwood came out. He held Andy's head while I dismounted. I gathered my saddlebags, thanked him, and headed inside. Of course, I went through the kitchen just to joust with Laurie. I stamped the snow from my boots and rattled the doorknob so she couldn't accuse me of giving her a fright, then went in.

A warm kitchen, full of the smells of dinner cooking, is a beautiful way to end a three-day journey through snow. I paused inside the door, just taking it in. That gave Laurie the chance to see me, and she positioned herself between me and the oven, holding a wooden spoon like a weapon.

"Huh-huh-huh," she chuckled triumphantly. "I'm ready for you, milord. You'll not be sneaking a peek in the oven tonight, unh-uh."

"Why, Laurie!" I protested. "Since when have I ever done such a thing?"

"Nearly every time you come through here instead of using the rear entrance like you should," she said. "I've heard all about what a naughty rascal you was as a boy. It's too bad I wasn't around then. I know just how to make naughty boys behave," she said, brandishing her wooden spoon but smiling broadly.

"But then we wouldn't have all this fun, Laurie," I said with a wink as I passed through to the hall.

I followed the sound of voices through the parlor to the study. Lucy and my father were there. He was sitting at the desk examining what looked like account ledgers. I dropped my bags with a thump to announce my presence.

Lucy came to me, embraced me, and kissed me. My father marked his spot in the ledger with his finger before looking up. "Hello, Caz."

"Duncan is checking my figures," Lucy said. "He turned the account books for the March over to me, and I have been keeping them. He already uncovered a big problem."

"Which is?"

"Since you arrived, Lucy has been paying all the household expenses out of your pocket," my father chimed in grumpily. "They should be charged to the household account for the March."

I smiled at Lucy to let her know she need not worry. Then I slid into the chair facing him. He looked up.

"Sir, who is Earl of the March?" I asked.

"I am," he answered testily.

"Exactly," I agreed. "If I were Earl of the March, I would fold my personal holdings into those of the March, wouldn't I?"

"Yes, when your day comes," he replied, implying he wasn't planning on stepping aside anytime soon (I have to say, I heartily approved of his attitude— so different from a few months before).

"I am not Earl of the March. Lucy is not Lady of the March. Our accounts are separate from the March. We chose to pay those expenses because we intend to make Easton Manor our home even before we inherit the title," I explained.

"We made the decision to engage Mr. Pruitt. We hired the staff. I don't recall that we asked for your permission or included you in the decisions. Do you?"

My father immediately grasped where my argument was heading. "You have a point," he conceded. "But staff wages, food, fuel, and all the other routine household expenses should be paid by the March, not by you. Just as the salaries of the armsmen, their armor and weapons, their food, their quarters, and all their other expenses are paid by the March."

"I agree," I said. "When we arrived, how much money was in the March's accounts?"

"Almost nothing," he admitted. "If you had not provided the loan…"

"So, when Lucy took over managing the household, there was no money in the accounts to do anything," I stated, "no repairs, no staff, no food, no fuel—nothing. The only choice was to use my personal account, and we did so gladly and eagerly, hoping to restore life in the manor to what it always should be. I'm guessing that, with the harvest in, our tenants are paying their annual rents?"

"Yes."

"And the March now has money in its accounts and can resume paying those expenses. Father, we are not going to demand recovery of the money we spent up to this point. If we did, the March would suffer. Think of it as a gift. Beginning with Morsug, the March can resume paying the usual expenses. Now that Veronica and her offspring are not bleeding the March dry, spending the money on who knows what—"

"Gambling and whoring," my father interrupted. "Several unsavory gentlemen have come to the manor in the last few months, looking for Edwin and Percival to settle their debts. Thank all the heavenly beings we have competent guards now."

"What do the guards tell these people?"

"That Edwin and Percival have changed residences, and we do not know where to find them."

"Good. With a fresh start, I have no doubt the March can accommodate the ongoing expenses," I said. "You will need to authorize Lucy to draw from that account if she will continue the manage the household—unless you want to?"

"Seven Hells! Absolutely not!" he exclaimed. "Lucy, we will go to the bank tomorrow. Now, what's in the tube?" he asked.

"Something to discuss after dinner," I said. "I came in through the kitchen, and I suspect we will be eating presently. One other piece of business before that, if you don't mind."

"Go ahead."

"We now have six unmarried armsmen living above the stable," I said. "I remember that being the case when I was a boy. How did grandfather prevent them from, how should I say this… from interfering with the maids?"

"He threatened to chop their balls off and send them to Bannock Hill to keep watch all winter," my father replied. "Please pardon my language, Lucy. I always wonder why he didn't do that to me."

"I'm sure he considered it," I replied. "You might want to make sure the men know that threat still applies before dinner. I don't mind if they entertain overnight guests, as long as none of them are Rose, Gladys, or Hazel."

"Right," my father agreed as he stood, then left, presumably for the stable.

Lucy came and sat in my lap, putting her arms around my neck. "Thank you," she said. "I would have been able to make the same points eventually, but it would have taken longer. So how was it?"

"Fenwick reminded me that you are another point up since it was pirates and not Pedersen as I thought," I said. "We were able to bring her back unharmed. Fenwick began showing her some attention on the return voyage."

"Really?" Lucy exclaimed. "Tell me more."

I shared with Lucy the points I made to Fenwick in our conversation. Lucy especially liked my "Faint heart never won fair maiden" remark.

"Do you know her that well?" Lucy asked.

"Actually, not well at all," I said, "unlike other damsels I have saved. Maybe I am thinking too highly of her, but she has faced danger—as you have—and it didn't turn her into a quivering wreck. She has thrown herself into her father's business, and he is obviously proud of her."

"Oh, I hope it works out. I like Fenwick, you know," Lucy said.

"I do, too," I agreed. "There's only one thing that bothers me."

"Go on."

"If I fall out of favor with the king, he will send Fenwick to kill me. If Fenwick falls out of favor, the king will send me to kill Fenwick. Fenwick knows this as well as I do. It adds a tinge of melancholy to our friendship," I said.

"Then the two of you should take care to stay in the king's favor," Lucy stated.

ABOUT THE AUTHOR

John Spearman (Jake to his friends and colleagues) is a Latin teacher and coach at a prestigious New England boarding school. This book is the fifth of the *FitzDuncan* series.

www.ingramcontent.com/pod-product-compliance
Lightning Source LLC
Chambersburg PA
CBHW061242310726
48971CB00007B/2183